POWDERED PERIL

A DONUT SHOP MYSTERY

POWDERED PERIL

JESSICA BECK

WHEELER PUBLISHING
A part of Gale, Cengage Learning

GALE
CENGAGE Learning

Detroit • New York • San Francisco • New Haven, Conn • Waterville, Maine • London

GALE
CENGAGE Learning

LIBRARY OF CONGRESS CATALOGING-IN-PUBLICATION DATA

Beck, Jessica.
    Powdered peril : a Donut Shop mystery / by Jessica Beck. — Large Print edition.
        pages cm. — (Wheeler Publishing Large Print Cozy Mystery)
    ISBN-13: 978-1-4104-5262-7 (softcover)
    ISBN-10: 1-4104-5262-X (softcover)
    1. Doughnuts—Fiction. 2. Coffee shops—Fiction. 3. Private investigators—Fiction. 4. Murder—Investigation—Fiction. 5. Large type books. I. Title.
PS3602.E2693P69 2013
813'.6—dc23   2012050390

Published in 2013 by arrangement with St. Martin's Press, LLC.

Printed in the United States of America
1 2 3 4 5   17 16 15 14 13

To my daughter, Emily

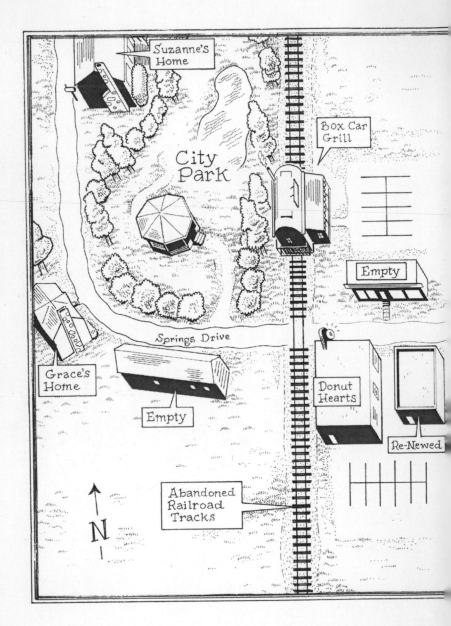

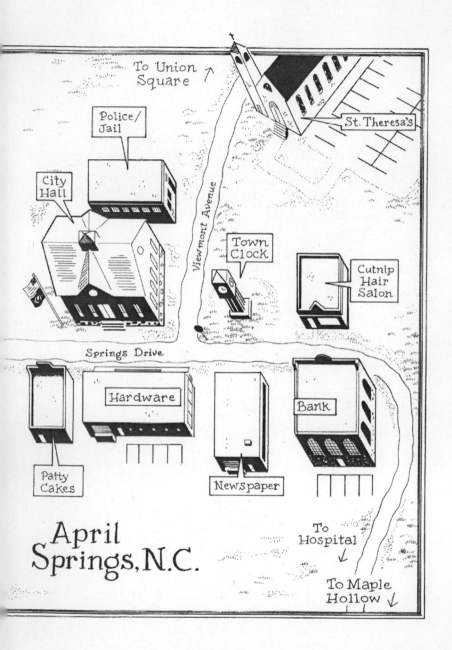

To Union Square ↑

Police/Jail

City Hall

St. Theresa's

Viewmont Avenue

Town Clock

Cutnip Hair Salon

Springs Drive

Hardware

Bank

Patty Cakes

Newspaper

To Hospital ↓

April Springs, N.C.

To Maple Hollow ↓

"Ich bin ein Berliner."

— Attributed to President John F. Kennedy
during a speech in Berlin, Germany
on June 26, 1963. Some believe it directly
translated into "I am a jelly doughnut,"
but others feel he correctly said in German,
"I am one with the people of Berlin."
You decide, but I love the idea that he
might have identified with donuts so much!
That's my kind of Commander in Chief!

CHAPTER 1

The dead body was hard to see at first in the deep shadows that surrounded it. Soon enough, as darkness faded into the edges of light, a false dawn would spread over the crime scene and reveal some of its secrets; photographs and videos would be taken, notes would be written, and the careful study of not only the victim, but the area around it, would occur. An amount of intense activity like no other would consume the investigators as they sought to solve the murder in the early hours of discovery.

But none of that would happen for hours yet.

For now, only one person knew about the crime, and they weren't about to tell anyone.

One thing was certain; the lives of the people in April Springs, North Carolina, would never be the same once they knew that murder had come back to visit their sleepy little town nestled in the Blue Ridge Mountains.

CHAPTER 2

My name is Suzanne Hart, and I've lost boyfriends in the past in as many ways as you can imagine; at least that's how it feels to me sometimes when I look back on my life so far. I hope I never lose my current beau, State Police Inspector Jake Bishop, but I can honestly say that I've never lost one to murder.

And hopefully, I never will.

I just wish I could say the same thing about a good friend of mine.

If I think about it, that's when everything started to fall apart in town, and it took all I had to keep the world from crashing down around me.

And more importantly, to save someone I cared for more than I could express.

It wasn't all that late in the day for most of the folks I knew, but for a donut maker, it may as well have been midnight. My crazy schedule often precluded me from staying up much past dark by the time April rolled around. I was just about to go upstairs for bed when the doorbell rang at the cottage I shared with my mother in April Springs, North Carolina. It was nearing seven in the evening, and I'd had another exhausting day making donuts by myself at my shop, Donut Hearts. Nan Winters, the woman I'd hired to replace my dear friend and longtime assistant, Emma Blake, was starting work tomorrow, and while I knew that I would miss Emma for a very long time, I needed *someone* there with me, because doing all the work at the donut shop alone was getting to be way too much for one person to handle.

I answered the door, ready with an excuse that would allow me to beg off and get my much-needed sleep, but all thoughts of rest vanished when I saw my best friend, Grace Gauge, standing there, an emotional wreck. It was pretty obvious that she'd been crying for a while, and it broke my heart to see her like that.

"Grace, what happened?" I asked as I stepped forward and wrapped my arms around her. She was the sister I never had, and I liked to think that I was the same to her. On the outside, the two of us were pretty different, Grace being blond and trim while I was a brunette with a bit more than my share of curves, but inside, we were two peas in a pod. She was my longest-lasting and dearest friend, and I hated seeing her so upset.

As I stroked her hair gently, I asked softly, "Are you okay?"

"Peter and I just broke up," she whimpered, and the tears started in full force. I could feel her shaking as she cried, and I held her tight, stroking her hair lightly, and doing my best to offer her what comfort I could.

"Come on inside," I said as there was a break in her sobs. She fought to catch her breath as she pulled away a minute later. "I can make us some coffee and we can talk all about it."

Grace wiped her nose with a tissue as she shook her head. "I shouldn't have come at all. I know it's getting late for you, Suzanne. You need your sleep. I just didn't have anyone else to talk to." She sniffed again, as though she were holding back more tears by sheer willpower alone, and then she added softly, "You don't have to worry about me. I'll be okay. I promise."

"Don't be silly. I wasn't going to go to bed for hours," I said as I led her inside into the living room.

She stopped dead in her tracks. "Don't lie to me, Suzanne, especially tonight. I've had just about all of that I can take from the rest of the world."

"Okay, I'm sorry; you're right. I shouldn't have said that. The truth is that I was heading off to bed when you rang, but I don't have to go to sleep this instant. I've got time to talk, at least a little bit, anyway." I had to get Grace talking. Once she started, I was pretty sure she wouldn't be able to stop until I had the whole story. If I paid for it later by being drowsy tomorrow at work, then so be it. Grace came first in my mind, on an equal level at the top of my life with Momma and Jake. Without any one of the three of them, my life just wouldn't be the same, and I knew it. There were people who floated in and out of my life and others who always seemed to hang just around the edges, folks I cared about, but those three were my core.

Grace looked around the cottage as she tucked the tissue away in her hand. In a low voice, she said, "I hate to be a pain, but is there any way that we can talk somewhere else? Your mother doesn't need to hear all of my problems."

"No worries," I explained. "She's off on

one of her dates with Chief Martin, so we've got time to talk before I have to go to sleep. Honestly, I don't expect them back for hours." I took her hands in mine and added, "Grace, I promise you that you've got my undivided attention as long as you need it. If I have to go totally without sleep tonight, you're worth it. I'll find a way to manage tomorrow."

"I'm not doing that to you, or your customers," she said. "I know how grumpy you can be when you're sleep deprived," she added, even managing a slight grin. It was good to know that her spirit was still in there somewhere, despite the temporary pall that hung over her.

"I'd say that was patently untrue if I could do it with a straight face, but we both know that you're right," I admitted. "I always shoot for seven-thirty as my bedtime, but how many times do I actually make it? Trust me; I'm wide awake. Even if you leave right now, there's no way I'm going to be able to go straight to sleep."

"Are you sure?" she asked hesitantly.

"Absolutely," I said as I settled down on one side of the couch.

She nodded as she sat beside me, and then she started to talk.

"I just found out that Peter Morgan is a

liar and a cheat," she said, her voice now strangely calm as she blurted the information out matter-of-factly. "I knew he seemed too good to be true when we first met, and in the end, it turned out that I had been right all along."

It wasn't a huge secret to the world that I'd never been all that big a fan of Peter's, though Grace had clearly been crazy about the man. I'd done my best to accept him, but it hadn't been easy. He'd been a little too slick for my taste, and a bit more manipulative than I'd liked, but I couldn't say that to Grace, especially now that he'd broken her heart and proven my doubts about him had all been right. "Why don't you tell me what happened?"

"At first, it was a lot of little things that didn't add up," she said. "He wouldn't answer his phone sometimes when we were together, and he'd be late for no real reason when we were supposed to have a date."

Surely there had to be more than that. "Go on," I said.

Grace bit her lower lip, and then continued. "I caught a whiff of someone else's perfume on his shirt collar last night. It might have been innocent enough, and I was going to do my best to forget it, but I couldn't. I decided that I was going to talk to him about it at dinner tonight. Something happened before that, though. About an hour ago, we were at my place getting ready to go out. We'd been sitting on the couch discussing where we were going to eat, and he'd asked to wash up a little before we left for the restaurant. While he was gone, I heard his phone ringing, and I realized that it must have slipped out of his pocket and was buried in a seat cushion." Grace looked at me intently as she added, "Suzanne, I wasn't snooping. Honestly, I didn't think a thing about it. When a phone rings, I answer it. It's some kind of compulsion I have."

"I don't see how anybody could blame you for that. Who was calling?" I asked. "Did you look at the caller ID?"

She nodded, and I could see her fighting back another onslaught of tears. I touched her shoulder lightly. "Grace, do you need to take a second? You don't have to tell me all at once, you know."

She took a few moments to collect herself, and then nodded. "It's okay. I'm fine. At least I will be." After blowing her nose, she explained, "It was Leah Gentry."

I knew Leah, and she wasn't one of my favorite people in April Springs. In her early twenties, Leah worked at her uncle's hardware store down the street from Donut

Hearts; there wasn't a man in all of April Springs she hadn't made a pass at at least once. I'd had my own run-ins with her uncle, Burt Gentry, enough times in the past to realize that bad attitudes must run in their family, and that particular apple was sitting pretty close to the tree.

"I hate to ask this, but could it have all just been innocent?" I asked, playing devil's advocate for a second. I wasn't at all interested in defending the man, but I didn't want Grace to jump to any conclusions either, at least not without knowing all of the facts.

"Actually, she tried to make it sound that way when I answered Peter's phone," Grace explained. "Leah made up something on the spur of the moment about a part he had ordered coming into the hardware store, but it was clear to me that she was lying. When I pushed her on it, Leah mumbled something incoherent and hung up just as Peter came back into the room. Do you want to know what his first reaction was when he saw me holding his cell phone? He looked angry and he tried to grab it from me. I held it away from him, though, and asked him about Leah. For a few seconds, I saw him searching for any excuse he thought I would buy, and as he tried to come up with something I might accept, I hit the menu button and checked his recent calls." Grace looked down at her hands, and then said, "I shouldn't have done that. I know that now. But I just had to know how big a liar he actually was."

I wasn't about to let Grace beat herself up for doing something to stand up for herself. "Are you kidding? I think that was brilliant. I'm not at all sure that I would have been smart enough to do that, not under those circumstances. What did you find in his records?"

Her voice died a little as she said, "Leah wasn't the only woman's name there, not by a long shot, though she was listed a dozen times. When I think about it now, I don't know how he had time to date me at all."

"What did you do when you saw that list of women?" I asked, dying to hear what had happened next. Well, that wasn't entirely true; I knew the end result. What I didn't know was how it had come about from that initial discovery to her sitting on my couch with me.

"I confronted him about it," Grace said, "and you won't believe this, but the jerk actually admitted it. I guess he just couldn't be bothered coming up with an explanation that I might swallow. Peter told me that he'd made a few mistakes in the past, but that I was important to him. He even promised me that he'd drop every one of the other women he was seeing in a heartbeat if I'd forgive him and try to work things out between us."

"But you couldn't do that, could you?"

Grace shook her head. "He's lied to me so much, how could I ever believe him again? I was about to break up with him right then and there when his phone rang again."

"Was it Leah calling back?" I asked. "She doesn't give up, does she?"

"No, but it was another woman."

"What did you do then?" I knew my best friend had a big and generous heart, but I also knew that if someone crossed her one too many times, she could be as hard as stone, and cold as ice.

Grace shook her head gently, as though she were trying to delicately dislodge a bad memory. "I opened the front door, threw his phone out into the front yard, and then I told him that we were through. I'm done with him, and he knows it."

"I still can't believe that Leah would do something like that to you," I said. "She's no one I'd ever be friends with, but there are rules about this sort of thing, you know? She had to know that the two of you were dating. It's not like it was a big secret or anything." I suppose the young woman was pretty, in a brassy kind of way, and some men seemed to enjoy her attention, but she couldn't hold a candle to Grace, inside or out. What would cause a man who had Grace's heart to go after a woman like Leah? He'd traded gold for lead, and my friend's heart was broken because of it.

"I'm not happy with her either, that's for sure, and I won't make a single excuse for her, but I can't help thinking that Peter's the real snake here." Grace hesitated, and then added, "You know what? If she wants him, she can have him. I'll be just fine without him. I don't have to have a man in my life." She broke down again, and as I hugged her, I knew that she had loved this man, and he'd betrayed her. I couldn't imagine how I'd react if I'd caught Jake doing anything like that, but then again, I couldn't even fathom the circumstances where he would think about it for one split second. Jake was many things, sometimes frustrating me beyond explanation, but he was loyal and trustworthy; I knew that in my heart.

It was close to eight when Grace finally

stood. Had we really been talking for over an hour? "I've kept you up long enough, Suzanne," she said. "You need your sleep."

"I'm okay, honest," I said as I stood. Unfortunately, a yawn slipped out just then, though I tried my best to kill it.

She smiled at me. "Suzanne Hart, you're the best friend I could ever ask for, but you're a terrible liar. It's time I leave you to your sleep. I'm feeling a lot better now."

"Is that really true?" I asked, looking deeply into her eyes.

She considered it for a moment before she answered. "Well, maybe not yet, but I will be. I'm going to go home, eat a pint of Ben & Jerry's, and then I'm going to watch sad movies until I fall asleep. Maybe I'll have myself a Nicholas Sparks marathon and cry out all of my tears. You can count on him for one thing for sure; somebody's not going to make it until the end."

We'd laughed in the past about how someone always seemed to die in one of the movies based on his books, but we were proud that he was from North Carolina, too, and we never missed reading his latest novel together in a kind of small, two-woman book club, nothing like the ladies I hosted at my donut shop. While that group thrived on serious discussion, Grace and I weren't above mocking anything we found scornworthy in any book we read. "That sounds great," I said. "I'd be more than happy to join you."

"You'd fall asleep before the opening credits of the first movie, and we both know it." Grace hugged me, and then said, "Get some sleep, Suzanne."

I couldn't deny that I was beat. "If you're sure," I said.

"Go on. You've been wonderful. It's great having you as my best friend."

"I think so, too," I said, and then realized how it might have sounded. "Reverse that. What I should have said was 'right back at you.' You know what I meant."

Grace smiled again, briefly, but it was there. Maybe I really had helped.

"Remember, call me if you need to talk," I said as I walked her out onto the cottage's front porch. "I don't care what time it is."

"I promise," she said, and then Grace walked up the road toward her house.

If I had it to do over again, I would have gone with her, and neither one of us would have gotten into the mess we ultimately did. But, hindsight is always twenty-twenty, so instead I watched her until she was gone, and then I went upstairs to bed. Jake was tied up on a case, so I knew he probably wouldn't have a chance to call. As much as I would have loved hearing his voice as a reassurance of what we shared after hearing of Peter's betrayals, I didn't need it. I trusted him with my heart, and with my life.

It was the only way I knew how to love, and I fully understood that Grace felt the same way, no matter what the consequences were. We both went all out when we were in a relationship, and while that meant we got hurt sometimes, like she had been tonight, finding real love was always worth the risk. This time, she'd gambled and lost, but I knew that she'd find it in herself to try again someday.

Grace must have found a way to make it through the night, because I didn't hear from her after she left my place. When I woke up the next morning, too early as usual, I quickly got dressed and headed to Donut Hearts to start working on that day's donuts with a little lighter touch to my step. After all, it was a big day for me. Emma's replacement, Nan Winters, was starting her first day of work. Sure, she'd trained with us for a few days before Emma left, but then she'd had to go visit an old friend while she had the chance before she started helping me make donuts six days out of every seven. With only one day off a week, she knew she wouldn't be getting any more time off for a while, so she'd taken advantage of it. I just hoped Nan remembered what Emma and I had taught her, but I had my doubts. Then again, maybe a fresh start would be better for all of us. I had resisted the impulse to pick up the phone and call Emma a hundred times since she'd been gone. In a way, I felt as though my own daughter were going off to school, and not just an employee. Honestly, she was much more to me than that, and everyone knew it. But I'd promised to give her a month of finding her way at her new school letting her get settled in and used to her new life before I started pestering her, and I was going to respect that. Emma had signed up for spring classes with the college's unusual schedule, and while I hated losing her too early, she had every right to go out into the world and find her own way.

I drove to Donut Hearts in the darkness, and as I went past the front of my shop, my headlights picked up something odd about the front of the building. My business was housed in an old railroad depot, and once upon a time the tracks had been right beside it. One of the reasons I'd bought the business was for the old weathered bricks up front. I wasn't sure if it was my imagination or not, but I could have sworn the bricks looked different somehow in the light from my high beams. I stopped and backed my Jeep up onto the grass of the nearby park, not really worrying about getting in anyone's way on Springs Drive, since most folks with any sense at all were home in bed instead of out on the road in the middle of the night.

When my headlights hit the building again, I saw that it hadn't been my imagination.

Someone had splattered bright yellow paint on the front of my building, obscuring not only the brick, but the new front window I'd just had repainted with our logo. My heart sank as I saw the mess. I was pretty sure the paint would come right off the window without too much of a fuss, but the bricks might be another thing entirely. I moved my Jeep into one of the parking spaces on Springs Drive, grabbed my flashlight, and then walked back toward Donut Hearts to see if things were as bad as I feared.

When I saw the paint-spattered bucket lying empty beside the front door, I figured it might be time to call the police. If the

vandals could be identified by their fingerprints, I wanted to make sure they were
caught and got what they deserved. If they
were arrested and convicted, and the judge
felt like giving them community service, I
would want to see if I could get the perpe-
trator assigned to me. By the time I got
done with them, they'd think twice about
vandalizing another business.

To my surprise, I got one of my friends
on the line as I dialed the police night desk.
I figured there was no reason to tie up 911,
since this was clearly not an emergency.
Whoever had defaced my building was long
gone.

When Officer Stephen Grant answered the
phone, I idly put a finger on the brick, test-
ing to see if it might still be damp.

No such luck. It was pretty clear that it
wasn't going to come off without a great
deal of work.

"Officer Grant, I've got a problem," I said
when he picked up and identified himself.

"Suzanne, is that you?" he asked. He
should know my voice by now. The man had
been in my donut shop, on official business
as well as during his free time, often over
the years. Even though he was a slim young
man, he had a surprising appetite for donuts, and we were slowly building a friend-

ship during his frequent visits to my shop. "You didn't lock yourself out of the donut shop, did you?" he asked hopefully. "Please tell me that I've got an excuse to leave the duty desk and come out there."

"As a matter of fact, you do, but it's nothing as trivial as that." That's when I realized that he shouldn't be working the night shift at all. There was only one explanation for that. "What did you do to get on the chief's bad side?"

After a brief hesitation, he said, "I made a crack about his disappearing waistline he didn't care for," Officer Grant admitted. Ever since Chief Martin had been dating my mother, he'd been on a constant diet, and so far, he'd lost two pants sizes, with no end in sight.

"And he punished you for that? I figure he'd be pleased that you noticed."

"Not so much. At least not the way he overheard me talking to another cop. Don't sweat it. It'll all blow over soon enough, but until it does, I'm riding a desk. Now, you didn't call here to listen to my problems. What can I do for you, if it's worse than a set of lost keys?"

"Somebody decided to redecorate Donut Hearts for me without even asking." Just talking to him on the telephone made me feel better somehow. I would have called Jake first if he'd been in town, but he was in Spruce Pine, and I knew that the cell phone reception in the mountain town was spotty at best.

"They didn't break your front window again, did they?"

"No," I said as I looked at the intact glass. At least there was that. "They did chuck a half-full bucket of paint on it, though, and the brick exterior, too."

That got his attention. "Is the bucket still there? We might be able to get some fingerprints off of it."

I looked toward the bucket again, and that's when I noticed something else. "I can do better than that," I said. "There's a set of footprints in the paint where whoever did it ran off. I just found them."

"Don't do anything crazy, Suzanne. I'll be right there."

"Can I at least go inside the shop and wait for you there?" I asked.

"I'd rather you didn't," he said. "Why don't you go sit in your Jeep until I get there so I can have a look around?"

I laughed. "We both know those flimsy windows I've got wouldn't stop a determined chipmunk, let alone a killer. I'll be all right where I am until you get here."

"Just stay out of sight, okay? It would be crazy to take any chances. I'm on my way."

"I've got nowhere else I need to be right now except inside making donuts," I said, and then realized that I had dead air on the other end of the line.

The police station was just down the road, so I figured that it wouldn't take Officer Grant long to get there. I decided to compromise somewhat, and moved away from the shop a few yards. Okay, I admit that my path of retreat led me beside the footprints I'd first seen in the spilled paint, and my flashlight tended to follow them with eerie precision, but I was careful not to step in the paint, so I didn't think he'd have anything to complain about if he found me doing a little snooping on my own. It was a warm early morning, and though it had cooled somewhat after hitting near eighty in the heat of the day, I still preferred autumn, winter, and spring. Folks still ate donuts yearround, but certainly not as many as they did when the weather turned cooler. Besides, I liked a nip in the air, which was one of the many reasons I'd refused to move to L.A. with my ex-husband, Max, the Great Impersonator, when we'd been together. Give me the changing of the seasons, and I was a happy gal.

I surely wasn't a fan of this warm early morning air.

As I searched to see where the footsteps led, the impromptu path got harder and harder to see in the tall grass, and unfortunately, soon enough the paint trail ended half a dozen steps toward the park. By the time Officer Grant showed up, I'd lost them completely.

He had his squad car lights all blazing, but at least he hadn't used his siren on his way here. I'd had more than enough of that kind of attention in the past, and I didn't need any more of it ever again.

I met him at the patrol car, shielding my eyes from the bright light. It was quite a change from my flashlight, with its dying beam barely able to light my way back to my vehicle. I'd have to remember to get new batteries for it. With only a few seconds of feeble light left, I shut it off and threw it onto the passenger seat of the Jeep.

"Where did you just go?" Officer Grant asked as he scanned the donut shop and the land around it with the monstrous flashlight-weapon combination in his hand. Honest to goodness, it was big enough to bring down a bear. He might have to do just that someday, since there had been a few bear sightings around the area over the past few months. It shouldn't have surprised anyone, as far as I was concerned. It just made sense to me. After all, we were developing more and more of the woodland creatures' natural habitat, so why was everyone so shocked when they started invading our turf?

"I followed the yellow brick road," I admitted as I pointed to the tracks. "Well, it's not a road exactly, it's more like a path, but it's yellow; there's no denying it."

Officer Grant fought back a grin, but I could still see it. This was serious police business; at least that was the way that he was treating it. I kept my other quips to myself as I asked, "May I go start on the donuts now while you search out here? I'm kind of tight on time because of the delay." I'd cut the shop's hours, working on donuts from three to six in the kitchen, selling them from six until eleven, and then cleaning up after everyone else went home. It made the day more reasonable, and I almost felt as though I could actually have a life of my own outside the donut shop, as much as I loved being there.

He considered it for a moment or two, and then nodded. "I can't see why not. Go on in. Lock up when you get inside, and I'll knock when I'm finished here."

I smiled my thanks and moved inside after unlocking the front door and carefully avoiding the spilled paint as I walked, though I knew it was dry. I noticed that the door handle had a splatter of yellow paint on it as well, and I was glad that the vandal hadn't had any red paint at his disposal. I wasn't sure I'd be as flip as I was being now if it had looked as though the front of my shop had been covered in blood.

Once I was inside, I put on the coffeepot and turned on the fryer, checked the messages on the machine, and then got started on the batter for the cake donuts. Nan wasn't due to report for another half hour, so I still had some time to myself.

I was so focused on making donuts that I barely heard Officer Grant as he pounded on the front door fifteen minutes later.

I opened the door and let him in, noting that he, too, had stepped over the dried paint. "Find anybody out there?" I asked as I relocked the door behind him.

"No, and the tracks died before I could trace them any farther into the park. They stopped before I even got to Trish's Boxcar Grill, so unless we find a pair of yellow-stained shoes somewhere, we're out of luck."

"What about fingerprints on the bucket?" I asked. "Do you think you'll be able to find any there?"

He shrugged. "I've already bagged it, but I wouldn't count on us having much luck. Unless the vandal is in our system, it will be impossible to track him down."

"Do you think it was a man, too?" I asked.

"Absolutely." He smiled at me as he asked, "Why do you think so?"

"Well, the shoe size, for one thing," I admitted. "Unless it was a really big woman I don't want to mess with, it had to be a guy."

He grinned at me. "Dead on, Suzanne. Keep that up, and you'll earn your Junior Detective badge yet." His smile faded quickly as he pointed outside. "I'm afraid it's a real mess out there. I don't have a clue how you're going to be able to clean it all up."

"Hey, as long as no one got hurt, I'm counting my blessings," I said. "Would you like some coffee before you go?"

He stifled a yawn, and then nodded. "I probably should say no, but honestly, that would be great."

I fixed him up with a cup to go, and then let him out the front door.

I'd be able to better assess things once it was daylight, but in the meantime, I had donuts to make. There was nothing I could do about what had happened, but I could do my job, and people around here depended on me. Letting them down wasn't going to happen.

CHAPTER 3

"Good morning, Nan," I said to my new assistant as she walked into the kitchen of my donut shop ten minutes later. To my surprise, she'd pounded on the back door that led to the alley to summon me, an entrance and exit I rarely used myself. Had she even seen the mess up front?

"We just use this door for deliveries. Remind me to get you a key for the front door," I said as I let her in and bolted it behind her.

"That would be lovely," Nan said as she put her apron on. I'm a morning person by nature myself, but this woman was just a little too perky for me. Emma was unbearable until she had her first cup of coffee, but it appeared that Nan woke up every day with a smile.

It was funny; Emma had only been gone a short while, but I already missed her more than I ever could have imagined. She'd been my right hand since I'd opened Donut Hearts, and having her gone felt exactly the same as missing my two front teeth. No matter how hard I tried not to think about her absence, I continually saw her shadow everywhere I looked. Emma was off to college, though, something she'd dreamed about since she'd first come to Donut Hearts, and now I had bright and cheerful Nan.

I didn't really want to bring up what had happened in front of the donut shop, but Nan was an employee now, and she deserved to know about it.

"Did you see the mess up front?" I asked.

"No, what happened?"

"Somebody threw a bucket of paint on the donut shop."

"Oh, dear," she said, clearly upset by the thought. Well, she wasn't the only one. "May I see it?"

"Why not?" We walked up front, and I flipped on the outside lights. "Do you need to go outside?"

She took in the smeared window and could see the paint on the ground through the glass front door. "No, there's no need. Suzanne, who would do such a thing?"

"It's hard to say."

That wasn't the answer she wanted,

clearly. "Do you have that many enemies?"

"That's not what I meant. It's just a random act of vandalism."

"Oh, well, that's better then, isn't it?" she asked as we walked back into the kitchen together.

"How do you figure that?" She was an odd bird, there was no doubt about that.

"Well, if you were being targeted somehow, this would just be the beginning, wouldn't it?"

What an unpleasant way to think about it. "Anyway, I just thought you should know. Now, are you ready to make some donuts?"

"I am," she said, and I decided to do my best to forget about what had happened.

Back in the kitchen, Nan looked at the counter at the bowls of batter I'd prepared and rubbed her hands together. "How lovely. Shall we begin?" She was a middle-aged woman with a distinctive mole on her left cheek and a nest of gray hair arranged haphazardly atop her head. From her ample and abundant figure, Nan was clearly a woman who had befriended more than her share of donuts over the years.

"I'm ready if you are," I said with the brightest smile I could manage.

"Let's do it then," she answered.

I looked around to see where she should

begin her tasks at Donut Hearts. "If you don't mind, could you get started on the first round of dishes?"

"That sounds perfect to me," she said as she started to put hot water into the sink. I had to give her credit. The woman was a dynamo.

She just wasn't Emma, but I couldn't hold that against her.

"I'm dropping donuts now, so you need to go in the dining room for a few minutes," I said a bit later. Nan smiled, dried her hands, and dutifully moved to the front.

Forcing the batter down into the dropper required me to swing the entire contraption like a pendulum, and it had slipped out of my hands once, hitting the plaster wall hard enough to leave a mark. I hated to think what might have happened if someone had been standing in its path, so that was one of my rules. Everyone but me had to evacuate the kitchen area when it was time to drop donuts.

After making my usual run of cake donuts, I fried up a batch of a new apple and orange cake donut recipe I'd been trying to perfect, and quickly doused them with icing the moment I pulled them out of the fryer. After taking a bite, I shook my head in disappointment. The donut was still too sweet, and not enough of the fruit flavor came through. It was back to the drawing board for this recipe.

"You can come back in now," I called out, and Nan reentered the kitchen.

I was about to throw out my latest failure when Nan surprised me. "You're not going to just chuck those, are you?"

"I don't have much choice. They aren't very good," I admitted. "Not every new recipe I try can be a winner." I'd have to make a note in my copy of my recipe book, and tweak the ingredients and proportions yet again. I'd lost the original recipe book once to dire circumstances, and now I kept a backup on computer and an extra hard copy at the house, too. At least I had kept my computer files current when Emma had been with me. Blast it all, I was going to have to find someone else to do that for me now that she was gone.

"Can I have a taste of one before you throw them away?" Nan asked timidly.

I shrugged. "Be my guest. I doubt you'll like them, though."

She picked a warm donut up, took a bite, and then nodded and smiled. "Wow, that is fantastic."

"Really?" I asked.

"It's the best donut I've ever had in my life. Suzanne, you're really good at this."

I couldn't believe that we were talking about the same donut. I reached over, pinched a piece off another one, and popped it in my mouth.

No, it was still too sweet for my taste.

"You really like it?" I asked. "Nan, you don't have to be nice to me. I'm not going to fire you for being honest about my donuts. In fact, I'm counting on it." Honestly, it would take more than I was willing to admit for me to get rid of her. Where else was I going to find someone who was willing to put up with the kind of crazy hours I worked?

"I love them. You should sell these. I'm guessing that they'll get even better with age."

I personally didn't think that I had that long. So much for using Nan as my taste tester. If she truly liked these donuts, I wasn't sure I could trust her judgment on anything. Not that I could tell her that directly. I had no intention of killing her spirit on her first day of work.

"Tell you what," I said. "Why don't we cut these up and offer them as free samples today? If enough folks like them, we'll put them in the rotation. How does that sound?"

"Like a winner," Nan said. She finished the donut she'd sampled, and then smiled again. "Suzanne, I truly do think that you've got a hit on your hands."

I personally thought that she was crazy, but I was going to keep that opinion to myself.

We had more donuts to make, more dishes to wash, and more tasks to perform before we were ready to open for business, and I had no desire to do any of it by myself again if I could help it.

My first customer of the day was not someone I particularly wanted to see, despite the gradual thawing of our past chilly relationship. Chief Martin looked grim as he walked into the donut shop, and I didn't even have to ask if he was there for some of our treats. Ever since the chief had left his wife in the hopes of pursuing and winning my mother's heart, he'd been on a diet, and the results were remarkable, there was no denying it.

I had a hunch why he was there. "Before you ask, I need to tell you that I have no idea who did it. I was hoping that you'd be able to find out yourself."

He looked as surprised as if I'd just handed him a hundred-dollar bill for no rhyme or reason. "How did you know?"

Chief Martin asked in a subdued voice. He was keeping the volume down, but there was no one in the dining room but me, since Nan was in back happily doing dishes.

What was going on here? "I reported it, remember? Officer Grant came by and made a report, didn't he?"

The light finally dawned. "I get it. You're talking about the paint out front."

"Of course I am," I admitted. "What else could it be?"

He shrugged, and a frown crept over his face. "Suzanne, I'm afraid that you need to come with me."

I couldn't believe it. It clearly wasn't a request. Chief Martin was actually ordering me around, something I didn't take lightly in my donut shop. Had he learned nothing in the years since he'd known me? "I can't do that, and you know it. It's Nan's first day, and I'm not about to abandon her here alone. If you think I'm going to shut the place down altogether to help find out who vandalized my shop, as much as I'd like to, I can't afford to just leave. If there's anything you need to ask me, or tell me, for that matter, we can do it right here just as easily as somewhere else."

"Are you sure about that?" he asked.

"As much as I can be," I answered.

"Okay then, we'll do it your way. We found your vandal thirty minutes ago."

I was delighted with the news, and curious why he wasn't more excited about solving a case, no matter how small it seemed. "That's great news, Chief. I'm sorry I gave you such a hard time, but that paint really wrecked my day. Give me an hour in the cell with whoever did it, and I'll make sure they've splashed their last bucket of paint."

"I wish I could, but I'm afraid that's not going to happen."

"Are you sure you can't let me have a crack at him first?" I asked.

"Trust me, I would if I could, but someone else beat you to it. He's dead, Suzanne. Someone murdered him."

I took a deep breath and studied his expression before I allowed myself to react. "He's really dead? You don't think I did it, do you? I don't even know who it was."

"Take it easy," he said. "I'm not accusing you of anything right now. The thing is, you're involved in this, whether you want to be or not."

I felt my chest tighten. "It's not someone I know, is it?" My mind raced through a list of my male friends, but I couldn't think of a single one who would want to deface my

45

storied old building. Worse yet, I hated to think that someone I knew had been murdered. It never failed to make me sick to my stomach when I realized just how capable some people were of ending their disputes with homicide.

"I'm sorry, but it is."

I couldn't take it another second. Why was he dragging this out? Was it Max? My ex-husband had done some idiotic things in his life, but trashing my building wasn't even in the realm of possibility. At least not if he was sober. "Don't keep me in suspense. Who is it?"

"Someone killed Peter Morgan between ten o'clock last night and five this morning," he said, and I felt my knees weaken, not because of my attachment to Grace's ex-boyfriend, but because I knew that if there was foul play involved, the chief would have to consider Grace first. The relief that it wasn't Max was tempered by the fact that it was still someone I knew, and that was hard to take, no matter how I felt about him. The chief went on to explain, "It looks like they hit him from behind with an old wooden post they found behind the Boxcar."

"Are you telling me that he was killed right over there?" I asked, looking out the front door toward Trish's diner. Sure enough, I could see that there was police tape strung up in the trees behind the Boxcar. The activity had been impossible to see from the kitchen, but once I knew what was going on, I couldn't miss it. It looked bad for my best friend, and I knew it. She'd been angry with Peter last night, and there was no telling what some folks thought she might be capable of if their relationship was torn apart.

I had to nip this in the bud right now.

"Grace didn't do it," I said defensively.

"Hang on a second. No one said that she did," the chief replied, holding his hands up as though he were trying to keep me at bay.

"That's good to know," I answered, mollified, if only for a moment.

"Don't read too much into that," Chief Martin said sternly. "She's a suspect, there's no way around that, but I'm not ready to say she's guilty until I have more information."

"Is that why you're here?" I asked. "Are you expecting me to help you hang my best friend for something she didn't do?" I was trying to keep my voice calm, but it was getting harder and harder to do.

"Nobody's getting hanged around here, at least not just yet," he answered, his voice indicating that his patience clearly was wearing thin.

"Then why are you here, Chief?"

"I thought you might want to come with me when I tell her the news," he admitted. "I wouldn't do it under ordinary circumstances, but I know how close you two are, and I'm sure she could use a friend when I tell her what happened. There's one condition, though."

"What's that?" I asked, immediately suspicious of the string Chief Martin was attaching to his offer. I knew that it had been too good to be true.

"You have to stay in the squad car while I tell her. After that, you can console her all you want to, but I need the first few minutes alone with her."

That was a reasonable request, but I wasn't certain that I could honor it. "How about if I stand on the porch with you, but I promise not to say anything?"

"Suzanne, this isn't a swap meet, and we're not bargaining. I need to speak with her alone, and if you're with me when I ring her doorbell, it's not going to help any of us, including Grace. So, what's it going to be? Will you stay in the car and wait until I'm finished with her, or do I go by myself?" He hesitated, and then added, "Don't think you can turn me down and then go to Grace's anyway. I'll have a man stop you before you get within a hundred yards of her place if I have to. This is just a courtesy."

I realized that was true enough. I liked a good fight as much as the next gal, but there really wasn't any reason for me to push him on this.

"You've got a deal. Give me a minute. I have to lock up the shop."

"What about Nan?" Chief Martin asked. "Can't she run things?"

"It's her first day," I answered as Nan herself came out of the kitchen.

"Did I hear someone mention my name?" She looked at the chief, and then said, "Hello, Phillip. How are you?"

"I'm fine, Nan. Suzanne, make up your mind. This won't wait. What's it going to be?"

I shrugged. How bad could it be? "Nan, I know this must sound crazy to you, but I need to go with the chief to help out a friend of mine. I'm perfectly happy to shut the donut shop for an hour if you'd prefer, and you can take a break. Don't worry, I'll pay you for your time."

"Is there any reason I can't run it for you in your absence?" she asked as she glanced at my cash register. "This is an 8200 model.

49

I've run one before."

"It's not fair for me to ask you to do that," I said.

Nan smiled broadly. "You're not asking; I'm volunteering. Go on, I'll be fine."

She'd been with me just a few hours, and now my new assistant was asking me to entrust my livelihood with her, all that I owned. Could I trust her? If not now, when, though? After three days? A week? A month? There was no time like the present to see if I could leave the shop in her hands. "If you're sure, that would be great. I really appreciate it."

"Go on. I can always call you if I get in over my head, but I don't think I will."

"Let's go," I said to Chief Martin, afraid that if I lingered too long, I'd change my mind. On the surface it didn't make any sense at all, but Grace was involved, so logic went out the window. I didn't have many good and true friends, though I had scads of acquaintances in our small town, and when one of them was in trouble, there was no way I wouldn't be there for them.

We got to the squad car, and I automatically headed for the backseat.

"You can ride up front with me, if you don't think it might ruin your reputation," Chief Martin said as he held the door open for me. It was something I loved about living in the South. No matter how we might have felt about each other, we still respected the unwritten rules that drove us all, and courtesy was one of them.

Driving to Grace's, I asked, "I'm curious about something. How can you be certain Peter was the one who painted my shop?" Before he could answer, I immediately did it myself. "Strike that. He had yellow paint on the soles of his shoes, and probably on his hands and clothes as well."

The chief glanced over at me for a second as he continued driving. "Suzanne, you told Grant that you didn't see anyone do it. How could you know all of that? You didn't find the body yourself and not tell anyone about it, did you?"

"Of course not," I said, though I couldn't fault the chief for jumping to a wild conclusion like that. I had meddled in police business a few times over the years, but I'd never done anything so overtly wrong before. At least not in my mind, anyway. "I saw the footprints in the paint, and from the way the paint was sloshed all over the front of the building, it would have taken a miracle not to get any on his hands or on his clothes. It just makes sense."

"Well, you couldn't have described him

better if you'd seen the man himself," the chief said. "You're pretty quick, aren't you?"

"Maybe I've been reading too many of my mother's mystery novels," I admitted. I wasn't all that excited to have the chief remembering the times in the past when I'd played detective myself. "You're going to take it easy on Grace, aren't you? Hearing about Peter's murder is going to be a real shock to her."

"I'll do what I can," he said as he pulled into her driveway, "but I have to talk to her first, and I don't have time to be gentle. That's why you're here."

"To help pick up the pieces after you're through," I said, without an ounce of anger in my words.

"I wouldn't put it like that exactly, but the gist of it is true."

"I appreciate you thinking of me," I said as he got out of the car.

He just nodded, and I had to fight the urge to leave the car as well and march right up those steps with him. A promise was a promise, though, even if I'd made it to our chief of police.

I saw Grace answer the door after a few minutes of ringing and knocking, and I rolled down the window so I could eavesdrop on their conversation. I'd promised to stay in the car, but I hadn't said a word about not listening in.

Luckily, I could hear them just fine from my vantage point.

"What is it, Chief?" Grace asked as she pulled her robe around her. Her hair was a bit of a mess, and she hadn't put any makeup on yet, but I still marveled at how pretty my friend was. It might have caused some jealousy and competition in some women, but I'd always been proud to have a friend like her. Going past the surface was what counted, and Grace was every bit as pretty on the inside.

"When was the last time you saw Peter Morgan?" he asked.

"Last night," Grace admitted. "Why? Did he say something to you about me?"

I knew right then that I should have called Grace and warned her that the chief was coming. Was that the real reason he'd brought me with him? If I was in the car with him, I couldn't call Grace without him knowing it. Then why had he told me in the first place? Maybe he'd seen me in the front of the donut shop when he'd been at the crime scene, so he was making a preemptive strike by including me in this interrogation. Or maybe he was doing exactly what he'd said, making sure Grace had a shoulder to cry on after she found out about Peter Morgan. I wasn't sure exactly what to believe, but I decided that until I heard otherwise, I was going to do my best to give him the benefit of the doubt, a real change of pace for me when it came to dealing with my mother's boyfriend.

"I need to ask a few questions before I answer any of yours. What time would that be?" the chief asked.

Grace started to get even more suspicious. "Chief, Peter didn't call you after he left here last night, did he? What a little weasel. He shows up on my front porch drunk, we have an argument, and the next morning, the chief of police shows up on my doorstep before seven. What a guy. I'm glad I slapped him last night, and I'm even happier that I didn't take him back when he begged me to. I'm better off without him."

"Did anyone see him leave here? And you never told me what time he left." The chief was persistent, I had to give him that.

"No one saw him here, at least not that I'm aware of. I thought I'd made it clear that I was finished with him earlier when I found out that he'd been cheating on me, but he just wouldn't leave it be. I admit that I was broken up about it at first, but the more I thought about it, the more I realized

54

that I was better off alone than having him in my life. He finally realized that I was dead serious somewhere around eleven," Grace said. "He kept mumbling something about Trish throwing him out of the Boxcar, and that he had to come here to make things right with me. Fat chance. Chief, that man's a liar, and if he told you anything different, you shouldn't be all that surprised." Grace glanced over at the squad car, but from where it was parked, I doubted she could tell that I was there, given the shade of the tree and the way the car was angled. "Is that him? Come on out, you coward," she shouted, and I ducked down a little in my seat.

"Go on, bring him over here," she said as she turned to the chief. "I have the right to face my accuser. Let's hear what the loser has to say."

"That's not Peter," the police chief admitted. "It's Suzanne."

"Suzanne?" Grace asked, clearly surprised by the information. "Why is she in your car? You didn't arrest her, did you? Whatever you think she might have done, she didn't do it."

I felt a rush of pride as my friend rose to defend me, not even knowing why I was there.

"Actually, I brought her here for you," the chief admitted.

Grace looked more confused than ever. "Why would you do that? As much as I'm happy to see her, I don't really need her for anything at this unholy hour."

I saw the chief tense a little, and I knew that he was about to tell her the news. Even as I was opening my door, I heard him say, "I'm sorry to be the one to tell you this, but Peter Morgan was murdered last night near the Boxcar Grill."

The look of shock on her face broke my heart. "He's dead? No. No. I don't believe you. That can't be."

"I know that it's a shock for you, but it's true."

"When did it happen?" I heard her ask as she began to cry. I hurried toward my best friend to offer any comfort that I could.

"Between ten last night and five this morning," the chief said.

"But I already told you. He left here at eleven, and besides a slap in the face, he was fine, if you don't count being drunk as something wrong with you."

The chief shrugged. "I have to ask these questions, Grace, but I'll do so as quickly as I can. Let me see your hands," he prompted, and Grace presented them just as I arrived.

I looked down at Grace's hands.

To my unending relief, there wasn't a speck of yellow paint on them.

Evidently, that wasn't what the chief was looking for. At least not just that.

"What happened here?" he asked as he pointed to a scraped area on one of her palms.

Grace looked at me oddly, but all I could do was shrug. She glanced down at her palm and said, "That? It's nothing. I got a splinter painting an old bench in my backyard yesterday. Why?"

"I'm afraid you need to come with me," the chief said.

"Why should I do that?" she asked, the concern thick in her voice. "What's this got to do with anything?"

"Whoever killed Peter Morgan used a wooden post on him," the chief said gravely. "We're going to the hospital so we can retrieve that splinter, and then we're going to go to my office and chat a little more."

"Suzanne?" she asked. "What's going on?" She was clearly in a state of shock after hearing the news about her ex-boyfriend.

"Can't she at least get dressed first?" I asked.

"Not until we get that splinter. I'm sorry. You'll need to make your own way back to the donut shop."

"I'll meet you at the hospital with some clothes," I volunteered as I ignored the police chief. "Don't worry, Grace, it's going to be okay."

She nodded slightly, but I could see in her eyes that she didn't entirely believe me.

If I was being honest with myself, I wasn't sure that I believed it, either.

THICK AND RICH OLD-FASHIONED BAKED DONUTS

As we've started eating healthier, we've changed some of our old-fashioned fried donut recipes to baked ones. Having a portable donut maker that produces mini-rounds has been perfect, but these donuts are nearly as good baked in muffin tins in a conventional oven. This is a delightful take on an old favorite, creating a donut that is dense and rich with subtle overtones.

Ingredients

Mixed
- 1 egg, beaten
- 1/2 cup sugar, white granulated
- 1/2 cup mashed potatoes
- 1/4 cup whole milk
- 4 tablespoons butter, melted

Sifted
1 cup flour, unbleached all-purpose
2 teaspoons baking powder
1/2 teaspoon nutmeg
1/2 teaspoon cinnamon
1/4 teaspoon salt

Instructions

In one bowl, beat the egg thoroughly, then add the milk, sugar, melted butter, and mashed potatoes. In a separate bowl, sift together the flour, baking powder, nutmeg, cinnamon, and salt. Add the dry ingredients to the wet, mixing well until you have a smooth consistency.

Using a cookie scoop, drop walnut-sized portions of batter into small muffin tins or your donut maker, and bake at 365 degrees F for 9–11 minutes, or until golden brown.

Yield: 8–12 small donuts.

CHAPTER 4

As soon as Grace and the chief were gone, I dashed inside my best friend's house and packed a small bag with a change of clothing and some makeup. There was no reason she couldn't look presentable, and I knew for a fact that some of Grace's confidence came from looking and dressing well. If it helped her, why not indulge the act? She could use every bit of self-esteem that she could muster at the moment.

I locked the door on my way out, and then hurried over to the donut shop to check in with Nan before I took off. I wasn't at all certain what I was expecting to find, but seeing the place full of happy customers hadn't been one of the thoughts passing through my mind.

Nan finished with her last customer, and then turned to me. "Back so soon?"

"Just stopping in, actually. Is everything okay here?" I asked.

"Better than that. Folks love your new donut, Suzanne. It's a real hit."

I'd forgotten all about my new creation, and nodded absently at the news. "That's nice. Listen, I hate to do this to you, but I've got a friend who needs me. I know it's lousy timing, and you have every right to say no, but would you mind watching the shop a little longer?"

"Go, don't worry about a thing here. We close at eleven, right?"

"I'll be back long before that," I said hastily.

"Don't worry if you can't make it. Everything is under control here."

I was suddenly very glad that I had Nan in my corner. I knew that I'd always miss Emma and the drama of her ever-changing love life, but it wasn't the worst thing in the world having someone a little older at the shop now who had a calmer perspective about everything.

I parked my Jeep in the ER parking lot, but I had a tough time finding Grace once I was there. I was starting to panic when my friend Penny Parsons saw me. Dressed in her disheveled scrubs, she looked as though she'd had a rough shift nursing, but it didn't stop her from smiling when she saw me.

"Suzanne Hart, what brings you to my corner of the woods?"

"I'm here looking for Grace Gauge," I said. Penny and I had shared some rough times lately, but we were back on solid ground now, something I was extremely grateful for.

"Why would she be here? Did something happen to her?" Penny asked, concern evident on her face.

"Not exactly," I answered. "She's here with Chief Martin so they can get a splinter removed from her hand."

"How bad is it?" Penny asked, clearly confused by my reply.

"The splinter? It's barely there. The mess she's in? I'm afraid it's quite a bit worse than that." I didn't want to go into much detail where idle ears could overhear our conversation. "It's a long story, and I'll tell you all of it sometime, but now I'm here with some clothes for her. I'm guessing that your shift is over, but is there someone I could ask for help tracking her down?"

Penny smiled. "Don't worry, this won't take a second. Stay right here."

She went to the front information desk, and then tapped a few keys on the computer before frowning and looking back at me.

"What is it?" I asked.

63

"Let me make a quick call first," she said.

Penny was on the phone for over a minute, and then finally hung up and walked back over to me.

"She's still here, isn't she?" I asked. Had the police chief already taken her away?

"Yes, but Chief Martin told me that I should tell you to leave the clothes with me, and he'd collect them shortly." She made no move to take the bag from my hands.

"We both know that I'm not doing that, though, don't we?" I asked with a smile.

"How could I take them, when I'm not still here?" Penny returned, with a wicked grin of her own. "Someday you really will have to tell me what this is all about."

"I've got a feeling you'll find out pretty soon without hearing it from me," I answered. "Thanks, Penny."

"What are friends for? I was glad to do it. Good night, Suzanne."

"Good night," I said, though it was just past eight in the morning. I thought I kept odd hours until I realized how many varying shifts Penny worked. At least my schedule was consistent from day to day.

Chief Martin came out ten minutes later, looking around for Penny.

When he saw me, he didn't exactly smile, but then again, he didn't run off in the other direction, either.

"Where's Penny?" he asked.

"She had to go," I replied. "Where do you have Grace stashed? I need to give her these clothes."

"Don't worry about it, Suzanne. I'll take them to her," he said as he reached for the bag.

I wasn't about to let them go, though. "Hang on a second. Is there a reason I can't talk to her myself?"

He was clearly getting exasperated with me, but I had to give him credit. He managed to hold it in check. "Suzanne, she's fine, but you can't go back in the restricted area where we're keeping her. We just recovered the splinter, so as soon as she gets dressed, I'm taking her to my office. There's nothing you can do here."

"You don't honestly believe that she killed him, do you?" I asked, fighting to keep my voice quiet.

He wouldn't commit to it, though. "Like I said, it's too early to say anything. Now, can I have her things? I thought you had a donut shop to run."

"Nan's handling it," I said. "How do you know her, by the way?"

He just shrugged. "Ask her if you want to know."

65

"Why are you being so difficult all of a sudden?" I asked.

"I'm sorry if I'm curt, but I don't have time for this," he said, and held out his hand again. "I've got a murder to solve. Now, if you want Grace to have that bag, hand it over. Otherwise, she can stay in her bathrobe until we're finished. I don't care much either way right now."

He wasn't bluffing; I could see it in his eyes. I gave him the bag, and as he walked away, I said, "Tell her to call me as soon as you're finished with her."

He didn't answer me, so at least it wasn't an outright rejection.

I thought about all of the things I could do just then, but then I realized that there was only one place I needed to be.

It was time to go back to Donut Hearts and see if Nan was still handling my shop without a bit of help from me, or if the sky was falling in on her in my absence.

I honestly wasn't sure which outcome I was hoping for. After all, I wanted to feel needed in my own place.

The shop was crowded when I walked in, but Nan didn't seem the least bit flustered. She smiled at me as she cheerfully waited on her next customer, and I moved in closer and stood just behind her. When she finished that order, I tapped her on the shoulder and said, "Thanks, Nan. I can take over now."

"Are you sure? I don't mind, honestly."

Her positive attitude about being in front was a real change of pace for me, since Emma hadn't been a big fan of waiting on customers, but I needed my work at the donut shop to get a little taste of normal back into my life. "Thanks, but I've got it. You're the best."

"It was nothing," she said as she stepped away and went into the kitchen, but I could see a slight grin on her face as she left.

"Who's next?" I asked, and started waiting on the rest of my customers.

Once there was a lull, I opened the kitchen door and called out, "Nan, do you have a second?"

"Of course," she said as she dried her hands on a dish towel and joined me. She nearly had the morning dishes finished, and I was really impressed with her efficiency. "What can I do for you, Suzanne? Is there somewhere else you need to go? I'd be happy to take over again. All you have to do is ask."

"I've got it covered. I just wanted to thank

you again for pitching in. I also want to assure you that this isn't going to happen very often."

"It was fun. Did you see the tray of samples I put out?"

I had to think about what she was talking about for a second, and then it hit me. "The orange and apple disasters. I remember."

"They were nothing of the sort," she said with a hint of reproach in her voice. "I hope you don't mind, but I took the liberty of naming them Orange and Apple Surprise."

"I don't mind one bit," I said. The only surprise to me was that anyone could choke a bite down, but maybe I'd been wrong. As shocking as it sounded, it had happened before, and probably would again. "Folks really liked them?"

"Well, not your crowd," she admitted, "but mine was delighted with them."

I had to smile at her description. "Funny, I didn't even know that I was part of a crowd. Do you mean brunette donut makers, or divorced women in their thirties who own their own businesses?"

Nan blushed a little, and I felt bad for teasing her after she'd stepped up and helped me out. I put a hand on her arm as I said, "I'm just having a little fun with you. I know what you meant. So, do you really think we should add them to the menu?"

"You'd do that, just on my word? That's so kind of you, Suzanne. Everyone told me how nice you were, but you're even sweeter than I imagined."

"Sweeter than those donuts?" I asked with a grin.

"Yes, of course," she replied, not getting the fact that I was joking around with her again. Emma would have laughed if I'd said it to her, I just knew it. Well, I couldn't expect them to be identical. Each had her own strengths and weaknesses, and I knew that I'd have to learn about Nan's quirks. I made a mental note to back off on my jokes, but I wasn't sure that I'd be able to do it. I had a habit of saying something if I thought it was amusing, and I knew that I couldn't stop completely, but if I could cut the quips in half, we might just make it.

I heard the door open, and I turned back to the front of the donut shop to wait on my next customer. Finally, someone I was truly happy to see.

"Mr. Mayor, may I buy you a donut and a coffee?"

George Morris, one of my true friends, smiled at me as he put a hand on the counter. He'd been walking with a cane since his accident, but this was the first time

I'd seen him out and about without even a hint of his former limp. "I'd love both, but I'm afraid that I'll have to pay for them. I can't take freebies anymore, Suzanne. I have to think about how it would look."

"Wow, being mayor isn't all that it's cracked up to be, is it?" I asked as I got him a coffee and a plain cake donut. Unless he told me otherwise, this had become George's favorite late-morning snack, and it was a rare day he didn't make it into the donut shop since he'd been elected.

"Well, I didn't exactly campaign for the job, so I didn't know what I was getting myself into," he said with a grin.

"Everyone's happy with the job you've done so far," I said.

"Well, Cam Hamilton didn't exactly set the bar very high, did he?"

"No, not so much," I said, remembering the former mayor for a moment, and then doing my best to forget about him.

As George paid for his order, I asked, "How's it going, seriously? Do you like being in charge of everything that happens in April Springs?"

"Don't kid yourself," George said as he took a seat by the bar where we could talk while I waited on other customers. "Most of the time I'm forced to act like a recess

70

monitor in grade school. I never knew how petty some grown adults could be, but I'm finding out."

"Well, I heard there was at least one perk," I said slyly.

"What, being the grand marshal at the Christmas parade? When you think about it, it really isn't much of a perk."

"I'm talking about Polly North, and you know it." Polly was a retired librarian who was now the mayor's receptionist. She'd done the job for Cam, and George had asked her to stay on to lend him a hand. If the rumors floating around town were true, the two of them were becoming more than just coworkers, though, and I only hoped that the whispers were true. They both deserved a little happiness in their lives.

"Polly is a valuable member of my team," George said. As I studied him a little closer, I could swear that I saw him blush a little.

"Is that all she is to you?" I asked with a grin.

He shook his head. "Suzanne, I don't have time for this nonsense. The reason I came by was to discuss what happened over there." As he said it, he gestured toward the Boxcar. Crime scene tape was still all around it, and it appeared that Trish wouldn't be opening in time for dinner, let

71

alone for her lunch crowd, something that I knew must have been killing her. It sounded harsh in my mind even as I thought it, but I was a little glad that Peter hadn't gotten himself killed in front of the donut shop. Not only could I not afford the bad press, but the karma wouldn't be good, either. I'd had enough dead bodies associated with my donut shop to last me a lifetime, and if I never stumbled across one again for as long as I lived, I would be just fine with that.

"Have you heard something?" I asked George as I walked over to him. I noticed that a few other folks in the shop were listening as well, but there was nothing I could do about that.

He shrugged. "It's an active police investigation, so I've tried to stay out of it, but if you want me to ask a few questions, I will. After all, what good is it to have a friend in the mayor's chair if you can't take advantage of it now and then."

"I appreciate the offer, but it's fine, really," I said. "Don't do anything on my account."

He wasn't about to accept that, though. He did look a little hurt as he explained, "Suzanne, don't dismiss me so quickly. I've got some real power now."

"That's just it," I said softly as I patted his hand. "I don't want to spoil your time in office by asking for favors. It wouldn't look right."

George appeared to consider that, and then he nodded solemnly. "I confess that I didn't think about it that way," he admitted. "Surely there's something I can do, though."

"Grace is involved up to her neck, so I'm going to help her clear her name. If we can think of something you can do that won't interfere with your job, I'll call you. Do we have a deal?"

"We do," George said, as Wayne Johnson came into the donut shop.

"Can I help you, Wayne?" I asked.

"No, but he can," he answered as he pointed to George. "What about that NO PARKING sign for my loading dock? When are you going to get around to it?"

"Wayne, I told you before. Those things have to go through the town council, and I only get one vote out of seven."

"Cam could have done it on his own," Wayne grumbled. "He wasn't afraid to throw his weight around. Why are you?"

"Because I play by the rules, for you, and for everyone else."

Wayne was clearly unhappy with that response. "So, you're telling me that if Suzanne here had a problem you could fix,

73

you wouldn't jump all over it, as close as the two of you are?" He hesitated, then turned to me and added, "No offense intended, Suzanne."

"None taken," I said, "mainly because I would never let the mayor do something he shouldn't just to make my life easier. Can you say the same thing, Wayne?"

He wasn't sure how to take that, and I could see him mulling it over in his mind. After a few seconds, a grin broke out on his face, and he said, "Well, it would be hard to do that with a straight face after what I just said." He slapped George on the back, and I could see my friend wince a little at the hard impact. "Forget what I said, Mayor. I'll be at the next council meeting and present my case just like everyone else. I've at least got your vote, right?"

George nodded. "If it's the same proposal you showed me last week, you do."

"That's good enough for me, then," Wayne said, and he left without buying so much as a single donut hole.

I looked at George and asked, "Is it always like this?"

"I swear, some days I don't even want to leave the office."

I grabbed a paper cup and filled it to the brim with more coffee. "Here you go. Refills are on the house, for you and everyone else."

He nodded. "Thanks for that." Before he stood, George leaned toward me and whispered, "Suzanne, I meant what I said."

"I know you did," I answered. "And I can't tell you how much I appreciate it."

George stood, steadying himself as he did, and then walked out with his coffee. I felt a little responsible, at least by proxy, for his new position, since my mother had steamrollered him into it, but I had to admit, it was good for him, and there was no doubt in my mind that George was going to be exactly what we needed in April Springs.

It was finally eleven, but I hadn't heard from Grace yet. I was getting worried as I locked the front door, but when my cell phone rang, I grabbed it quickly, hoping to hear what was going on with her. I didn't even look at my caller ID when I answered it.

"Grace? Are you okay?"

"It's me. What's wrong with Grace?" Jake asked.

"Jake, it's great to hear your voice. How are you? How's the case going?"

"Not great," he admitted. "It feels like everyone in town wanted this guy dead, and I'm having a tough time narrowing my suspect list down to one page. How does one man make so many enemies in one lifetime?"

I knew a little bit about the case he was working on. "He owned half the town, right?"

"More like most of the county," Jake admitted.

"There you go," I answered. "Money can cause more problems than it solves."

"Suzanne, answer my question. What happened to Grace?"

I took a deep breath, and then I asked, "I don't suppose there's any way we can postpone this conversation to another day, is there?"

I heard him laugh, but there wasn't a lot of joy in it. "Do I really even need to answer that question?"

"No, I know you. You'll find out in a few minutes if you don't hear it from me, so I might as well tell you myself. Someone killed Peter Morgan by the Boxcar Grill, and Chief Martin's been questioning Grace about it all morning."

There was enough silence on the other end of the line that I began to worry that we'd lost our connection. "Jake? Are you still there?"

"I'm here," he answered.

"You got awfully quiet," I said.

"I was just considering the possibilities," he replied, and I could hear the state police investigator in his voice. "Do you need me there? I might be able to pull a few strings and get out of this case if you want me there with you."

"It's sweet of you to offer, but for now, maybe you should just stay right where you are."

After another long pause, he replied cautiously, "The more I think about it, the more I believe you just might be right."

I was sensing a trend here that I didn't like. "Jake, you don't think Grace actually killed him, do you?"

"Suzanne, I don't have any of the facts about the case. How could I have an opinion?"

"Because you know Grace," I answered. "What's your gut tell you?"

"That I don't have enough information. I know that you love Grace like a sister, and I'm just about as fond of her myself, but you know my theory. Given a hard enough push, anyone can commit murder. Anyone."

I knew on a rational level that Jake felt that way, but I didn't want him to be a cop right now; I wanted him to be my boyfriend. "Okay, stop being an investigator and start being the man who loves me. Now, what do you think?"

"She didn't do it, and I'll do everything in my power to help you prove just that," he answered without even hesitating.

"That's better," I said.

"You know what I said before was true as well, though, right?"

I grinned, and I was certain that he had to be able to hear it in my voice. "Let's not spoil the moment, okay?"

He laughed genuinely, a sound I'd grown to love. "Got it. Call me if you uncover anything, and Suzanne, do me a favor, okay?"

"What's that?"

"Somebody killed Peter, and they aren't going to be pleased when the two of you start poking around into what happened."

"What makes you think we're going to investigate?" I asked as innocently as I could manage.

"Oh, I don't know, maybe based on your past behavior?" he asked, and I could almost hear the smile in his voice.

"I never go looking for trouble," I said, trying to defend myself.

"But it still manages to find you, doesn't it? I meant what I said. Don't take any chances with this. It could get bad in a hurry."

"Don't worry. We'll be careful," I said.

"Good. It took me too long to get you into my life. I'd hate to start over now."

"That makes two of us," I said.

I was about to add something else when I saw Grace walking up to the donut shop. "Grace is here. I've got to go."

" 'Bye," I heard him say as I shut my phone.

I was finally going to hear what Grace had been through, and maybe we could come up with a plan together to clear her name.

CHAPTER 5

"Grace, are you okay?" I asked as I threw the door open and let her in. She looked like she was about to cry, and from the look of her reddened eyes, I imagined that she'd shed more than a few tears already today.

"I'm managing, and that's the most I can hope for, right?" she asked as she stepped into the shop.

I locked the door behind her just as Nan came out front.

"I thought we closed at eleven," Nan said as she spied Grace, and it wouldn't be too hard to see that something was wrong. "I'm sorry, I didn't mean to interrupt."

"You're fine," I said. I needed some time alone with Grace, so I added, "Why don't you go ahead and take off? I'll finish the dishes, balance the register, and then I'm getting out of here myself."

"The kitchen's already clean," she reported. "All I have out here yet to be

80

washed are the trays and a few mugs."

"I can easily take care of the rest myself. You did great work, Nan," I said. "You deserve a bonus for what you did today."

She looked pleased by the praise. "Please, it was nothing. I'll see you in the morning." Nan pulled off her apron, then nodded to Grace as she left, but I wasn't certain my best friend had even seen her.

Once the door was locked, Grace looked at the large front window open to all of Springs Drive.

"What are you going to do about that?"

I honestly hadn't given it much thought, though I knew that I should. "I'm working on it."

Grace nodded absently. "Could we talk in back, Suzanne?" she asked. "It's so public out here, I feel as though I'm on display."

"Absolutely."

As we walked toward the kitchen, I saw her looking at the leftover donuts. "Grace, have you had anything to eat today?"

"There wasn't a chance," she admitted.

"Then let's grab you some donuts and coffee. Would you like anything in particular?"

"I'm so hungry, I'm not all that picky," she said, and then must have realized how it sounded. "You know what I meant."

81

"No apologies needed," I said as I grabbed her three donuts and a large mug of coffee. Grace was usually a very careful eater, limiting herself to a single donut on rare occasions, but I knew that she could use a boost right now, and I happened to sell them in my shop. I carried her donuts in back, and we took up the stools I kept there for the rare occasions I had company in the kitchen of the donut shop.

I waited until she'd eaten two donuts, and then asked, "How bad was it?"

She sat there in silence for ten seconds, and then admitted, "Honestly, it's all a blur right now. I can't believe Peter's gone, but it's even worse having folks think that I had something to do with it."

"No one thinks that, Grace," I said, doing my best to reassure her.

"What did I say last night? Don't lie to me, Suzanne. Just about everyone who isn't in this room right now thinks so."

I ticked off on my fingers as I said, "I know George believes you, I'm certain Momma does, and Jake even offered to drop the case he's working on and come here to help us find the real killer."

"Wow, that's sweet of him. Okay, I have three allies in the town I grew up in. That's better than I hoped."

"You have more than that," I said. "Just wait. You'll be amazed by how many people are going to be willing to support you."

"And even more surprised by how many want to stick a knife in my back the second I turn around," she added.

"Hey, don't dwell on the negative. I need you at your best if we're going to find whoever killed Peter."

"That's the real reason that I'm here. Are you sure you don't mind helping me?" she asked.

"Grace, I would do anything for you; you should know that." I loved that we were finally going to do something about this. Peter had been dead less than twenty-four hours, but I felt as though we'd been fighting the stigma of his murder for weeks. "We need to make a plan first, and then we can get started. First off, do you have any ideas about who might want to see Peter dead?"

She looked saddened by the question. "That's just it. I don't get it. I can't think of anyone who would want to kill him."

I looked into Grace's eyes, and it seemed as though she honestly believed it. I knew that Peter could be charming when it suited his purposes, but I also realized that there had to be a great many people who weren't all that fond of him. "This is important. I know how you felt about him, but you need to look at this as objectively as you can."

"Where do I even start?" she asked. The tears started for a second, but she quickly stopped, wiping her eyes as she looked at me.

"Well, you said you found out he was seeing Leah Gentry. I'd say she's as good as anyone to consider as a possible suspect."

Grace didn't even pause to think before she spoke. "Leah might be a snake, but I can't see her killing him. I can't imagine *anyone* hating him enough to do it."

We weren't getting anywhere. "Grace, maybe I should do this on my own. I've got the feeling that your heart's not in it. I understand completely, but if you want me to investigate, I can't keep worrying about how you're going to react to every suggestion I make. We have to both treat this as dispassionately as we can."

"I can do that, Suzanne," she insisted.

"I'm sorry, but I'm not so sure that you can." They were tough words to say, but we had to hash this out right now before I was going to get myself involved in another murder investigation. It was just too risky to do it halfway, so unless I had free rein, with a little help from my friends, I wasn't sure I could do it.

"Leah could have killed him," Grace said with a nod. "Especially if she thought he was dumping her for me. I know most folks think she's harmless, but she's pretty tough, too. If he broke her heart, she might want to see him dead."

"Okay," I said. "That's good. Now, who else do we have?"

Grace took time to ponder my question now, and after a full minute, she said, "Suzanne, I'm not a big fan of gossip and rumors, but I've heard talk behind my back about Peter when we were with some of his so-called friends. It turned out that he wasn't the angel I might have made him out to be in my mind."

"I'm listening," I said, and I grabbed a pen and an old order pad.

The first thing I did was jot Leah's name down, and beside it I wrote "Scorned Love."

When I stopped writing, Grace said, "Well, Peter's brother, Bryan, has to go on our list. The two of them never got along, that was no secret, but there was more animosity between them than I realized at first. Bryan confronted Peter once when we were out on a date in Hickory, and I thought the two of them were going to come to blows in the street, it got so bad."

That was interesting. "Were they fighting

about anything in particular?"

"From what I could tell, it was all about money," Grace admitted.

I kept waiting for her to add more, and after a minute of silence, she said, "When their grandfather died, Peter was the executor for the estate. Bryan claimed that Peter used that as an excuse to gut the inheritance of everything valuable, and then split the little bit that was left with him. It was supposed to be over two hundred thousand dollars when all was said and done."

That kind of money would make a good motive for murder in a great many people's eyes. "Was there any truth to it?"

Grace just shrugged. "Peter admitted to me later that he took more than his share, but only after his brother threatened to take him to court over a new truck their grandfather had just bought. Bryan thought Peter should pay it off, and then sign it over to him, but Peter wouldn't do it."

"Why would he, if it was part of the estate?"

"From the way it was explained to me, it didn't make any sense to me, either, but that's what Peter told me, and at the time, I believed him."

I added Bryan Morgan's name to our list, and put "Money and Bad Blood" after it.

"Who else should we add?" I asked.

"Honestly, Suzanne, there's no one else I can think of," she said as she drained her coffee. "I'm getting more. Would you like some?"

"No thanks, I'm good."

Grace went up front to refill her mug, and I started thinking about motives folks had for murder in general. Unfortunately, I'd run across a few cases in the past, and it all seemed to boil down to a handful of reasons like love, greed, and envy. The list didn't cover everything, but it was a good place to start.

When Grace came back into the kitchen, I asked, "I've been curious about something for quite a while. What exactly did Peter do for a living?"

"He said he was in investments, but I could never really pin him down beyond that. Whenever I tried, he always said that he liked to keep his business life separate from his personal life, and like a fool, I trusted him."

That was interesting. "Did he work alone, or did he have a partner? I know he was out of town on business quite a bit lately."

Grace looked as though she wanted to cry again, but she held back her tears, and I was proud of her for the way she was handling my line of questioning. I knew that it had to be tough on her, but I couldn't pull any punches just because she was my friend. Especially not because of that.

"I'm beginning to wonder if that was true at all," she finally admitted. "There's a good chance he was just using it as an excuse to see someone else without having to constantly lie to me about what he was doing and where he was going. I'm beginning to wonder if there was anything he told me that was true."

I hated being in a position to defend a man I hadn't liked, but he hadn't been completely rotten. "No matter what else he did, he clearly cared about you," I said.

"Do you believe that?"

"I do," I said. "Peter may not have been perfect, but he showed excellent taste when he started going out with you."

"Why doesn't that give me any comfort?" she asked.

"Give it time; it might offer you some somewhere down the road. Now, let's focus on my last question. Did he have a business partner?"

"I'm not sure you could call him that, but Peter did talk to a man named Henry Lincoln quite a bit on the phone, and it always sounded like it was business to me."

"Do you happen to know where he lives?" I asked as I jotted his name down on our list.

"Union Square, I think," she said.

I looked over the three names we had listed, and realized that we had covered quite a bit of ground. There were three solid suspects we could interview, and there was no time like the present to get started. "Are you up for a little question-and-answer session with these folks?"

She nodded. "I'm ready."

"Okay, but we need to clear something up first. You need to hold back and not say anything when I'm interviewing these people. I need for them to not suspect that I'm grilling them, and besides, you might be able to pick up on something I miss if you stay neutral."

"I'm not going to do anything to rile anyone up," she said.

"I hope not. Remember, if any one of them senses that we're actively investigating Peter's murder and not just being friendly and chatting with them about someone we all knew, we're not going to get a thing out of them." Grace frowned a little, so I added, "Are you sure that this isn't going to be too tough on you?" The last thing I wanted to do was put my friend through something that might not be productive at all, and just end up causing her even more pain.

"I'm sure," she said. "I hate the way that Peter was treating me behind my back, but I cared for him, maybe even loved him before I found out the truth. Suzanne, I need to figure out what happened to him, and why." She hesitated for a moment, and then added, "To be honest with you, in a way, I feel responsible for what happened to him."

I was shocked to hear her say that. "Just because you broke up with him? He was cheating on you, Grace. You need to remember that. Nothing that happened to that man was your fault."

Grace shook her head, and then took a moment before she spoke. "If I'd handled things better with him he might not have gotten drunk and put himself in a position where he was vulnerable to being attacked."

"You had every right to end your relationship with him," I said, doing my best to reassure her. "You know that, don't you?"

"On one level, I suppose I do. But in my heart, I can't really be sure until I find out why Peter was murdered. If it's not because of me, I can let it go."

"And if we discover that your worst fears are true and it *was* directly related to your breakup? What happens then?"

She shivered for a few seconds, and then Grace said, "Then I'll deal with it, and do my best to move on. At least then I'd know one way or the other. Sometimes I think it's the mystery of it that's tearing me up so bad."

"Then let's go find out who did it," I said.

As we left Donut Hearts, I asked, "It's your call. Who would you like to tackle first?"

She pointed down the street to the hardware store. "I know that neither one of us is a big fan of Burt Gentry, but there's no use putting it off. We need to speak with Leah, and she just happens to be the closest one of our suspects."

I looked around at the casual shoppers on Springs Drive and realized that though my work was finished for the day, quite a few shops were still open for business. It wouldn't do to have too big an audience when Grace and I spoke with Leah, though. I didn't want to have to censor my questions, and more important, I didn't want Leah filtering her replies just because of who might be standing close by. Public opinion could turn on a dime sometimes in our little town, and if Leah was innocent, we would be putting her in a position where she'd have to defend herself to everyone who walked into the hardware store, whether she was the murderer or not.

"You know what? I'm worried that the hardware store might be crowded at this time of day. We could always wait outside for her to take her break," I said.

Grace shook her head. "I understand why you're worried, but honestly, if we delay this for even ten minutes, I might lose my nerve. Let's go, Suzanne. We can worry about the consequences later."

"If you're sure, then I'm ready."

"Lead on," she said.

"Good afternoon," Leah Gentry said automatically when we walked into the hardware store, even adding a smile as she said it. But that vanished quickly enough when she realized who we were. At least there weren't too many customers nearby to listen in on our conversation.

"Got a second?" I asked, trying to be as upbeat as I could. I wanted to do my best to put her at ease. It might be the only way we'd get anything out of her.

Leah looked as though she wanted to turn and run away, but it was clear that she had a job to do, so she really didn't have much of a choice. "Actually, I'm kind of busy right now," she said.

I looked around and saw that the front was nearly empty. I decided not to point that out to her, though. "This won't take long. We just want to speak with you about Peter Morgan."

"Would you keep your voice down?" Leah asked, looking toward the back where her uncle's office was located.

"Burt doesn't know that you were seeing Peter Morgan, does he?" I asked. So far, Grace was keeping quiet. I just hoped she'd be able to stick to it and not butt in.

It was a direct hit. "My personal life isn't anybody's business but my own," she said, a little too defiantly for my taste.

"It might have been before, but a man's been murdered, one you were known to be seen with around town. I think your uncle might find that interesting in and of itself."

I started for the office, but Leah put a hand on my arm. "You can't do that."

"Sure I can," I answered, keeping my voice cheery. "Leah, there's something you need to understand. I'm talking to someone here today. It's your choice. Is it going to be you, or your uncle?"

"You need to focus on your friend there. She was the one dating him," Leah said as she pointed to Grace.

"We've already discussed that," Grace said. I could tell she wanted to say more, but she kept her cool, something I was very grateful for.

"Last chance," I said as I pulled away from her and started for the back.

Leah glanced at the clock on the wall, and then said, "Meet me by your shop in ten minutes. I'm due for a break then, and we can talk in private."

"You're not trying to get rid of us, are you?" I asked.

She sounded frustrated as she explained, "I'll talk to you both, but it's going to be on my terms."

I thought about pushing her a little harder, but then I decided that it wasn't that important to me to win every battle. "You've got ten minutes. In eleven, I'm coming back here, and you won't be happy with the way I act, trust me."

She gave me a wicked look for a split second as Grace and I walked out, but I didn't care. I'd gotten under her skin and had found a pressure point I could use to get her to talk to me, and I was going to make use of it. It might not make me popular with her, but I couldn't worry about that at the moment.

Grace and I waited outside by Donut

94

Hearts, and as I looked at my watch every thirty seconds, Grace said, "Don't worry. She'll be here."

I was beginning to have second thoughts about leaving Leah at the hardware store, so Grace's encouragement was welcome. "What makes you so sure?"

"She puts on a brave front, but she's afraid of Burt, and I doubt she'd welcome any new source of irritation between them if she can help it."

"What do you know about it?" I asked as I watched a handful of birds fly in and out of a nearby maple tree. Was there a nest there? From the air traffic, I wondered if there was more than one.

"Let's just say that I've heard that he doesn't approve of the way she conducts her personal life. I'm not exactly his biggest fan, but even I don't blame the man. He's worked hard to build up the family business, and he doesn't want any scandals threatening it. I'm willing to bet that Leah's going to do everything in her power to appease him now that her actions have bitten her on the tail."

I looked at my watch again, and saw that Leah had one more minute left on my deadline.

I started walking toward the hardware

store, and Grace looked perplexed. "Is her time really up?"

"She's got one minute," I explained, "but I plan to cross that threshold the second the clock runs out on her," I said.

"Do you really think that Burt will be able to tell us anything if Leah won't talk to us?" Grace asked.

"I don't know, but I'm not letting Leah get away with lying to me like that. If I have to take Burt's abuse, so be it, but I meant what I said. Someone's going to answer for her behavior. I demand satisfaction."

"Get in line," Grace said.

"I didn't mean it that way," I said, sorry for my choice of words. It had to be hard for Grace to do what we were doing, especially without complaint.

She shook her head briefly. "I'm the one who's sorry. I'll try to keep quiet, but I can't make any promises."

"I don't blame you a bit. Let's keep poking around and see what we come up with."

I took a deep breath, checked my watch one last time, and saw that Leah's deadline had officially passed.

Was she still in the hardware store, or had she skipped out the back way to avoid us completely?

CHAPTER 6

Burt was at the register reading a magazine about guns when we walked into the hardware store, and he didn't look all that surprised to see us.

"Where's Leah?" I asked.

"Why do you want to see her?" Burt asked, not even trying to be cordial.

"We have some unfinished business to discuss," I replied.

"Sorry, but she's gone," he said as he turned his attention back to the magazine. It was pretty clear that he wasn't sorry about it at all.

"She was supposed to meet us in front of the donut shop twelve minutes ago," I said. "Do you know if that's where she's headed?"

"Nope," Burt answered.

What was going on here? Was she honestly leaving me to talk to her uncle? What did she have to hide that was so bad she'd incur

Burt's wrath and lecturing? "Does that mean you don't know where she is, or are you saying that she's not going to meet us?"

Burt finally put his magazine down. "Suzanne, she's not here. That's really all that matters when it comes down to it, isn't it? Was there something else that I could help you with?"

I'd threatened to talk to Burt about his niece if she skipped out on me, but it had been an idle threat, or so I'd thought. I had no choice now, though. I had to follow through. "We're looking into the murder of Peter Morgan," I said, "and I just found out that your niece has been dating him in secret on the side."

Burt shook his head. "It never was much of a real secret." He glanced at Grace as he added, "I'm sorry about that, but I didn't have anything to do with her stepping out with him."

"It wasn't your fault," Grace said.

"No, but it was my niece's doing, and she knows better than to act that way. She was raised better."

"We really do need to talk to her," I pushed.

"Like I said, I can't do anything about that," Burt said.

"Well, if she won't talk to me, I'm guessing the police chief is going to want to have a word with her." I wasn't sure if Chief Martin knew about Leah's relationship with Peter, but if he didn't know at the moment, he was going to find out pretty quickly from me.

He shrugged. "What can I say? He can look for her all he wants to, but she's gone," he said. "I'm not exactly sure what I can do about that."

"Could you at least tell us where she might have gone?" Grace asked. "Please? It's important."

He pushed back a little from his seat. "Ladies, she needed a break from April Springs, and truth be told, I'm not exactly sure when she'll be coming back, and I'll tell the police chief the same thing if he comes by to ask about her."

"You sent her away, didn't you?" I asked, the hunch strong in my gut. "You didn't want your niece answering any of my questions, did you?"

Burt just smiled for a brief moment, and then he went back to his magazine, dismissing us completely. What was so fascinating about handguns and rifles to him, anyway? If Peter had been shot, I might consider it a clue, but anyone could have hit him in the back of the head with a piece of wood.

This was worse than useless. We left the hardware store, and for some odd reason, Grace was smiling. She held up her hand for silence as she dug into her purse, found a notepad, and jotted something down. When she was finished, she looked up at me. "I don't think we're going to need Burt's cooperation after all."

"Why do you say that?"

She showed me her pad, which now had three telephone numbers written on it.

"What's that?"

Grace explained, "While you were talking to Burt, I was memorizing the numbers displayed on the phone that was sitting on the counter in front of him."

That was news to me. No wonder she'd been so quiet at the end of the conversation. "I didn't know anything was displayed there. How on earth did you remember all three numbers?"

"That was what I was chanting to myself until I could write them all down. I hope they're right."

I nodded. "I'm sure they are. I'm just not certain they'll do us any good. He could have just as easily called three customers for all we know."

"Maybe, but I'm willing to bet that one of them gives us a clue as to where Leah is.

Should I dial them up and see?"

I stopped Grace just as she pulled her cell phone from her purse. "Hang on a second. You don't want to do that."

"Why not?" she asked.

"What if you're right and one of those numbers can tell us where Leah is? Do you really want your name and number displayed on one of those phones?"

She frowned as she put her phone away. "You've got a point, but what are we going to do? I haven't seen a pay telephone in donkey years, so it's going to be hard to call these numbers without them knowing who we are."

"I'm sure we'll think of something," I said.

"I've got it," Grace answered after ten seconds. "We'll give them to Jake and have him check them out for us."

"I'm not sure that we should do that just yet. I'm not about to drag Jake into this without more reason than that. He's got a case of his own he's trying to solve, remember? We're going to have to find another way to check these out."

She nodded. "Fine, but we need to come up with something quickly. When Leah ran like that, she went to the top of my suspect list; how about you?"

"She's definitely gotten my attention." I

hesitated, and then asked, "Was it me, or was Burt a little too happy about his niece's absence? I got the distinct impression that she left at his request."

"You weren't imagining it," Grace said. "He was clearly trying to protect her."

"From me, or the police?" I asked.

"I don't know."

"Make me a copy of those numbers, would you? I've got an idea."

Grace looked puzzled as she processed my request, but then she jotted them all down and handed the list to me. "You know you're not going to do any digging without me, right?"

"Trust me, I'm not trying to cut you out of the loop. I just needed these written on something I can pass along to someone else."

"Would you care to share with me exactly who this someone else might be?"

"I can do better than that," I said. "You can come along, too."

As we parked in front of city hall, Grace asked, "You're not going to ask George to do it, are you?"

"No, I told him we weren't going to involve him unless we had to. As far as I'm concerned, he and Jake are both off our list of resources. I do know someone else who might be able to help us, though." Instead of going to George's office upstairs, we made our way down the steps to the Board of Elections.

If anyone could find out who those numbers belonged to, it had to be Hillary Mast.

"What can I do for you, ladies?" Hillary asked as we walked into her office.

"We need your help," I said as I slid the list of numbers across the desk to her. "Is there any way you can tell us who has these phone numbers?"

She didn't even glance at the list, but instead kept watching us. "I have to ask you something first. Is this official city business?"

"No," I said. "It's just a favor for two friends."

Hillary frowned. "Well, I'm sorry, but I can't use city computers to help you."

I reached for the numbers as I said, "That's fine. Thanks anyway. We understand."

She stopped me before I could retrieve the list. "However, I was about to take my break, and no one tells me what to do when I'm on my own time." She reached down and brought up a notebook computer, opening it in one fluid motion. After a few moments, Hillary took the list, typed in the first number, and then said, "It will just take a second."

Grace looked at me. "I could have done that myself."

"But there's no need to," Hillary replied. "I'm doing it for you." She looked at the screen, and then said, "The first number belongs to Cutnip."

Why would Leah be talking to someone at the local beauty shop? I kind of doubted that Burt would call them unless he was looking for his new wife, but then again, I knew that Marge wasn't a big fan of Cutnip's identical styling results.

"What else do you have?" I asked.

Hillary didn't even have to type in the second number. As she looked at it, she said, "This one came directly from upstairs," she said, a little surprised.

"From any telephone in particular?"

"Unless I'm mistaken, and I know that I'm not, this is the mayor's direct phone number," she admitted.

Was George following up on the case himself, even though I'd asked him not to? Our next stop had to be upstairs so we could ask him, but there was one more number on the list.

"And how about the last one?"

Hillary punched the number in, and then said, "Whoever owns it is in Montview," she said. "Someone named Ida Belle. Here's the address," she said as she copied it down on the back of our original paper.

As she wrote, I asked, "I'm curious; is there some kind of secret database you can tap into to find those numbers?"

Hillary laughed. "It's called a reverse directory. It's amazing how much information is out there if you just know where to look. Is that all I can do for you?"

"Thanks, you've been a big help," I said.

"Posh, it was nothing," Hillary replied.

"I wouldn't say that. It's good for half a dozen donuts and a big cup of coffee, any time you want to come by to claim it."

Hillary laughed. "I've been offered a great many bribes over the course of my time here, but I have to admit, never donuts."

"More's the pity," I said. Then it hit me what she'd just said. "Hey, it's not a bribe. It's just the only concrete way I have to thank you for helping us."

"In that case, I'll see you tomorrow morning before work," Hillary said. She glanced at her watch, and then said, "If I hurry, I'll still have just enough time to eat lunch." She looked at each of us in turn, and then added, "All I have is a ham sandwich, but

I'd be glad to split it three ways if you'd care to join me."

"Thanks for the offer, but we're in kind of a rush," I said.

As we started for the door, she said, "Tell the new mayor I said hello."

"What makes you think that's where we're going?" Grace asked.

"Please, ladies, I'd be disappointed in you both if you weren't planning to see what that telephone call was all about. You *are* investigating the murder, aren't you?"

"We might do a little digging," I admitted.

"Well, I sincerely hope that you find Peter's killer. It's all rather unpleasant business, isn't it?"

"There's no doubt about it," I said.

As we headed up the steps to George's office, I told Grace, "I've never heard anyone refer to murder as unpleasant business before, have you?"

"It's a great deal worse than that, isn't it?" Grace asked. "Suzanne, we need to focus on the fact that we're doing this for a reason. I hated the way Peter and I left things, and now neither one of us will ever have the opportunity to make it right again between us. I'm not going to let a few roadblocks stop us."

"Grace, are you serious? Do you really believe that you might have gone back to him after he lied to you?" I asked, having a hard time buying it.

She thought about it before she answered, and when she finally did, the weight of the world was in her words. "I don't guess we'll ever know the real answer to that, will we? Suzanne, you forgave Max a great many things after you split up, remember?"

"I might have," I conceded, "but I never did manage to forgive his tryst with Darlene. I kicked him to the curb the moment I found them together, and I haven't looked back."

"And you can't ever see it in your heart to forgive him?" she asked.

"There's no reason to now. I've got Jake, and I'm happy," I said.

"But what if you didn't have him in your life and Max came knocking at your door?"

"I honestly can't say, but I'd have to guess that I doubt I would answer it. I'm sorry. I know some folks find a way in their hearts to forgive a cheating spouse. I just don't think that I'm one of them."

"I guess my point is that you can never say never, not as long as you both are still alive."

I didn't want to think about my marriage

to Max anymore.

We were at George's office in another two minutes, and I was surprised to see that Polly wasn't at her desk. George's door was ajar, and as I knocked, it swung open. George was sitting at his desk, with Polly leaning over his shoulder showing him something written on a piece of paper in front of them. They looked rather cozy together like that, but I knew better than to tease either one of them about it, and I had a hunch that Grace did as well.

Polly looked almost guilty as she stood up and moved away from the new mayor as though he were radioactive. "I have calls to make. Just let me know when you've signed them, sir."

"I keep telling you, it's George," my friend said.

"Not when you're in this office. I didn't agree with Cam Hamilton on a great many things, but I do believe the mayor should be treated with respect while he's sitting behind that desk." She turned to us and asked, "Is there something we can do for you?"

"We need a second with George, er, his honor," I said.

That was going to take some getting used to, but Polly had a point. George was already working hard for the folks of April Springs, and he deserved a little respect for it.

Polly turned to him and asked, "Is that acceptable, sir?"

"Sure, I have a minute," George conceded as he started to stand.

"But just that," Polly said. "You've got a zoning meeting downstairs, and you can't be late."

"Why not?" George asked.

"Because you're the one who's running it," she replied.

George nodded, and Polly left us.

The second she was gone, I asked, "You're not investigating Peter's murder on your own, are you?"

"What? Of course not. I told you that I wouldn't, and I meant it."

"Then why did you speak with someone at the hardware store today?" Grace asked.

"Hang on a second; it's bad enough following the logic behind one of your questions, let alone both of you together. Teaming up against me just isn't fair."

"The hardware store, George," I said flatly.

"I don't know why it's such a big deal. If you have to know, I needed a new washer for one of my faucets at the apartment, and they called me back to tell me that they'd have to order one special," he answered, clearly perplexed by the line of questioning.

"Did you speak with Leah, or Burt?" I asked.

George frowned for a second. "What is this about, Suzanne?"

"Trust me, it's relevant. We're interviewing suspects," I admitted.

"And you think I killed Peter?" he asked, clearly bemused by the very thought of it.

I shook my head. "Of course not."

He nodded, and added a smile as well. "I thank you both for that. Then you must believe that Burt might have done it."

"No, we were thinking more along the lines of Leah," I replied.

George shook his head. "Okay, you just lost me again. Why would she kill Peter? I just don't get it."

Grace answered him in a halting voice. "Not a great many folks know this, but they were dating on the side. If there was a rift between the two of them, she might have a motive for killing him."

"I'm sorry, I shouldn't have said that," George answered, slumping back down into his chair. "I didn't know."

"There's no reason you would," Grace said. "So, which one did you speak with?"

"It was Leah," he admitted.

"So, it was nothing about the murder, then?"

"No, sorry to disappoint you," George said. "Are you two sure you don't want my help?"

"You can't," I said as Polly walked back in.

"I'm sorry," she said as she tapped her watch, "but you really do have to go."

George nodded and stood again. "I have to go. Listen, if you two get yourselves in trouble, call me," he said as he walked out of his office.

We all watched him go, and then Polly said, almost to herself, "I'm worried about him. He's working too hard."

"It's got to be a tough job," I said.

She looked at me as though she'd forgotten that I was there. "It can be, if it's done correctly. I'm afraid Cam let a great many things fall through the cracks during his tenure, and George is trying to fix them all himself overnight. I keep telling him it can't be done, at least not without a great deal more time than he's got, but he won't listen to me."

"He can be a stubborn man, but he's worth it," I said.

"I'm sure I don't know what you mean," she said, though I saw her cheeks redden slightly. "Now, if you'll excuse me, I've got to get back to work myself."

After we left city hall, I pointed to the hair salon. "We're this close. We might as well see why someone at the hardware store called them."

We didn't even have to go inside to ask. As we got to the front door of the beauty salon, Marge Gentry nearly knocked us over as she walked out.

"Hi, Marge. How are you?" I asked. Things had been dicey between us since I'd treated her like a murder suspect, and though she claimed that she'd forgiven me, I wasn't sure that was entirely true.

"Suzanne. Grace," she replied curtly as she tried to brush past us.

"How have you been?" I asked, refusing to move so that she'd have to talk to me.

"Fine," she replied.

How was I going to be able to stop her long enough to see if she'd just called her husband? I was still struggling for an answer when Grace said, "Your hair looks lovely today. Achieving that splendid look must take forever in a chair. Sometimes I wonder if it's worth looking so glamorous, don't you?"

I didn't know how she could compare

Marge to herself, and even more perplexing, Marge seemed to accept it at face value. "We do a great deal to look presentable, don't we?" As she said it, she shifted her glance to me. Hey, I was just a donut maker. There was no real reason to get glamorous, especially when Jake was away working a case. It was not the time to defend my style choices, though.

Grace asked, "Does Burt ever get impatient waiting for such perfection?"

I bit my tongue to keep from barking out a laugh, but Marge just smiled. "As a matter of fact, he called the parlor twice today wondering when I'd be finished. I keep telling him that looking nice takes time."

"He'll be happy enough when he sees the results," Grace said, and Marge hurried off to the hardware store with a smile.

"How did you do that?" I asked once she was gone.

"What, get that information out of her?"

"No, I'm talking about keeping a straight face the entire time you said those things," I admitted.

"Hey, I didn't lie. She looked nice, Suzanne. There's no harm in telling her that."

I just shook my head and smiled. "You really are a saleswoman at heart, aren't you?"

"Don't forget, I'm in the beauty business myself," she answered. "Making women look good is directly tied into my livelihood."

"I get it," I said. Grace had finally gotten tired of wasting her samples on me, since I was a minimalist kind of gal myself. Her makeup, on the other hand, was always expertly applied, to the point where I couldn't see that she was even wearing any. I suppose it had to be attributed to her skilled touch. If I wore that much makeup myself, I'd look like a recent graduate from clown college. At least Jake liked me just the way I was.

"So, we have one more name on our list to speak with today, and one more telephone number to investigate. Would you care to take a drive?"

Grace nodded. "It's the best lead we have about where Leah might have gone. Do you think it's just another routine part order from the hardware store, or are we going to uncover something about the girl herself this time?"

"There's only one way to find out," I admitted. A thought suddenly occurred to me. "Hey, isn't Montview near Spruce Pine?"

"It's just a few miles away," she said, and

then it dawned on her. "You want to see Jake while we're there, don't you?"

"It crossed my mind," I admitted. "Would you care?"

Grace thought about it a second, and then shrugged. "If we track Ida Belle down first, I don't see why we shouldn't pay your boyfriend a visit." After another moment, she added, "Why don't you see if you can track him down in Spruce Pine, and I'll tackle Ida myself."

"No, it can wait," I said.

"Don't you trust me, Suzanne?"

"You I'm fine with," I admitted. "It's the bad guys I'm not so sure about. I'd never be able to forgive myself if I let you go there alone and something happened to you. We've had close calls before, and we shouldn't push our luck if we don't have to."

"Okay, I'll admit that I'm happier if you go with me, but I wanted to make the offer."

I hugged her. "I appreciate that. If we find Jake, that would be great, but it's not why we're going to Montview. We need to see if this woman knows something about Leah that we don't."

"Do you think she might implicate her in the murder?" Grace asked as we got into her car and started driving.

"I honestly can't say, but I would like to cross her name off our list if we can. We've got a few other suspects to follow up on, but I have a feeling that Leah might be the key to this."

A TASTY CHILLED DONUT

The reference to chilled in this recipe name is to the time the donut spends in the refrigerator after the dough is created. Two hours may seem like a long time, but it allows all of the ingredients to blend well together, so I recommend that you don't skip this step. It produces a nice fried donut that's rich enough to be decadent without too much of the guilt, but they are donuts, after all, right?

Ingredients

Mixed
1 egg, beaten
1/2 cup sugar, white granulated
1/2 cup heavy cream
2 tablespoons butter, melted
1 teaspoon vanilla extract

Sifted
2 cups flour, unbleached all-purpose
1 teaspoon baking powder
1/2 teaspoon cinnamon
1/4 teaspoon nutmeg
A dash of salt

Instructions

In one bowl, beat the egg thoroughly, then add the cream, sugar, melted butter, and vanilla extract. In a separate bowl, sift together the flour, baking powder, cinnamon, nutmeg, and salt. Add the dry ingredients to the wet, mixing as little as possible as you go.

Cover and chill the dough in the refrigerator for two hours.

Roll the chilled dough out on a lightly floured surface 1/4 to 1/2 inch thick, then cut out donuts and holes with handheld cutter.

Fry the dough in hot canola or peanut oil (370 degrees F) for two to three minutes on each side. Drain, then top with powdered sugar immediately or let cool and ice.

Yield: 8–12 small donuts.

CHAPTER 7

"Are you sure this is the address Hillary gave us?" I asked as I looked at the house number we'd been hunting for in Montview.

"It says so right here," Grace said as she eased her car beside the property. It was a rundown place with chipping yellow paint all over the wood exterior. Weeds grew throughout the yard, and the once-white picket fence was now a dingy shade of gray from dirt and neglect. The only vehicle parked in the stone driveway was an old Chevy from the sixties with faded paint and bald tires, and I wasn't exactly sure that it even still ran.

"We need to be as polite as we can when we approach Ida," I said. "We're just here looking for information about Leah. Maybe this is another dead end, but it might be exactly what we're looking for. Once we find Leah, then we can start digging into the possibility that she killed Peter."

"Then I suppose there's no way to find out but to knock on the front door and ask for her," Grace said.

We climbed the porch steps together with more than a little trepidation, and I could swear I felt the entire structure sway with every footstep.

I knocked on the door, and then put on my bravest face.

No one answered.

I knocked again, this time louder, as Grace yelled, "We need to speak with you."

I was about to tell her that it was no use when a cherry-red Trans Am came racing from the back of the house and through the yard on the other side, nearly taking out a section of fence as it swept past us.

I only had a quick glance, but that was all I needed to see who was driving so recklessly.

We'd come hunting for Ida Belle, but instead, we'd found Leah.

Now if we could only catch up with her.

The girl surely liked to run, if our contact with her so far today was any indication.

"How fast should I go?" Grace asked as we tried our best to follow Leah down the pot-holed road. We'd both raced to Grace's car the second we realized that it was Leah driving, but by the time we got in and took off after her, there was no sign of the young woman anywhere.

"I don't even know which way to go," I admitted as I scanned all around us for any sign of her car. The Trans Am would have been tough to hide, but I didn't see it anywhere. It was clearly fast, and the driver obviously wasn't intimidated by the thought of getting a speeding ticket.

"You might as well just pull over," I said reluctantly as we hit Main Street. There wasn't a car like Leah's in sight, and I'd counted at least four different turns she could have taken in the time it had taken us to go after her.

"It's no use. There's no way we can find her now."

"I don't think it's as dire as all that. We still have Ida," I said. "Why don't we drive back there and see if she's at home? Maybe she'll be able to tell us why Leah ran away like that."

"Then again, maybe we should wait around here for a while," Grace suggested.

I didn't understand her line of reasoning at all. "Why would we do that? We can't give Ida the opportunity to get away, too."

Grace just shrugged. "Okay, if that's what you want, we can go back to Ida's right now.

I just thought you might like to see Jake for a second before we did that, though."

I looked to where she was pointing, and saw my boyfriend coming out of a diner called the Three B's.

"On second thought, you're absolutely right," I said with a grin as I jumped out of her car and hurried toward Jake, who still hadn't seen us.

I nearly knocked him down with my embrace, and after a long kiss, it took us both a second to catch our breaths before either one of us could talk.

"Jake, what are you doing in Montview?" I asked my boyfriend when we finally got untangled. "I thought you were working on a case in Spruce Pine."

"I was following up on a lead here, so I decided to have a quick bite while I had the chance. You haven't been stalking me, have you?" he asked with a grin.

"You should be so lucky," I answered with a smile of my own. "This is just serendipity at its finest."

He smiled that quick grin of his that I loved so much. "Seriously, what's going on?"

Grace had stayed in the car to give us some privacy, something I appreciated even more at the moment. "We're here following up on a lead about Peter's murder."

"All the way up in the mountains?"

I nodded. "We found out that Burt Gentry's niece was dating Peter on the side, along with who knows who else. We tried talking to her in April Springs earlier, but she ran out before we could make any progress. I got the distinct impression that Burt was behind her fleeing."

"And you two tracked her all the way up here," Jake said. "I'm curious about how you managed that."

It was time to confess. "When we realized that Leah had skipped out on us, we talked to Burt about where she might be. Grace saw the phone at the front desk at the hardware store, and the display showed the last three outgoing calls. One call was to Cutnip, another was to George's office, and the third led us up here to a woman named Ida Belle. When we knocked on her front door, Leah tore out past us in her Trans Am."

"I'm guessing that you didn't catch her in Grace's company car."

I shrugged. "We tried to follow, but she was too fast for us."

Jake nodded. "She's certainly not going out of her way to make herself look innocent, is she?"

123

"Not so far. Why else would she run?"

Jake chuckled softly. "Suzanne, you wouldn't believe some of the things that can make people bolt. Who knows why she ran off like that?"

"So, you don't think this makes her look at least a little bit guilty?"

He held up his hands in surrender. "I'm not saying that at all. You're right to keep after her. All I'm saying is don't assume anything. Get the facts, then figure out what they mean." He glanced at his watch, and then added, "I have half an hour before I need to meet up with one of my suspects. Would you like me to come with you to the house and flash my badge? It might just help loosen this woman's lips."

"You'd really do that for me?" I asked. Jake hadn't always been behind my impromptu investigations, but lately he'd become more supportive as he saw that I didn't take too many unnecessary chances, and that I was actually pretty good at what I did. I suppose there was also a chance that he was just appeasing his girlfriend, but whatever the reason, I was glad to have him in my corner.

"All you have to do is ask," he said. "I've got a stake in keeping you healthy, remember? The quicker you solve this case, the sooner you're out of danger from the killer."

I was tempted to take him up on his offer, but I hated to use Jake unless I really needed him, and I thought Grace and I could handle this, at least so far. "Thanks, I can't tell you how much I appreciate your offer, but I think we'll be okay, at least for now."

He nodded. "Good enough." There was none of the foolishness where he tried to talk me out of my position. That was one of the things I loved about Jake. He respected my opinion, and was always willing to accept my decisions, even if he didn't necessarily agree with them. I could tell that Jake was about to add something else when his cell phone rang. He glanced at the number, and then said quickly, "I'm sorry, but I've got to take this. I'll call you tonight, okay?" He kissed me briefly, and then answered his phone, still smiling at me. The news he got must not have been good, though, because his grin quickly faded into a frown. "I don't care what he thinks is going to happen, we're talking, and I mean right now."

I waved to him as I walked back to Grace's car and got in the passenger seat.

"That must have been a nice surprise," she said with a fleeting grin.

"For both of us," I said. "So, what do you

125

think? Should we keep searching around town for Leah's car, or should we go back to Ida Belle's house and see if we can get anything out of her?"

"I say we go to Ida's," Grace said. "You saw how fast Leah was driving. She could be in Tennessee by now. As much as I love this company car, there's no way we could catch her, even if we knew where she was going, which we don't."

As we drove back to Ida's house, Grace said, "It's really too bad Jake's working a case. It would be nice to have him with us."

"He offered," I admitted.

"And you didn't take him up on it?" Grace asked as she glanced over at me.

"I don't want to take advantage of him," I said. "You understand that, don't you?"

"Completely," she answered. "He's one of the good ones, isn't he?"

"I think so," I said. I reached over and patted her shoulder, and Grace looked at me again for a split second, but then she turned her attention back to the road. A great deal had gone unspoken between us in those few moments, but that was just one of the things I loved so much about our friendship. So much could go unsaid, but still be understood.

To my surprise, when we pulled back in

front of Ida's place, an older woman was out cutting the grass with an old-fashioned reel mower. My grandparents had used one when I was a kid, and I earned a dollar whenever I cut their grass. It was some of the hardest money I'd ever earned, though, since the gears were rusty and the blades were always dull.

I got out before she spotted us, with Grace quickly on my heels.

"You're Ida Belle, aren't you?" I asked as I approached her. The mower stopped suddenly, since it didn't rely on an engine to push it forward, but I'd still managed to sneak up on her.

"Why? Who are you?" she asked as she let the mower fall where it stood.

"I'm Suzanne Hart, and this is Grace Gauge. We're friends of Leah." I'd said it before I had a chance to think about the ramifications.

"That's a lie," Ida said flatly. She was an older woman wearing a faded housedress and worn slippers, not the most appealing attire I'd ever seen, and her hair was up in honest-to-goodness curlers that looked as though she'd had them at least fifty years. "Don't try to fool me. You two are the reason Leah ran away."

She started back toward her front door,

but I stepped in front of her before she could make it. I wouldn't stop her from going back inside, but I needed her to know that we weren't just going away. "We're here to help her if she's innocent of murder, not turn her over to the police."

"Murder?" Ida asked, stopping dead in her tracks. "Who said anything about murder?"

"Just out of curiosity, what exactly did Leah tell you when she showed up?" Grace asked.

"My niece told me that some crazy woman thought that she was seeing her boyfriend behind her back, and that she needed to lay low until things blew over," Ida replied. "Nobody said anything about murder. I'll kill Burt when I get my hands on him."

"You're his sister?" I asked.

"Yes, though I'm not exactly proud of it. Now, let's start over from the beginning. Who exactly was murdered?"

"My boyfriend, Peter Morgan," Grace said. At that moment, she got a little wobbly, and I reached out to steady her. Ida's harsh expression dissipated instantly, replaced by concern. "Dear child, you must be in real pain. Would you like to come inside? I've got fresh lemonade."

"That would be great," Grace said, and

we found ourselves being led into Ida Belle's home. I wasn't sure if Grace's attack had been sincere or planned, but either way, we were getting our audience with Ida Belle.

Inside was like stepping into a different world. The rooms were all clean and neat, decorated in a style older than I liked, but still a pleasant place to be. She must have noticed my reaction to her furnishings.

"I like a neat house," she said with a touch of a grin. "I had a young man who came around and did my yard work and kept things up outside, but he's gone away to college, and I can't find anyone to replace him."

That made me think of Emma, and I felt the hole where she'd been in my life again. "I understand completely. My assistant just left to go to school. It's tough, isn't it?"

"Mitch is a good boy," Ida said. "I honestly don't know how I'm going to manage without him." After a moment's pause, she said, "Now, let's see about that lemonade."

"Would you like some help in the kitchen?" I asked her.

"No, I can manage just fine by myself; thank you for asking, though."

Grace and I exchanged glances, but we didn't have time to talk. Ida popped back in the living room with three glasses and a pitcher full of glorious-looking homemade lemonade. After she'd poured and served for all of us, we tasted it together. It was the best lemonade I'd ever had in my life, and Momma made a mean batch herself from time to time.

"This is delicious," I said. "What's your secret?"

"I use real natural sugar instead of processed," she said happily. "It makes all the difference in the world."

I planned on passing that tip on to Momma myself.

Grace took another sip, and then said, "Thanks. I'm feeling better."

"I'm sorry for your loss," Ida said. "I don't know what happened to Leah, and I'm done making excuses for the girl. Until she was fifteen, she never gave any of us one lick of trouble, but as soon as she started getting interested in boys, that all changed. I've talked to that child until I was blue in the face, but nothing ever did any good."

I was about to ask her where Leah might be when my hand slipped as I was reaching for my glass, and I accidentally knocked it over. There wasn't much liquid in the glass, but I still felt terrible. "Do you have a towel I can use to clean this up?"

"There's a dishcloth in the kitchen," Ida

said as she started picking up ice cubes. "There, that should do it."

I went into the kitchen and found the cloth as promised, positioned near the trash can. I glanced inside, not because I was snooping, but because it was where my line of sight went naturally.

What I saw there was a game changer in our investigation.

At the top of the trash can was an opened box for a home pregnancy test.

If I had to guess, I'd say that Leah just might be pregnant, and I had a strong suspicion about who the father might be.

All in all, it might just be enough of a motive to kill a man.

I forgot all about the spill as I held the recovered box up to Ida. "Ida, is Leah pregnant?"

Ida took the box from my hands as though it were the most valuable thing on earth. "Were you snooping around in my kitchen, Suzanne? Was that spill really an accident, or did you just use it as an excuse to snoop?"

"It wasn't planned," I said. "And I wasn't snooping. This was on top of the trash. Honestly, it was kind of hard to miss."

She softened then, and I could feel some of the starch go out of her. "I'm sorry. I shouldn't have accused you like that. Leah's got me in such a state right now, I don't know how to act."

Grace asked softly, "Is she pregnant with Peter's child?" The words came out as though they wounded her with each syllable.

"No, dear, it turned out to be a false alarm," Ida said in a comforting manner that surprised me. "She thought she might be with child a few days ago, but she took another test when she got here, and she's not having a baby."

"But she thought she could be?" I asked.

"I'm shamed to admit that she did," Ida said. "Like I told you before, the girl's out of control. I doubt she could narrow her list of suspects of possible fathers to the fingers on one hand, if you want to know the truth. When her parents died, she turned to Burt and me for support, but it was never enough for her."

"I'm sorry about that, but I'm betting that Peter was at the top of her list," I said.

"I admit that she's mentioned him a time or two," Ida said as she finished wiping up the spill. She took the towel, and the discarded box, back into the kitchen.

I followed her, with Grace close behind.

"You know her better than we do. Is there

a chance in your mind that she could have killed him?" Grace asked, her voice heavy with the weight of what had happened.

After hesitating longer than I could have imagined, Ida said, "I've been asking myself the same question ever since you told me that the man was dead, and to be honest with you, I don't have an answer one way or the other. The old Leah couldn't have done it, but it feels as though I hardly know this girl anymore, and that's the honest truth."

The front door opened, and Leah herself walked in. She was clearly angry, and had worked herself up into quite a state. "I saw your car out front. You can't just barge in here like this. You both need to get out, or I'm going to call the police."

Ida snapped, "Young lady, you'll do no such thing. They are my guests, not yours, and they'll stay as long as I please."

She looked shocked that Ida had taken our side. "What did they tell you? Never mind. Whatever they said was a lie," Leah protested.

"Are you claiming then that your special friend, Peter Morgan, isn't dead?" Ida asked, staring hard at her niece.

"It's true that he's gone," Leah said, "but I didn't kill him."

"Then why did you run?" Grace asked softly. I was amazed at how calm her voice was, especially under the pressure she had to be feeling.

"I didn't want to, but Uncle Burt saw us talking, and he made me come here when I told him that you weren't finished with me. He said that if I talked to you again in his hardware store, he was going to fire me. What choice did I have?"

"Why would Burt care if you talked to us, anyway?" I asked, honestly curious.

"He said you were both snoops, and that if you got started on me, the whole town would believe that I was a killer. He said I'd be washed up then, and would have to go somewhere else and start over."

Given my history with the man, I could almost understand where he was coming from. "We're looking for the killer. If you didn't do it, you don't have anything to fear from us."

Leah took that in, and then turned to her aunt. "What do you think, Aunt Ida? Should I believe them?"

"If it were me, I would," Ida said after a moment's consideration.

Leah nodded, accepting her aunt's judgment. "Okay, we can talk. You just can't tell my uncle that we spoke."

I had no problem making that particular promise. "We won't say a word to him." That didn't mean he wouldn't find out somehow, particularly if Leah was a killer, but I'd keep my word. Burt Gentry wouldn't hear it from me.

Leah sighed loudly, and then said, "Honestly, it will be a relief getting this off my chest. I've wanted to tell someone since I found out that Peter was dead. I just didn't know who to talk to about it."

"We're good listeners," I said.

Leah nodded, and then began to talk.

CHAPTER 8

"First, I'm really sorry for what I did to you," she said as she turned to Grace. "You deserved better than that, and I feel worse than you can imagine. You have to understand something, though; he told me he was single and unattached, and by the time I found out about you, it was too late. The man was like heroin to me. I tried to give him up, but I couldn't do it. I just wasn't strong enough."

I wasn't sure how Grace was going to react to the way Leah was justifying her behavior, but after a moment, my best friend just nodded, and then she said, "I knew how Peter was when he wanted something, believe me. He could be the most charming man in the world when he set his mind to it."

"And the cruelest when he was finished with you," Leah said.

Grace looked surprised by that statement.

"He was never like that to me."

Leah snorted. "That doesn't surprise me one bit. It's because you were his public girlfriend. Peter paraded you around out in the open, but he hid me in the shadows."

"You're not actually blaming *me* for that, are you?" Grace asked.

"Of course not," she said quickly. "You just don't know how much I envied you."

Ida said, "Stop stalling, Leah, and tell them what you know about the man."

I looked at Ida and offered her silent thanks. I wasn't sure how long Grace was going to be able to keep it together without falling apart, and I didn't want Leah to push her any more than she had done already.

The three of us looked expectantly at Leah, and after nodding briefly, she began to tell us what she knew about the many secret lives of Peter Morgan.

"I'm not quite sure where to start," Leah said, "because some of the stuff I know might be uncomfortable for you to hear, Grace."

"I can take whatever you have to say," my best friend said, and I was never more proud of her. "We can't find his killer unless we know about all of his misbehavior."

Leah accepted that after a moment, and nodded once. "Okay. The main thing that set me off four days ago was when I found out about Kaye."

"What are you talking about?" I asked. "Who's Kaye?"

"Kaye Belson," Leah explained. "She lives in Union Square, and I'm not surprised you don't know about her. After all, you didn't even know about me."

"Tell them why you were so upset," Ida urged her niece. "When you called me, you were in tears."

"I thought I might be pregnant with his baby," Leah said, "and Peter was cheating on me with her." I was amazed that she actually had the nerve to claim offense, since she was doing the exact same thing to Grace. "I nearly blew my stack when I found out."

"If he cheats *with* you, he'll cheat *on* you," I recited. It was one of Momma's favorite sayings, and I'd learned it well enough as a teenager to keep me from some bad situations. Maybe that was why catching Max with Darlene had stung so much. I was loyal to a fault, but sadly, my ex-husband couldn't say the same thing.

"Suzanne, there's no need to beat her up about it," Ida said. "I'm sure Leah feels bad enough as it is."

"It's okay," Leah said. "She's got a point.

I probably deserved it."

"What do you know about Kaye?" Grace asked.

Leah let out a big breath of air. "Well, the first thing is, she's got a temper; I know that much myself."

"What do you mean?" I asked her.

Leah looked sheepish as she admitted, "I borrowed Peter's telephone once so I could check my messages at home, and I happened to see a text from some random girl. I decided to look her up and tell her that she was messing with the wrong man. When she answered, I told her who I was, and why I was calling. I was expecting her to feel guilty, maybe even apologize. Man, she was furious! I thought she was going to pop my ear drum before I hung up on her."

"What did Peter have to say when you told him you found out about Kaye?" I asked. I was curious to see if he'd try to deny it, or maybe even justify it by claiming that he could do what he wanted to without asking anyone else's permission. They sounded like equally plausible scenarios.

I was wrong, twice, though.

Leah explained, "He told me to get over it, that he had enough on his mind without worrying about how I felt about anything. I couldn't believe how rude he was to me."

Rudeness was the least of Peter Morgan's character flaws. "Was she mad enough to kill him when she found out about you?" I asked.

"I wouldn't put it past her," Leah said.

"Is there anyone else who might have wanted to see Peter dead?" Grace asked. I didn't know how she was keeping it together, but her voice was calm and steady as she spoke.

"Peter had his share of enemies, trust me," Leah admitted. She asked Grace, "You know about those yourself, right?"

"Indulge us all and tell us anyway," Grace said.

"Let's see. We have to start with his brother, Bryan. Those two were not fans of each other, no doubt about it. There's his business partner, Henry Linx, or was it Lincoln? I don't know, it was something like that. They were having a battle of their own, let me tell you. Henry accused Peter of stealing from him, and the last time I saw them together, Henry was ready to put Peter's head through a wall. The thing is, after Henry left, Peter was laughing about taking advantage of him. He said if the man was too dense or weak to spot a bad deal, it wasn't up to Peter to protect him."

Grace looked puzzled, and I was sure I

knew why without even asking. She hadn't seen this side of Peter at all. He must have been on his best behavior with her, but clearly he didn't care that much about protecting Leah from his true self. "Anyone else?"

"That's all I know about, but the one you should really ask is Rose White. She's constantly nosing around in Peter's business. If anybody knew his enemies, it would be her."

"His landlady?" Grace asked. "Really?"

If she hadn't said something, I would have done it myself. I had never heard of the woman before.

"Trust me, she always wanted to be more than that with Peter. You had to have seen the way she looked at him," Leah said to Grace.

"We only met once," Grace admitted. "Peter said that he was a very private person, and that he didn't want to rush things between us by bringing me to his apartment."

"He never had that problem with me," Leah admitted, and then realized how it must have sounded. "Listen, I'm sorry. That was out of line."

"Leah, watch your step," Ida said sharply.

"Hey, I apologized, didn't I?" she asked.

"Is there anything else you can think of that might help? When was the last time you saw Peter, Leah?" I asked.

"It was yesterday at lunch, if you can believe that. Just think. Twenty-four hours ago, he was still alive," she said. Was that a tear coming unbidden down her cheek? Could it be possible that the girl honestly missed him, even after all of the things she'd discovered about him lately? The heart is a strange thing, and no one knew that better than I did.

Leah continued, "I'm sorry to say that we had a huge fight, and now I'll never be able to make things right with him." She looked at Grace and asked, "Were you two on good terms the last time you saw him?"

"Not particularly. I broke up with him yesterday afternoon, and then I slapped him and threw him out of my house last night."

Leah frowned. "It's too bad."

"What's that?" I asked.

"Peter died without knowing that anyone loved him," Leah said so softly that I almost didn't hear her. "No one should have to die like that."

Ida stood, and we all followed suit. She hugged her niece, and then said, "I'm proud of you, Leah. I know all of that couldn't have been easy for you."

"It was the right thing to do, telling the truth," Leah said. She looked at Grace, took a step forward, and started to hug my friend. Grace caught onto what she had planned instantly and stepped away from her embrace. "I'm sorry. I don't mean to be rude, but it's just a little too soon for that."

Ida tugged on Leah's arm and pulled her back. "We understand. We're finished here. My niece and I need to spend a little time getting reacquainted."

"You're not coming back to April Springs?" I asked, curious about why she'd stay in exile after our conversation.

"Uncle Burt doesn't want me back at the hardware store, so maybe I'll stay here a while and see what pans out in Montview."

"I'm sure I can find you a job nearby," Ida said. "You could always stay with me."

From Leah's expression, it was clear that she hadn't counted on being put to work again, especially so soon. "Thanks, that would be great," she said, if a little half-heartedly.

We left them there to sort out their problems. As Grace and I got back into her car, she drove half a mile down the road, and then pulled over unexpectedly.

"Is something wrong? Did you forget something?" I asked.

143

Instead of answering, Grace turned to me, and then buried her head in my shoulder, sobbing and trying to speak through her tears. "Suzanne, how could I have been so blind? I didn't even recognize the man she was just talking about."

"You can't blame yourself. He fooled everyone," I said as I stroked her hair. I was proud of how long she'd held out, but this was good, too. Grace needed to get this out of her system, and I knew it was the only way she'd ever manage to move past her time with Peter.

"He didn't fool you, though, did he?" she asked through her tears. "You knew he was rotten from the start, didn't you?"

I could have lied to her again right then, and maybe I should have, but we'd been friends for too long for me to do that comfortably, and she'd already called me out for lying twice before. Besides, she'd been deceived enough lately, and I wasn't about to add any more deception if I could help it. "I admit that I wasn't a big fan of the man, but I had no idea just how wrong he was for you."

"I don't know how I'm ever going to be able to trust a man again," Grace said as she pulled away and dried her eyes.

"Once upon a time, I felt the same way

about Max, remember?" I asked softly. "That's okay for a while, but it's not a good way to live the rest of your life. If I hadn't been open to new possibilities, I never would have found Jake."

"You got lucky there," she said as she blew her nose.

"I'm not denying it," I replied. "But you'll get your own run of good luck yourself, I can feel it in my heart."

"I don't know if that's true or not, and honestly, right now, I don't care." She glanced in her vanity mirror and said, "Look at me. I'm a mess."

I had to laugh. "Funny, you're still more put together than I am," I said.

She laughed a little, an encouraging sign. "Let's just say that we're both pretty and move on. I'm ready to tackle our next suspect, if you have the time."

I studied my friend with concern. "Are you sure you're up to that? Maybe we should just take the rest of the night off. By the time we get back to town, it's going to be too late to do much of anything."

"If you're game, I think we should try to tackle one more suspect today. Truth be told, I'd like to get the taste of what we just heard out of my head."

"Don't worry about me; I've got lots of

time," I said. If the worst thing that happened today was that I missed out on a little sleep, it would be a very good day indeed. "What did you have in mind?"

"I'd love to talk to Rose White after what Leah just told us," Grace said. "Besides, Peter's apartment is on our way back home, so we don't even have to take a detour."

"Then let's go have a chat with her," I said.

As Grace drove to the outskirts of Union Square, we chatted quite a bit, but Peter's name never came up again. It was almost as though she were trying to forget what we were doing, if only for a few moments, and if that was her plan, I was game as well. This was tough on her, and if there was anything I could do to make it any easier, I would.

Grace pulled up in front of a very nice apartment complex with over forty units in the three buildings. I'd never seen it myself, so I was glad that she knew where to go. The buildings were all made of red brick and black wrought iron, and I had no trouble seeing Peter Morgan living there. We walked up to the manager's apartment, clearly marked by a sign on the walk and on her door, and rang the bell.

It was time to see if we could get some

146

answers out of the woman.

"May I help you?" a pleasant-looking woman in her early forties asked as she answered the door. She was wearing a nice summer dress and sandals, and her makeup was nicely applied, if a little subdued. From what Leah had said, I'd been expecting some kind of vamp or siren. Instead, she looked as though she'd just come from shopping at the grocery store or a meeting at the PTA.

"Hello, Ms. White. I'm not sure if you remember me," Grace said as she stepped forward, extending her hand. "I'm Grace Gauge and this is my friend Suzanne Hart. I was a friend of Peter Morgan's."

"Of course," she said, sympathy flooding her face. "And please call me Rose. You must be heartbroken. Would you like to come in?"

"That would be nice," I volunteered. It would be much easier to get her to talk to us in her apartment, rather than out on the sidewalk.

We walked in, and Rose offered, "I was just about to have a cup of tea. Would you care for some?"

"That would be nice," I said, "but please don't go to any trouble for us."

"Nonsense," she said with a smile. "It's

just hot water and a bit of loose tea, after all. Make yourselves comfortable. I'll be right back."

Rose entered the small kitchenette, and I looked around the living room. The woman kept the place immaculate, something I'd never been able to manage, whether living with Max, or Momma. There was a nice display of photos arranged neatly on a table by the window, and I studied them in turn, searching for Peter, or some sign that any of what Leah had told us was true. Surely if the woman had the kind of obsession for Peter that Leah had talked about, there could easily be some evidence of it. I didn't find any shots of Peter, but there *was* someone featured in one of the frames that I couldn't believe. I was about to remark on it to Grace when Rose came back into the room carrying a tray with an elegant ceramic teapot and a lovely set of cups and saucers.

"Here we go," she said as she put the tray down on a different side table. "I took the liberty of including a few cookies as well."

They looked delicious, and clearly home-made. "Did you bake these yourself?"

Rose laughed lightly. "I wish I could admit that I had, but Mrs. Myerson in unit 14 is a fabulous baker, and she considers it her sacred duty to keep me from losing the last four pounds on my diet."

"Trust me, you don't have to tell me about temptation. I run a donut shop." I'd gotten the reference in on purpose to see how she would react, but there was no change of her expression when I'd said it.

"You must have more willpower than I do," she said. "How would you like your tea?"

"Two sugars, please," I said.

"That sounds good to me, too," Grace said.

After the tea had been sampled and the cookies tasted, Rose said, "It really was quite a shock around here when we learned about Peter. The police left here a few hours ago, and I spoke to a man named Chief Martin. He seemed nice enough."

I kept my comments about our police chief to myself as Rose added, "I suppose I'll have to go through Peter's things and pack them for his brother now that the apartment's been released by the authorities. I admit that it's not a service I usually perform, but he's paying me to do it and I can't afford to turn down the money."

"Has Bryan even been here yet?" Grace asked.

"No, but when he called to hire me just a few minutes before the police left, he told me to have everything packed by six P.M. tonight. I'm doing my best to give him the benefit of the doubt, but he was rather abrupt with me. Honestly, I'll be hard-pressed to have it done in time."

"We can help," I blurted out. Helping Rose sounded as though it would give us the only chance we'd have to dig for clues through the things the police hadn't confiscated, and I hoped that Grace wouldn't mind me volunteering for such an intimate task.

"Thank you for your generous offer, but I could never ask that of you," Rose said, dismissing the idea as quickly as I had presented it. While she was still being pleasant, there was no doubt in my mind that her refusal had been full of steel.

"Please?" Grace asked in a pitiful voice. "It might help me to come to terms with what happened to my love. There's a key chain that I gave Peter that holds a special fondness in my heart. I'm sure Bryan wouldn't mind if I took it. It's just a trinket, but it would mean the world to me."

"I'm not sure," Rose said, her voice clearly wavering.

"It's really important," Grace pleaded. "If you think it would help smooth things over, I can call Bryan myself."

Rose couldn't refuse her; I could see it in her eyes. "Are you certain that it won't be too painful for you?"

"I may shed a few tears, but it's the right thing to do," Grace said.

"And I might just cry a little along with you," Rose answered. "Peter and I were friends, not just acquaintances. We shared more than cups of tea and stories from our past, I can tell you that. I'll miss him."

I could see that she was telling the truth. It was clear that Rose had been fond of Peter, but I had to wonder about Leah's interpretation of the relationship. Was it possible that Leah had seen it through her own eyes, where no relationship she had with a man could be simply a friendship?

"Then we should get started right now if we're going to meet Bryan's deadline," I said as I put my teacup down.

"I have to admit, it will be much nicer having company doing such a painful task," Rose said.

As we left the apartment and headed upstairs, I said, "It must be tough being in charge of everything around here all by yourself."

"There are times it's trying, but in the end, I wouldn't trade it for the world," she said. "I get to know so many nice people;

it's almost like we're all family here."

Was this woman just a little too good to be true, or was I being cynical about her attitude? I honestly wasn't sure, but I'd get Grace's take on it later. While I might be the better investigator between the two of us, she was the better judge of character and sincerity. I wasn't sure if working in sales had made her that way, or if she'd gone into sales because of it. Either way, I usually trusted her instincts.

As Rose started to unlock Peter's door, I heard Grace take in a deep breath. I grabbed her hand and squeezed it gently, hoping to give her some kind of reassurance.

"My, they left it in quite a mess, didn't they?" the manager said as she looked around the living room.

I went to see what Rose was talking about, and saw that the apartment had been thoroughly wrecked. I'd seen searches the chief led before, and they had never looked like this.

"Hang on a second," I said. "I need to make a call before we go in."

As much as I hated admitting to the chief that I was investigating Peter's murder, this was too important to pass up. I dialed his direct number, something I had because of his relationship with my mother, not as

152

some kind of special favor to me.

"Martin," he said. "Make it quick. I'm about to go into a meeting."

"It's Suzanne Hart," I said. "You searched Peter Morgan's apartment earlier, right?"

There was no happiness in his voice as he answered. "Suzanne, I swear, if you're meddling in another one of my murder investigations, I'll lock you up."

"Do you really think Momma would stand for that?" I asked as sweetly as I could manage.

I wasn't the least bit surprised when he immediately backed down. "Make it quick. What do you want?"

"Grace and I came by his place to get something of hers that Peter had. It's all perfectly innocent," I explained. "When the manager opened the door, we discovered that his apartment was a wreck. You're usually neater than that when you search a place, aren't you?"

He hesitated for a moment, and then admitted, "When I left it, everything was as neat as a pin. How bad was the place tossed?"

I looked around the room again and said, "If whoever did it didn't find what they were looking for, it wasn't for lack of trying."

He said, "Both rooms?"

"I don't know. We haven't been in the bedroom."

"Don't go back there," he shouted loud enough to hurt my ears. "I'll get a patrol officer in town to check it out. Hang on a second."

I put my hand over the phone and told Rose softly, "Close the door."

She did as I asked, and as we moved away from Peter's apartment, Chief Martin asked, "Are you there?"

"We're outside now," I said.

"Stay there. An officer named Trout will be right there. He searched the place with me earlier. Call me back after he's gone."

I was about to agree when he hung up on me.

"What happens now?" Rose asked. She didn't seem on edge at all, as though this were a regular part of her duties.

"We wait," I said simply.

It wasn't long, though. Less than four minutes later, an officer arrived.

"I'm Trout," he said. "Chief Martin's already apprised me of the situation." He tried the door, but it had locked itself automatically. "Keys," he commanded, and Rose opened the door for him before stepping back.

Trout went in with his gun out, was gone

154

maybe ninety seconds, and then came back and rejoined us. "It's all clear. Nobody's there."

"Thanks for checking," I said.

"That doesn't mean they won't be back," he added. "Want me to stick around?"

"No thanks, we'll be fine on our own," I said. There was no way I wanted a cop there watching us while Grace and I searched the place ourselves.

"Fine then," he said, and I swear he saluted us with two fingers to the brim of his hat before he drove off.

Rose said, "My, that was certainly exciting." She looked at me and added, "You must have a great deal of influence with the police. Is it because of the donut shop?"

"I don't follow," I said, though I knew full well what she was implying. I hated the "cop and donut love" stereotype as much as the police did. Officers like Stephen Grant were always welcome in my place, and I was happy he wasn't afraid of the stereotype.

Rose looked at me a little oddly. "You know, it's like the old joke that the safest place to be when there's trouble is at a donut shop, because that's where all of the cops hang out."

I didn't want to tell her that I'd been robbed myself, so I gave her my weakest smile, and then dismissed it.

As we reentered the apartment, I looked around and said, "We're going to need boxes in order to do this properly."

"I have some downstairs in the storage area," she admitted.

"Well, if you go get them, we can get started."

Rose looked reluctant to leave us, but she soon realized that I was right. "I'll be back in two shakes."

After she was gone, I looked at Grace and said, "We've got maybe four minutes before she's back. If Peter was hiding something incriminating that he didn't want anyone else to find, where would it be? I mean, a place that hasn't already been tossed."

Grace frowned for a moment, and then smiled with determination. "I'm not sure if we'll find anything, but I've got an idea."

As she walked into the kitchenette, I had to wonder what could be hidden there that hadn't already been searched. Boxes of cereal were opened and spread out on the countertop, and sugar and flour were both in the sink where the containers had been emptied.

Grace ignored all that, though. She went directly to the oven, though the door itself was open, as well as the storage area beneath.

Instead of searching one of the places that had already clearly been inspected, she reached up under the overhead hood and removed the filter.

Something fell out as she did, and I caught it just before it could hit the cooktop.

FRIED APPLE RAISIN DONUTS

We enjoy these donuts two times a year in particular, in the autumn when the apples are harvested, and again around the holiday season. They go perfectly with that cup of eggnog, and as an added bonus, they're fairly easy to make. Sometimes we substitute dried cranberries for the raisins, giving them a more festive, and slightly exotic, taste.

Ingredients

Mixed
1 package quick-rise yeast, 1/4 oz.
1/2 cup whole milk, warmed
1/2 teaspoon sugar, white granulated

Sifted
1 cup flour, unbleached all-purpose
1 tablespoon sugar, white granulated
1/2 teaspoon cinnamon
1/4 teaspoon nutmeg
A dash of salt

Extras
1/2 cup diced and peeled apples, Granny Smith
1/2 cup raisins or dried cranberries

Instructions

Add the yeast and sugar to the warmed milk, then stir together until dissolved. Let it stand as you sift together the flour, sugar, cinnamon, nutmeg, and salt. Add the yeast/milk mix to the dry ingredients, then once blended together, add the diced apples and raisins/cranberries. Knead the dough on a lightly floured board 4–8 minutes, until the dough bounces back at the touch.

Spray a bowl with nonstick cooking spray, then cover and put the dough in a warm place until doubled, about an hour.

Roll the dough out on a lightly floured surface 1/4- to 1/2-inch thick, then cut out donuts and holes with handheld cutter.

Fry the dough in hot canola or peanut oil (370 degrees F) for two to three minutes on each side.

Drain, then top with powdered sugar immediately or eat as they are.

Yield: 8–12 small donuts.

CHAPTER 9

I examined what I'd caught, and saw that it was a carefully wrapped packet. As I studied it, I had to wonder how it could fit between the fan and the filter. Then I noticed that Peter had removed the fan blades entirely, so that the motor would still turn, giving it the illusion of working properly, but no air would be circulated.

What was so important that he had to go to that measure to hide it?

"How did you know about this?"

"Peter always bragged about how clever he was. In a way, he told me himself."

"I don't follow," I said.

"He once said in passing that if he ever had anything he wanted to protect, he'd give it to his biggest fan. After he said it, he laughed more than he should have, and it sort of stuck with me."

"You are a clever woman, have I told you that lately?" I asked. I started to open the packet when Grace asked, "May I?"

"Of course," I said. It was a small enough consolation. I figured Grace had a better reason than I did to be curious about what Peter had been up to, and she had the right to discover first what he had hidden so carefully.

As she opened the packet, I watched over her shoulder to see what might be there.

The first thing I saw was a wad of hundred-dollar bills, banded tightly together.

"How much is there?" I asked.

Grace thumbed through the bills. "It looks like three grand in cash."

"Why would someone hide that kind of money in a kitchen?"

"It could be that he didn't like to have all of his money tied up in banks," Grace said.

"Maybe," I replied, though I doubted that had been the real reason. More likely it was getaway money, but I was going to keep that to myself for now. "What else is in there?"

She took out the folded document, and at first I thought it might be a letter, but as Grace opened it, I read over her shoulder and saw that it was something completely different.

It was simply a list.

■ ■ ■ ■

"Is that all there is?" I asked.

Grace shrugged, so I picked up the wrapping to make sure we hadn't missed anything. Sure enough, stuck to the bottom of a piece of tape was a small, stubby key. I finally worked it free, and I held it up in the air to study it a little closer. "We've got a key."

Grace looked up, clearly surprised. "Where was that hiding?"

"It was in the packet, but the more important question is, where's the lock it opens?" I studied the small key. It had a black plastic grip, and printed on it was the word "WINGATE," along with a number, 282.

Grace took one look at it and said, "It's the key to a safe."

"What makes you think that?"

"I used to have one myself," she admitted.

"A key or a safe?"

She shrugged briefly. "Both, I suppose."

"I didn't know that."

"Well," Grace said with the flash of a smile. "I don't tell you *everything* about me."

"What happened to the safe?" I asked.

"Do you still have it?"

"Sure, it's still at the house, but I stopped using it. As a matter of fact, I emptied it out years ago," she admitted. "I didn't feel good having my valuables at the house. I figured my bank account came with a free safe-deposit box, so why not use it?"

I looked around. "Well, clearly Peter didn't feel that way. Do you think whoever searched the place found his safe, but not the key?"

"If they did, they wouldn't necessarily need a key to open it. The safes these keys fit are small, and I'm willing to bet that they aren't impossible to break into without a key, if you're motivated enough."

I looked around at the wrecked apartment. "I can't imagine that whoever did this tore the place up looking for a key. I've got a feeling that the safe is still here."

I was interrupted by someone at the door, and then I heard Rose come in with the boxes she'd promised to retrieve. I'd forgotten all about her!

Grace made the money and the letter disappear, and I slipped the key into my pocket.

Rose spied the filter lying on the stovetop, and then looked up at the vent. "What happened here?"

"I'm guessing the fan's broken," I said, stating the obvious. "Can you believe it?"

Rose looked at it carefully. "This was done intentionally."

"Well, we didn't do it," I said. "We saw that the filter was loose, and when we tried to put it back in place, it just fell onto the stovetop." That was a big fat lie, but I wasn't about to admit to Rose what we'd just found.

She considered it for a moment, and then shrugged. "Well, I hate to do it, but it has to be fixed. I'm going to have to take the cost of repair out of Peter's security deposit." Rose looked around, and then added, "You didn't make much progress while I was gone, did you?"

"We needed the boxes, remember?" I asked as I took one from her. "We can all get started now. Thanks."

"Thank you," Rose said. "I'm sorry if I snapped at you earlier. This is all a little too much to take, and I'm more on edge than I realized."

"I'm just glad we were here to help," I said.

As we worked to gather Peter's things together and box them, Grace and I kept searching for something else of importance, including the missing safe, but if anything important or significant was there, we missed it. Nor did I believe that Rose had found anything. I'd made it a point to keep an eye on her, just in case she stumbled onto something that could help us solve Peter's murder, but she didn't have any more luck than we did. As we all worked, I was dying to see the list Peter had hidden so carefully, but that was going to have to wait until Grace and I were alone. In a depressingly short period of time, we had Peter's things boxed up and ready for his brother. We'd filled several trash bags as well with the flotsam and jetsam we all seem to accumulate in our lives, and we set these out in front of the apartment, to be hauled to the Dumpster.

Once the fan blade was replaced and everything had a good cleaning, the apartment would be ready to rent again, and I didn't doubt for a second that Peter Morgan's memory would quickly fade from the place. It was sad in a way that I didn't want to think about too much.

We were stacking the four boxes of Peter's things outside the apartment when we heard a booming voice from below us say, "What do you think you're doing?"

It seemed that Peter's brother, Bryan, had arrived, and he was none too pleased to find

165

Grace and me there.

"I asked you a question. What are you two doing here?" Bryan asked as he stood over us. He was a big man, and while his brother had had a grace about him that even I had to admit was charming, Bryan had none of it. It was dislike at first sight between the two of us, and I imagined Bryan got that reaction more often than not whenever he met new people.

Grace didn't seem to mind him at all, though. She hugged him as she said, "Bryan, I'm so sorry for your loss. I can't believe he's gone."

The gruff exterior crumbled, if only for a moment, before he spoke. He looked down at her awkwardly, and then finally managed to free himself from Grace's embrace. "He told me you broke up with him, Grace. He was pretty shattered about it all when he called me."

"He made a mistake," Grace said. "That doesn't mean that I didn't love him in my own way. There was always the chance we could have fixed things between us, but someone's robbed me of that opportunity now."

Was Grace telling the truth, or was she just trying to get on Bryan's good side? In

166

my heart, I had a feeling that Grace wasn't lying. It had to have been tougher on her finding out about Peter than I'd realized, even though I'd reacted differently when I'd discovered Max had been cheating on me.

"You're right. It's too late for all of that now, isn't it?" He didn't say it with malice, but I had to wonder how Grace would take it as he turned to me. "Okay, I buy that she's got a reason to be here, and so does Ms. White. Why are you here?"

"I'm a friend of Grace's, and I wanted to help. I'm Suzanne Hart," I said as I extended my hand.

He took it briefly, but there was no warmth in his handshake. "I know who you are," Bryan said. "You're that donut lady."

I'd been called worse in my life, and it was certainly descriptive of what I did for a living, but I still didn't like the way he'd said it. "That's right, I'm the donut lady."

"This is none of your business," Bryan said flatly.

"Hey, I don't have any desire to step on anyone's toes here. I was just trying to lend a hand," I said. There was nothing to be gained by me hovering around, so I touched Grace's arm and said, "I'll see you in the car."

"Thanks for helping," Rose said, clearly

trying to smooth things over. "Your assistance was greatly appreciated."

"Glad I could pitch in," I said. I turned to Bryan and added, "I'm sorry for your loss."

He just nodded, so I walked back to Grace's car to wait for her.

At least that's what I wanted all of them to think. There was a space under Peter's apartment I'd seen earlier, a breezeway where I could stand out of sight and still hear their conversation. Maybe Bryan would be a little more open if he thought that I was really gone.

"She really was just trying to help," Grace started off, but Bryan wouldn't let her continue.

"Whatever. I say this is none of her business, but she's gone, so it doesn't matter anymore," he said.

As he reached down to collect two of the garbage bags, Rose said, "You want the boxes. That's just what needs to be thrown away."

"This stuff didn't come from his apartment?" Bryan asked.

"Of course it did, but it's nothing you'd want to have. It's trash."

"If it's Peter's, then I'm taking it, too," Bryan said firmly.

"Suit yourself," Grace said. "Would you

168

like us to give you a hand loading it up?"

"I can handle it myself," Bryan said.

"If you don't need me then, I'll be going now," Grace said. I heard footsteps on the stairs, and for a moment, I worried that I was about to be caught eavesdropping by someone other than my best friend, but happily it just turned out to be Grace.

"Hey," I whispered. "Over here."

Grace had been intent on leaving the complex, but I finally managed to get her attention. She veered over and joined me from my vantage point.

"I thought you were gone," Grace whispered.

"I thought I might hear something if I stuck around," I answered in kind.

Upstairs, I heard Rose say to Bryan, "You didn't need to be so rude to them. They were just giving me a hand."

"That's not their jobs; it's yours," Bryan said gruffly.

"And it's finished now, so you don't need me anymore," Rose said.

I could hear her walking away when Bryan spoke up. "What about my deposit?"

"What? As far as I'm concerned, you didn't make one; your brother did."

"I'm his only family," Bryan said. "Everything he had is mine now."

Rose's voice rose. "Mr. Morgan, I indulged you by letting you collect your brother's things out of sympathy, but I'm beginning to believe that I made a mistake. Please put everything back into the apartment. When you present a legal document that gives you access to your brother's things, I'll release them, but not until then."

I thought Rose was nuts to confront him like that, but I did admire her spirit. "Who's going to stop me from just taking everything anyway?"

Her voice stiffened. "Detective Newberry lives in Apartment Number 8. He is probably still sleeping since he works the night shift, but I'll wake him if I must."

The length of silence was unbearable, and I had to wonder who would back down first. Feet stomped on the steps now, and only Bryan's pause saved us as we hurried away.

"You didn't win anything here, lady," I heard him say. "I'll be back."

"I'll be here waiting," she said, and Grace and I hustled out of there before Bryan could catch us.

As we raced back to Grace's car, I said, "Good for her. I love it that she didn't let him bully her."

"I'm not sure how much good it did, though," Grace said. "Bryan's right. He was

Peter's only living relative. I can't imagine the circumstances where he won't get everything."

"Maybe so, but it's going to be done by the book. When he asked about the security deposit, I had a sick feeling that Rose was about to tell him about the altered fan."

Grace nodded. "I was holding my breath, too. The last thing I want is Bryan Morgan discovering that we found Peter's secret stash."

We got into her car and drove a few miles when I said, "Speaking of our discovery, may I see the list we found?"

Grace nodded as she pulled over into a nearly empty parking lot for an auto parts supply house. "I've been curious about that myself, but I wanted to make sure we got far enough away from the apartment complex."

As she pulled the note out, I leaned over so that we could both see what Peter had written there.

I had to believe it was important.

Why else hide it along with the cash he'd squirreled away?

As we both studied it, I saw that it was a list of names, a real mess, with new ones added and old ones struck out with pen and pencil. It was clear by the state of it that Peter had kept it for a long time before he decided to hide it. A thought suddenly struck me. Could we be certain that it was his list to begin with?

"Is this Peter's handwriting?" I asked Grace.

"It is, no doubt about it," she answered. "I can't figure out why he kept it, though."

"It's pretty clear, isn't it?" At the head of the page, written in large block letters, the words "RAT LIST" were written. "Did you know about this, Grace?"

She shrugged. "I knew that Peter was a fool for lists, but this is a little hard to take, don't you think? Who does this kind of thing, anyway?"

"I'm not the one to ask," I said. "It makes for some pretty interesting reading, though, doesn't it?"

I took the paper from Grace, with her approval, and started reading it a little closer.

Brother Bryan was first on the list, no last name needed. It had been crossed out a number of times, and from the look of it, Peter's brother had bounced in and out of favor with him since the list had been started who knew how long ago.

As I read down the list of names, I saw our other suspects mentioned there, and more. Besides Leah Gentry and Henry Lincoln, I was surprised to see Kaye Belson and Rose White, but nothing prepared me for the final two names I found written there. I nearly dropped the paper when I saw the name Nan Winters. What had my new assistant done to get on Peter's bad side?

But nothing compared to how I felt when I saw the last name on the list. It was the worst one for me to read, though I shouldn't have been surprised to see it.

Grace Gauge's name was written all in caps, and struck through just once with red ink, a very final slash.

"Nan's on his list?" Grace asked. "I don't understand that at all."

"You didn't realize that they knew each other?"

"I didn't have a clue. I'm amazed that I knew anything Peter ever did. How about you? Did she say anything to you when she found out about Peter's murder?"

I shook my head. "No, but I've certainly got a few things to talk to Nan about when she comes into work tomorrow."

"What else besides Peter?" Grace asked as she started driving again.

"That's right, I never got a chance to tell you. One of the photographs in Rose's apartment was of her and Nan together.

They looked pretty chummy."

Grace slowed a little, and I had to wonder if she even realized that she was doing it. "Your new assistant is in this up to her ears, isn't she?"

"Either that, or it's an awfully big coincidence, and you know how I feel about those."

Grace asked, "Are we going back home now?"

"I suppose we could, but I thought we might see if we can find Kaye Belson, since we're already in Union Square. From the sound of it, she and Peter had a bit of a love-hate relationship going on. Is that okay with you?"

"Suzanne, I'm grateful for every second you can spare me. I need to find out what happened to Peter, despite how we ended things. It's the only way I'm ever going to be able to put this all behind me."

"I'll give you every moment I can," I said. "You know that. How are you handling things? You seemed a little too brave to me a few times this afternoon."

She sighed. "I'm walling it off, if you want to know the truth. The less I think about my emotions, the better off I'll be."

"It's okay to express your feelings, you know."

174

Grace shook her head. "There will be plenty of time for that after we solve his murder. When we've caught the killer, I'll let myself wallow a little. I could use some company then, if you're interested."

"I'll be there. You can count on me, along with cookies, ice cream, soda, and anything else you can name."

"How about a dozen donuts?" she asked with a slight smile.

I laughed. "You name the variety, and they're yours."

"Let me think about it," Grace said.

We made it to the downtown area of Union Square, but neither one of us really knew where to go from there. "Any ideas about how we might find Kaye?" Grace asked me.

"We've got a ready source here we shouldn't discount. I say we talk to the DeAngelis ladies and see if they can help." Angelica DeAngelis and her three daughters; Maria, Antonia, and Sophia, ran Napoli's, the best Italian restaurant in ten counties. I'd grown quite fond of their family over the years, and I believed that the feeling was mutual.

Maria was at the front door, and her smile blossomed as Grace and I walked in. Each daughter was lovely in her own right, true reflections of their mother's beauty. "Ladies. It's so very nice to see you. I have a perfect table for you."

"We're not here to eat," I admitted. "We wondered if we might ask you a few questions."

Maria lowered her voice. "I'll do what I can, but Momma is in one of her moods. It would help if you had a little something, you know? She loves feeding you, Suzanne. It might just cheer her up."

I looked at Grace. "What do you think? I *am* hungry."

"I can always eat, especially if it's here at Napoli's," she replied.

"Okay, but we're in a time crunch," I said to Maria. "Could we keep it simple?"

"Two spaghettis, no extras, maybe a little wine; how does that sound?" Maria asked.

I had dreams sometimes of DeAngelis pasta, so it was an easy sale. "Done."

"Then I'll be right back," she said after she seated us at a table near the kitchen. Maria disappeared through the swinging door, and Grace said, "Actually, I kind of forgot how hungry I was."

"If you're hinting around that you want my spaghetti, too, sorry. You're out of luck."

She grinned for a moment, and I could see something of my friend buried under

176

her grief. "I'll try to control myself."

Maria came back out with two glasses of wine and matching plates of pasta on a tray. A patron across the room complained, "Hey, that's not right. They just got here, and we haven't even been served yet."

"They made their arrangements earlier," Maria said warmly. "Don't worry; your food will be out shortly."

The man wanted to be angry, that much was clear, but Maria's charm seemed to melt away his temper. "That's fine; I'm sorry for the complaint."

"We're just happy you're dining with us this evening," she said as she bathed him in her warmest smile.

"You're good," I said softly as Maria served us.

"Men are like puppies," she said lightly, "All they really long for is a warm smile and a little praise. Who doesn't like to feel special?"

I nodded. "I know I always feel like a VIP when I'm here."

"That's because you are," she said. "Momma has given us all standing orders that you are to be pampered whenever you visit us. The family owes you a great debt."

I thought back to the small service I'd done for them once. "It's not necessary."

"Speak for yourself," Grace said as she looked at her plate. "I'm glad to finally get a perk for being your best friend."

Maria laughed. "I imagine there are more than just your visits here. Now, you wanted to ask me a question."

I looked back at the impatient patron. "You can get his food first, if you'd like."

Maria shook her head. "He can wait another moment."

"Okay. Grace and I were wondering if you know someone in town named Kaye Belson."

Maria's smile faded, if just for a moment. "May I ask why you're interested in her?"

"We believe she might know something about Peter Morgan's murder," I admitted. I might dance around the truth with some people, but the DeAngelis clan deserved my honesty, and I was going to give it to them unless there was an extremely compelling reason not to.

She looked taken aback by the news. It was a rare stumble for her, and Maria quickly recovered. "It is Sophia you need to speak with."

"She knows her, then?"

"They are best friends, much like the two of you," Maria admitted, "though we sometimes worry about how close they've become."

She hurried back to the kitchen, and I took a bite of pasta while I could. If Sophia got upset by our questions, we might have to make a quick getaway, and I wasn't about to pass up a plate of their pasta as a sacrifice for our investigation. I would try to have both if I could.

Sophia came out a minute later, carrying the patron's food on a tray. She served it a little haphazardly, and then took a seat at our table. "You wanted to talk to me?"

"I'm sorry. There's no easy way to say this. We need to speak with Kaye Belson."

Sophia's expression clouded over, and I could see her mother in her just then. Of all the DeAngelis women, Sophia showed her emotions most openly. "What's that got to do with me?"

"We heard you two were best friends," Grace said.

Sophia turned to her. "The key word in that sentence is 'were.' It's definitely in the past tense."

"What happened between you two?" I asked, curious about what could split up such close friends.

"When she started dating Peter Morgan, I couldn't tolerate her behavior anymore," she said, not able to make eye contact with either one of us as she said it.

"It's okay, Sophia. We weren't married," Grace said softly.

"Maybe not, but you were committed to each other, and Kaye knew it when she took up with Peter. I tried to tell her it was wrong sneaking around with him like that, but she wouldn't listen to me. I really am sorry."

Grace patted Sophia's hand. "You don't owe me any apologies. Is there anything you can tell us about her?"

"She's pretty; there's no question about that. Up until the past three months, Kaye had a really level head about it, but when Peter started showing her some attention, she changed. All it took were a few soft words, and she was lost to him."

"Peter could be very persuasive," Grace said. "Do you think Kaye will talk to us about her relationship with him?"

"Alone? Not a chance," Sophia said.

"Would you come with us, then?" I asked softly. It was a great deal to ask, and I knew it, but we needed to talk to Kaye.

"Is it that important to you?" she asked, clearly reluctant to acquiesce.

"I wouldn't ask otherwise," I said.

"Let me talk to Momma," she said, and stood abruptly.

When Sophia was gone, I said, "I'm not sure how this is going to go, so if you'd like a last bite, I'd take it right now."

I did as I advised Grace, and we were finishing up when Angelica came out. A few diners tried to catch her gaze as she came out of the kitchen, but her attention was focused solely on us. "Suzanne, is what Sophia just told me true?"

How did I know exactly what her youngest daughter had just said? "We need her help. I'm sorry to ask, but there's no other way."

Angelica pursed her lips, and then asked, "This involves Peter Morgan's murder, doesn't it?"

I nodded. "It does, but I don't think there's any chance your daughter is in danger. If you're not comfortable with her going with us, though, I completely understand."

Angelica shook her head briefly. "Nonsense. The DeAngelis women don't back down from danger, not for our friends. I just want your assurance that there's no other way."

"I can't do that," I said. "Grace and I haven't even spoken with Kaye yet. We just have your daughter's word that she won't talk to us. We can try to see her ourselves first."

"Sophia said that Kaye wouldn't speak with you without her?"

"She did, but it's fine," I said as I stood, with Grace following. "Dinner was wonderful." I took a twenty from my wallet and pressed it in her palm. "Thanks so much."

I was nearly out of the dining room when Angelica caught up with us. "Suzanne, don't leave. I didn't say no."

"You didn't say yes, either," I said. "Angelica, I get it, I honestly do. You have every right to look after your daughters."

"Wait here," she commanded us, and I didn't have the nerve to disobey.

"How long do we wait?" Grace asked.

"As long as it takes," I replied. There was no way I was going against Angelica's order. Her friendship, not to mention her food, meant too much to me. Besides, I would never be able to face Jake again if I got us banned from our favorite restaurant.

Angelica came out two minutes later with Sophia in tow.

"She'll take you to Kaye," Angelica said.

"Are you sure?"

"Just keep her safe," Angelica said.

"Momma, I'm old enough to watch out for myself," she protested.

"I know you are, but indulge your mother," Angelica replied. "And don't linger. We need you here tonight."

Angelica kissed her daughter's cheek, and Sophia immediately rubbed the lipstick off.

Once we were outside, I asked, "Where should we start looking for Kaye?"

"We don't have to look far," Sophia admitted. "I know exactly where she is."

CHAPTER 10

"Sophia, what are you doing here?" a pretty young woman asked as we walked into the Laundromat just down the street from the restaurant.

"You need to talk to these women and answer their questions, Kaye," Sophia said.

"Why should I?" she asked as she looked at us. There was no recognition when she glanced at me, but the moment she saw Grace, her face reddened considerably.

"Because we used to be best friends, and Momma won't be pleased if you say no," Sophia replied. "Do you really want to risk being banned from our restaurant?"

Evidently the threat was taken to heart. "What do they want to know?"

"Ask them, not me," Sophia said. She moved to one side, picked up an old magazine, and took a seat. The Laundromat was mostly empty, so we had privacy for our conversation.

"What can I do for you?" Kaye asked with a clear and confident voice.

"We need to talk," I said.

"About Peter," Grace added.

"I don't know anyone named Peter," she said in a tone that no one would believe.

Sophia coughed once, and Kaye looked over at her guiltily.

"Funny, we found out that you were dating him when he was murdered," I said. "I'm sure the police would be happy to talk to you if you don't want to have a friendly little chat with us." It was an outright lie, since what Chief Martin did had nothing to do with my actions, but did Kaye know that? I doubted it.

"So, maybe we went out a few times. It was all just for fun," she added, and then looked at Grace. "The truth is, he loved you, not me. I was just something for him to do on the side."

I couldn't imagine knowingly being anyone's spare, and I was about to say just that when I remembered why we were there. I wasn't trying to reform this girl's character. I was looking for information.

"I heard you were a little more passionate about things than that," I said.

Her lips formed two thin lines as she shook her head. "I've got a bit of a temper,

185

and I show it too much sometimes," she admitted. "I didn't kill him, though."

"Do you have an alibi for last night and early this morning?" Grace asked.

"I was home alone," she said.

"That's tough to prove," I said.

She looked as though she honestly didn't care. "I don't have to. I didn't kill Peter. He didn't mean that much to me, and I sure didn't care enough about him to go to jail over the guy."

I wasn't sure how to respond to that when Sophia spoke up. I hadn't even realized that she'd been listening to us, but evidently she hadn't missed a word. "Kaye, tell them the truth."

Kaye looked at her former best friend with resentment clear on her face. She finally admitted, "Fine, have it your way. If you want the truth, I was with someone else."

"We need a name," I said.

"He's married," Kaye admitted. At least she appeared to be ashamed of the fact, but that did nothing to appease Sophia. She threw the magazine down on the floor, and then stormed up to her former friend. "Married? Seriously? Have you just made up your mind to be a tramp for the rest of your life?"

I thought Kaye might explode at the accusation, but instead, she nearly collapsed in Sophia's arms. "I've been a fool, and I know it. What happened to Peter was awful. I never should have gone out with him, and I made an even bigger mistake right after that. Sophia, I'm so sorry. You were right, and I was wrong. I miss you so much. Can you ever find it in your heart to forgive me?"

Sophia's own anger dissipated like morning fog. She embraced her friend as she began to cry as well. "Hey, come on. Take it easy. You're forgiven." She pulled away a few seconds later, and then asked, "You've really changed? You're finished with older men, and married ones, too, no matter how old they are, right?"

"I swear," Kaye said.

"Okay," Sophia said.

I hated to interrupt their tender moment, but I needed to know Kaye's alibi. I was about to ask her for the man's name when Sophia caught my gaze and shook her head subtly. I decided it could wait. "Thanks for your time. Let's go, Grace."

I led my friend away, who looked surprised by our departure. "Suzanne, she could have just as easily been lying to us."

"I know that. Sophia will find out what we need to know a lot easier than we'll ever be able to."

"How can you be so sure of that?" she asked.

"If she doesn't, we can ask Kaye ourselves later," I said. "I'm afraid that if we push her right now, we might never find out who she was with."

Grace was clearly unhappy with my answer, but she accepted it. "I know it's getting late for you, but is there any chance we can make time to speak with Henry Lincoln since we're in town anyway?"

I glanced at the dashboard clock. It was nearing seven, and getting closer and closer to my bedtime. I had to be up in seven hours, and we weren't even in April Springs yet. Then again, what was a little sleep compared to my friendship? "Sure, why not?"

Grace nodded. "Thanks. I'll make this all up to you someday. I promise."

"Grace, you don't need to thank me. We're in this together. Let's go see if we can find Mr. Lincoln and see what he has to say about Peter."

It was not to be, though. Henry Lincoln wasn't at his office when we checked his address in the telephone book, and his residence was unlisted. "We can pop back into Napoli's and see if Angelica knows where he lives." I yawned as I said it, though

188

I'd tried to squelch it.

"No, it can wait until tomorrow," Grace said. "You've got to get up early."

"I can handle it," I insisted, though my statement was broken up by another yawn.

"We're going back to April Springs right now," Grace said. "We've got a better chance of finding him tomorrow."

"Okay, we can come back here right after I close tomorrow at eleven," I promised.

The next thing I knew, Grace was shaking my shoulder. "Suzanne, wake up. We're here."

I looked up to see that we were parked in front of the cottage I shared with Momma. "When did we get back into town?" I asked as I unbuckled my seat belt. "Sorry. I didn't mean to fall asleep on you."

"You were snoring," Grace said with a smile. "You really are beat."

"You know what? I'm suddenly refreshed. Would you like to come in for a bit? You shouldn't be alone tonight."

"I'm fine by myself," Grace said firmly, and I knew not to push it.

"Call me if you need me, then," I insisted.

"I appreciate the offer, but I'll be all right. See you tomorrow."

"Good night, Grace."

I stood there watching her until she drove away. She wasn't that far up the road from me, but it might as well have been a thousand miles. I could tell that Grace needed to be alone, and I would respect that unless she called me. She'd been great with me when I'd needed time alone after my marriage to Max fell apart, and I was going to do the same for her now.

I thought Momma might still be out on her date, but I was surprised to find her in the living room when I walked in, reading her latest mystery. She was a huge fan of cozies, and was now ripping her way through a series of culinary mysteries.

"What happened, did you finally run out of crafting mysteries?" I asked with a smile when I walked in.

"No, but I thought I'd pick one of these up and see what all the fuss was about."

"And what's the verdict?" I asked as I sat down with her.

"I like it, but there's just one problem."

"What's that?" I asked.

"They all make me hungry," she admitted. "If I keep reading them, I'm going to gain a hundred pounds."

We both knew that my mother was exaggerating, since that would mean that she'd have to double her weight. Momma was slight in stature, but what she lacked in bulk, she more than made up for in sass. "I thought you had a date tonight."

"I did, but Phillip was so preoccupied with Peter Morgan's murder, I cut it short so he could get back to the office."

"Has he found any leads yet?" I asked, trying to sound as nonchalant as I could.

Momma laughed loudly. "Suzanne, you know the rules. If he wants you to know something, he'll tell you himself."

I had to smile. "Sorry. Old habits die hard."

"How is Jacob these days?"

"Busy solving crimes," I said as I reached for the light blanket we kept on the back of the couch. It wasn't the least bit chilly, but I still liked having a little weight on me.

"Such is our lot," Momma said. She glanced at the clock, and then asked, "Shouldn't you be asleep by now?"

"Normally, yes," I said as I stretched a little. "But I just had a nap, so I'm good."

"Where on earth did you take a nap?"

"I didn't plan on it, but Grace drove us back from Union Square, and I just nodded off."

Momma smiled. "Did you manage to visit Napoli's while you were there?"

I looked down at my shirt, but couldn't

see any evidence. "How did you know?"

"Don't worry, I'm not psychic. I knew you had to eat somewhere, since you're clearly not hungry right now."

I shook my head. "How do you know I'm not hungry?"

She laughed again. "Because there's a pie in the fridge from yesterday, and you haven't made a move toward it since you walked in the door."

"Guilty as charged," I said. "Grace and I both had spaghetti."

"How is she holding up?" Momma asked as she finally put her book down.

"I don't know," I answered after a moment's thought. "She's keeping everything together a little too well, to be honest with you. We asked some pretty tough questions today that had to have killed her inside, but she didn't even blink. I'm a little worried about her."

"Should you go see her right now? Being in that house alone can't be easy for her right now."

"I offered, but she declined," I admitted.

Momma's left eyebrow arched, but she didn't say a word. She knew that Grace and I would work it out between us, and she wisely stayed out of it.

"Would you like to tell me about what you

discovered today?" Momma volunteered. "I'm an excellent listener, and it might help you crystallize your thoughts."

I usually bounced ideas off Grace, but that was clearly not the best idea right now. "You don't mind? We uncovered some unsavory behavior today."

"I believe I can take it," she said, hiding her light smile.

"There's just one more item to discuss, then. This thing between me and the chief of police works both ways. If I want him to know something, he'll hear it from me and not you. Agreed?"

"Of course," she said. "I respect your privacy, Suzanne."

I nodded. My mother's word was golden, an unbreakable vow, and I knew that I could trust her with anything. "Well, it turns out that Peter was more of a snake than we realized. He was seeing two other women on the side besides Grace, and those were just the ones we've found so far."

"Who are these ladies?"

"I don't know that I'd call them ladies," I said. "They're more like girls that Peter took advantage of. Leah Gentry and Kaye Belson are both barely out of their teens, and Peter used them, then tried to throw them away."

"Emotions run deep in the young," Momma said. "And passions can be stronger than reason. Do they have alibis?"

"We're working on that," I admitted.

"Who else is on your list, then?"

I thought about it, and then said, "Well, his brother is a bully who hated his brother for his own reasons, and we've also heard rumors that Peter and his business partner were having troubles."

That piqued her interest even more. "Name, please?"

"Henry Lincoln," I admitted.

She nodded. "I thought so. I happen to know Henry."

That was news to me, but then again, my mother was known for keeping her business life one big secret. She owned buildings and businesses in town that even I didn't know about. "What do you know about him?"

Momma shook her head. "He tried to coerce me into a business relationship a few years ago that I wasn't interested in."

It was my turn to look surprised. "Do you mean that he actually tried to bully you?"

"I know, it would have been amusing if it weren't so completely delusional. I'd watch him if I were you, Suzanne. Even when he smiles, you still can't see his teeth. The man's a shark. Would you like me to question him for you?"

Momma had not really gotten directly involved in my investigations in the past, and I was reluctant to start now. "Let's see how it goes first when Grace and I talk to him," I said.

She nodded her agreement. "If you need me, just remember, I'm here. So, who else are you considering?"

"That's the thing. There's a handful of folks who are on the perimeter, and I don't know what to make of them yet. So far, we've got his landlady, Rose White, though I find her an unlikely murderer, and one more even stronger suspect."

My mother sat there patiently, and I finally managed to speak. "Momma, it looks like my new assistant is thick in the middle of this murder case. Every time Grace and I look somewhere, the woman turns up."

That got her attention. "Nan Winters? Are you serious?"

"I know, it sounds crazy, right? But there's no denying it. I saw her in a photograph on Rose White's end table, but that could be written off to coincidence. What's really incriminating is that her name was on the list we found in Peter's apartment."

She looked concerned when she heard

that. "Hold on. When were you in his apartment?"

"That's right, I haven't gotten to that part yet. We were at Rose's place asking some questions, and there was an opening when we had a chance to volunteer to help clean out Peter's apartment."

"And you couldn't say no, of course," my mother said with a smile.

"You bet we couldn't," I said. "Anyway, Grace and I were in the kitchen while Rose was fetching more boxes, and we happened to find his secret stash, or at least, one of them."

"Drugs?" Momma asked, a frown on her face.

"No, nothing like that. We found three grand in hundreds, a key to a personal safe, and a well-worn list of names. All of them had been crossed out at least once, and some of them had been struck through a number of times."

"And Nan's name was on his list?"

"Yes, along with his brother, his business partner, his landlady, and three women."

"Including Grace, I'm willing to wager."

"Hers was the last one written there," I admitted.

"Well, you've certainly been busy today, haven't you, Suzanne?"

"Funny, when I recap it for you like that, it sounds as though we've made some real progress, but I'm not all that sure. It seems as though we've just been spinning our wheels all day."

"Be patient," she said. "You know how these things work. You collect as much information as you can, and then you evaluate it."

"You don't mind me investigating this murder?" I asked. Sometimes my mother had a tendency to be overprotective when it came to me and my safety.

She shook her head. "I'm willing to make an exception in this case. This is for Grace. You're obligated to dig into the man's murder. Just be careful."

I was about to answer when my telephone rang.

"It's Jake," I said, not able to keep the happiness out of my voice.

"Take it upstairs, and then have sweet dreams," Momma said.

"Hey, Jake," I said as I answered, climbing the stairs to my bedroom two at a time, winking at Momma before I disappeared. "I'm so glad that you called."

"I hated leaving you today like that without even getting a kiss good-bye," he admitted. "Sorry about that."

"There's no need to apologize," I said. "You had business you needed to take care of. How did the interview go?"

"Honestly? I might as well have skipped it, for all the good it did me. The guy clammed up, and now I'm going to have to find some kind of a lever to pry him open."

"You're good at that," I said. "I'm sure you'll figure something out."

"I just wish I had as much faith in myself as you do. How's your investigation going? Did you ever catch up with Leah Gentry?"

"We did. Do you really want to hear about it right now?" I knew how Jake could be when he was working a case. He didn't like to have too much information about anything that didn't relate directly to his own investigation.

"Could we postpone the recap until tomorrow night?" he asked sheepishly. "I've got a bone I'm chewing on, and I'm close to figuring it out. I just know it."

"I'm happy to wait until then. I just went through it all with Momma, so I don't need to rehash it with you."

He laughed. "Have I been replaced?"

"Not a chance," I said. It was so good hearing his voice. "Any possibility we can get together soon?"

"Why do you think I'm working so hard

on this case? The second I'm finished, I'm on my way to April Springs."

"Then start detecting, sir," I said, not able to check my grin.

"I'm doing my best. Good night, Suzanne. I love you."

"I love you, too." As we hung up, I knew that I'd never get tired of saying it.

CHAPTER 11

When I got to the donut shop the next morning, something looked out of place as I drove past the converted railroad station. Once again, I backed my Jeep up and put the headlights onto the front of the building in order to get a better look. The paint was gone, both from the window and the bricks! How had that happened? Had Jake taken care of it, or maybe even Momma? Whoever had commissioned the work deserved a great deal of thanks from me. I'd been dreading hiring someone to clean up the mess, and some mysterious benefactor had taken care of it for me.

A little later, I had a conversation that I wasn't looking forward to, but had to have nonetheless. "Can we talk?" I asked Nan when she came into the shop five minutes before her shift was due to start. I hadn't been able to sleep very well knowing that we'd be having this conversation, so I'd come in early and made the cake donuts already. It gave us half an hour before we needed to start the yeast donuts, and I was ready for her.

"I've got coffee," I said as I handed her a mug.

"Is something wrong?" Nan asked worriedly. "You're upset about the front, aren't you?"

"What are you talking about?" I asked.

"I have a nephew who does building restorations," she confessed, "so I asked him to take care of the shop front as a favor to me. I know I should have asked you first, but I didn't know where you were, and I don't have your cell phone number. I'm sorry. I should have asked permission first."

"No, it's not that at all. I love that the mess is gone. Thank you for handling that for me."

Nan didn't look all that pleased by the praise, though. "If I'm doing something I shouldn't, just tell me so I can fix it. I don't want to lose my job, Suzanne."

"Take it easy," I said. "This isn't about work."

She looked confused. "What's it about, then?"

"Peter Morgan," I said.

Her face went pale at the sound of his

201

name. "What a terrible thing."

At least she wasn't denying knowing the man. "I'm not trying to interfere with your personal life, but there are some things I need to know. If you don't want to answer my questions, you don't have to, but you should know that it's important to me that we have a bond of trust between us, since we're going to be working so closely together. Is that reasonable?"

"I suppose so," she said. It was clear that she wasn't all that comfortable with the situation, but then again, neither was I. There was no way around it, though.

"Let's get this over with then, shall we?"

"I'd appreciate that," she said.

"First, I saw your photo when I was at Rose White's place yesterday. I didn't realize that you two knew each other."

"We used to be friends," she admitted.

"Did you have a fight recently?"

"No, nothing so dramatic as all that," she said. "We just drifted apart. It happens sometimes to the best of friends."

Okay, I suppose I could buy that. "Then let's talk about Peter."

"What about him?"

Was she really going to make me ask? "How did you two know each other?"

"I used to babysit him when he was just a

boy," she admitted. "We stayed in touch over the years. It's as simple as that."

If I hadn't seen Peter's Rat List, I would have believed it. Nan was that good.

There was only one problem, though.

I had seen her name stricken boldly through in Peter's hand.

"From what I've heard, I'm inclined to believe that there's more to it than that," I said, a little more forcefully.

"Why would you say that? Who's been talking about me behind my back?"

There was no way to dance around it now. No one knew that we'd found Peter's hidden list, but there was no way I could push Nan any more without disclosing the fact that we'd found something that the police had missed in their own search. "Your name was on a list of his, and there was a rather bold line struck through it, as though he were angry with you when he did it."

Nan looked a little flustered by this information. "I admit that we had words the last time we spoke, but it wasn't serious. Peter and I had an honest and direct relationship. It wasn't unusual for us to disagree, but in the end, we were important to each other, and we'd grown to value each other's opinions. At least I believed that we had."

It was certainly a spin I hadn't expected.

The only other person who could confirm it was now dead. If Nan was telling me the truth, it was impossible to prove, but if she was lying to me, it was the perfect strategy. What it all boiled down to was simple.

Did I trust Nan, or not?

I didn't have an answer, at least not at the moment.

Nan started to stand as she asked, "Are we finished here? We both have donuts to make before we open."

I made no move to stand myself. "There's no need. I came in early, so the cake donuts are all finished."

She looked surprised. "Surely there are dishes to be done, though."

"I finished the first round," I said.

"Suzanne, I realize you don't know me all that well, but I'm a good person. I had nothing to do with Peter's murder. In my own way, I'm mourning him nearly as much as your friend Grace is right now."

I kind of doubted that, but I didn't feel I could call her on it. For all I knew, she could be telling the truth.

She stood and looked down at me. "Was there anything else?"

"Just one thing," I said. "How long have you known the police chief?"

Nan just shook her head, refusing to

answer my simple question, and she went into the kitchen. Evidently, I'd finally pushed her too hard. My first instinct was to go into the kitchen and apologize immediately, but I didn't give in to it. I didn't want to assure her that everything was all right, mostly because I didn't believe it. I found myself wishing yet again that Emma had never left, but that was pointless. My life had moved forward, and I had to do the best I could with the way things were now.

When I went back into the kitchen, I saw Nan take something from her purse. To make matters worse, she looked guilty when I spotted her.

"What's that in your hand?" I asked. Could it be a gun? Was she about to punish me for my nosiness? I braced myself for what might come next, and was relieved when Nan held up a cookie cutter in the shape of a heart.

"I couldn't resist when I saw it yesterday. It's for you," she said as she offered it to me.

I took it, and saw that the edges were strong and rigid. It was the same size as my regular donuts, but the heart shape was quite pretty.

Nan explained, "You should have at least one donut heart for sale every day. At least that's what I think."

"It's an intriguing idea," I said. "Thank you."

"I got a smaller cutter for the center hole, too," she said, and presented that as well.

"Great. We can make filled donuts, and rings as well. That really was very thoughtful of you." I felt like a real heel.

I started the yeast donut dough, and as I did, Nan managed to make herself busy around the kitchen. We didn't speak of our earlier conversation, and that was fine with me. Nan had given me her answers, and I was going to have to accept them, at least until I found out they weren't true.

As the yeast dough proofed, I started making notes in my recipe book about ways to use the new cutters. Emma and I had always taken our breaks together outside, no matter what the weather, but Nan had declined, choosing instead to work at a Word Search Puzzle at one of the tables instead. When the proofing timer went off, I started working out how to incorporate my initial design. It took a few tries to drop the hearts into the oil without them collapsing in on themselves, but once I got the knack of it, two dozen plain donuts came out rather nicely.

After they were iced immediately upon removal from the fryer, I took a bite of one and smiled. "It tastes just as good as the others."

"And why wouldn't it?" Nan asked curiously.

"You never know in this business what is going to make a difference. These are good. It's going to be nice offering them."

"We can fill the whole donuts with raspberry filling," Nan suggested. I must have frowned a little at the suggestion. Nan asked, "What's wrong with that idea?"

"Do we really want people to bite into a heart and have red filling ooze out?"

Nan shrugged. "It might be off-putting at that," she admitted. "Still, you could use lemon or custard if you'd like."

"Why don't we start with lemon filling?"

We finished working, making rounds with the rest of the dough. I had rolling cutters that allowed me to cut out a great many donut rounds in the same time it took me to cut out only a few of the hearts. They would make a nice accent shape to what I usually offered, but they'd never replace the rounds.

Once the sales shelves were stocked, we were ready to open, though we were still ten minutes ahead of schedule. I thought about delaying our opening, and then decided against it. If I couldn't open my own donut shop capriciously every now and then, what was the point of being my own boss?

In the end, it didn't matter. None of my customers came in early. Apparently I'd already trained them too well to go by my new hours.

"Good morning, sunshine," my ex-husband, Max, said as he came into the donut shop a little past our regular opening time.

"What are you doing up this early?" I asked, in total and complete shock. I couldn't have been more surprised if he'd walked in wearing a dress. "Or have you even been to sleep yet?"

He looked smug as he said, "I've changed, Suzanne. No more late nights for me. I'm turning over a new leaf."

"Who is she?" I asked. It all suddenly began to make sense. My ex-husband was a handsome devil, stress the devil part, and I knew that he could make mountains move if he wanted to impress a new woman in his life. Unfortunately, he required a constant stream of them, since he kept getting bored and discarded them nearly as quickly as he attained them.

"What are you talking about, Suzanne?"

"Max, I know you too well to believe that

208

you're doing this on your own. There's a woman behind it."

He shrugged. "What can I say? Michelle likes the mornings, and I've really gotten to like them myself. Hey, it's a good thing that I can still change, right?"

During our marriage, I'd begged him to keep more normal hours so we could actually do things together, but he'd claimed that his inner muse wouldn't allow it. I could have taken a jab at him right then over his sudden and unexpected change of heart, but I was finally getting past all of that. While he still wasn't my favorite person in the world, I didn't wish him ill, either. Well, not all of the time, anyway.

"Congratulations," I said with my brightest smile. "It sounds like you're growing up."

He held his hands up as though he were warding off evil. "Hey, let's not go too far. I'm willing to admit that I can change, but I'm not all that sure I'm maturing." His grin was infectious; it always had been. There was an easy charm to my handsome ex-husband; even I couldn't deny it.

"Baby steps, right?" I asked. "Can I get you something, or did you just come by to show off that you were out and about this early?"

"Actually, I'd like two coffees to go, and

four plain cake donuts."

As I filled his order, I said, "You really are changing. No glazes, icing, or sprinkles?"

He patted his stomach. "No, I'm trying to lose a few pounds. I've got some auditions coming up in a few weeks in L.A., and I want to be ready."

As he paid for his order, I said, "Good luck."

"Do you really mean that?" he asked.

"Of course I do. I'm glad you've found someone."

He nodded, and I saw the trace of a smile on his lips. "That's good to hear. Suzanne, I'm sorry about what happened between us. You deserved better than I gave you."

Wow, he really was growing up. "It's okay, Max. It's water under the bridge, over the dam, and all of that."

"I mean it, though," he said. "I'm glad you've got someone in your life, too."

"From the sound of it, we're both doing all right for ourselves," I said.

Max nodded, and then left the shop.

As he was going, George came into Donut Hearts. Max held the door open for him as he entered, and George did a double take as he stepped through.

"Was that Max? What was he doing here this early?"

"He's got a date," I said.

"At six-fifteen?" George asked as he stared at his watch. "It had to be a sleepover."

I laughed. "Is that what you crazy kids are calling it these days?"

George turned the slightest shade of red, and I killed my laughter. I didn't want to tease him any more. "You're up early, Mr. Mayor."

"It's George, please," he said as he took a seat at the counter. "The only folks around here who call me Mr. Mayor are the ones who want something from me."

As I got him a cup of coffee and a donut, I asked, "How do you know I don't want something myself?"

He took a bite of donut, followed it up with a sip of coffee, and then said, "Because you wouldn't beat around the bush about it, Suzanne. You'd come right out and ask me."

"True, I've never been known for my subtlety. How's the job going? Momma kind of hung it on you at the last minute, didn't she?" My mother had been the leading candidate throughout the election until she decided that George would make a better mayor. She ran a silent write-in campaign behind my back, and no one but George was more surprised than I was when he won the job.

My good friend shrugged. "Most days I'm grateful that she did. I've been able to make some big changes already, and I'm just getting started."

"Glad to hear it," I said. "What demons will you be battling today?"

"I'm going through zoning waiver applications before the council meets this morning," he admitted.

"Yes, that must be exciting stuff," I said as I topped off his coffee. It was good having George back in the place, and I hoped things would settle down enough for him to spend some real time taking up his regular spot at my counter.

"You'd be surprised," he said as he finished his donut.

"How about another one? It's on the house."

"We both know that I can't," he said as he reached into his wallet and hauled out another dollar. "But I'm still a tad hungry. Make this one strawberry iced."

I grabbed one for him and laughed. "Living on the edge, aren't you?"

"Hang on a second. I changed my mind."

"Hey, I was just teasing, George." Wow, had he lost his sense of humor under the stress of his office?

"That's not it. What are those?" He was pointing to the donut hearts I'd just made.

"They're brand-new. What do you think? Are they too cutesy?" If anyone would give me his real opinion about them, it was George.

"Seeing them there, I kind of wonder why you never made them before. I'll take one of the filled ones, if you don't mind. Lemon sounds great to me."

I got him one, and watched him smile when he picked it up and took a bite. "Just as good as ever," he admitted. "I like these. You should make more."

"I would, but it's a pain to cut them individually by hand," I admitted.

"Don't you cut all of them yourself every morning?" He looked surprised by my admission.

"Sure, but I have a cutting roller made out of aluminum with the shapes raised on them. I can cut a full batch of donuts in the time it takes me to make half a dozen of these."

"That makes sense," George said. He finished his second donut, and then asked, "Is there any way I can get this to go?"

"I can transfer it to a paper cup, or you can just take the mug and bring it back the

213

next time you come in. I trust you. After all, you're the mayor."

"I am, at that." He stood, and then shook his head.

"What's wrong, did I forget something?" I asked.

"No, but I did. How's the investigation going? I've gotten so caught up in my new job that I forgot about my old one." George had helped me out in the past with my investigations, and I'd paid him in coffee and donuts. It had been an arrangement that had suited us both. I got excellent inexpensive labor, and George got to feel useful again after his retirement. The donuts were just icing. I hoped that someday we could go back to our arrangement.

"That's okay. I know how busy you've been."

He sat back down. "Never too busy for my friends," he said. "Tell me what you've been up to, Suzanne."

After I brought him up to speed, I was surprised to see him smiling at me. "What's so funny, George?"

"You never were one to waste time, were you?" he asked. "I can't believe how busy you've been."

"Grace is holding it together, and to be honest with you, I'm trying to get this murder solved before she falls apart. We've had to ask some tough questions, and it couldn't be easy to hear the answers we've been getting."

George nodded. "It must be tough on her." He was clearly about to say something else when the front door of the shop opened, and two men in business suits came in.

"Mr. Mayor, we figured we might find you here."

George didn't look at all pleased that he'd been found. "What made you come to that conclusion, Anthony?"

"We checked your apartment, but you were already gone," another one said. "We need to talk before the meeting. It's important."

"I'll be in my office in ten minutes," George said flatly. "We can talk then."

They were startled by his response, but one finally managed to find his tongue. "Yes, of course. That would be fine. We'll see you there."

After they were gone, I said, "Wow, you don't pull any punches, do you?"

"They expect business as usual, but the sooner they realize that there's a new sheriff in town, the better off everyone will be." He picked his mug up again, then stood. "Sorry, I wish I could stay longer."

"You've got important work to do," I said.

"Don't remind me."

After he was gone, Nan popped out of the back. "Was that the mayor?"

"Yes, he's an old friend," I admitted. "Do you know him?"

"No, not personally, but I wouldn't mind meeting him." There was more than a little casual interest in her statement, and I wondered if my assistant might not have a little crush on our new mayor.

"The next time he comes in, I'll bring you out front," I said, though I wasn't really sure how I felt about the prospect of getting them together. I probably didn't need to worry, though. It appeared that George and his new secretary were getting along just fine, and I didn't want to have any part in spoiling what could be a budding romance between them.

Nan smiled, and then went back into the kitchen. I kept looking outside, wondering where all of my customers were. It happened that way sometimes, when folks seemed to decide to take a break from donuts all at the same time. I knew that it was just a coincidence, but it couldn't keep me from feeling a little paranoid anyway.

By ten, things began to pick up, and when we locked the front door at eleven, we'd nearly made up for the earlier lull.

Not a single heart-shaped donut was left in the case.

Maybe Nan was on to something, but only time would tell.

LIGHT AND AIRY BAKED CAKE DONUTS

I came up with this recipe and wasn't sure what to call it, so I decided to be literal and just say what they are. These are delicious as they are, but when they're topped with sweet orange marmalade, they hit another level entirely!

Ingredients

Mixed

1 egg, beaten
1/2 cup sugar, white granulated
1/2 cup buttermilk
1/8 cup canola oil
1 tablespoon butter, melted
1 teaspoon vanilla extract

Sifted

1 cup flour, unbleached all-purpose
1 teaspoon baking powder
1/4 teaspoon nutmeg
1/8 teaspoon salt

Extras

Sweet orange marmalade as a topping

Instructions

In one bowl, beat the egg thoroughly, then add the sugar, buttermilk, canola oil, melted butter, and vanilla extract. In a separate bowl, sift together the flour, baking powder, nutmeg, and salt. Add the dry ingredients to the wet, mixing well until you have a smooth consistency.

Using a cookie scoop, drop walnut-sized portions of batter into small muffin tins or your donut maker, and bake at 365 degrees F for 6–10 minutes, or until golden brown. Top with marmalade while the donuts are hot.

Yield: 6–10 small donuts.

CHAPTER 12

"I'm not too early, am I?" Grace asked when she knocked on the front door of the donut shop a few minutes after I'd closed.

"No, you're right on time. I have to balance out the register, and then I'll be ready to go."

"Is she still back there?" Grace asked in a hushed tone.

"No, Nan's already gone," I admitted. "Why do you ask?"

Grace shrugged, but there was no denying how relieved she looked by the news. "Her name just keeps coming up in our investigation. It's kind of odd, wouldn't you say?"

"Do you think she actually might have had something to do with Peter's murder?" I asked. "I had a long conversation with her this morning, and it's looking less and less like coincidence that she's involved. She was Peter's babysitter when he was young, did you know that?"

"No, not a clue. Do we know that it's actually true?"

I admitted that I didn't, and she followed up with another question. "How about her relationship with Rose White? Did she explain that to your satisfaction?"

"They were best friends who had a falling-out," I answered.

Grace wasn't buying that, though. "If that's true, why would Rose still have a photo in her apartment that shows the two of them together? That certainly seems odd to me."

"Maybe," I admitted. "You're not a big fan of my new assistant, are you?"

"I don't know if I am or not. I just think we need to dig a little deeper, and get someone who can verify what she's told you."

I thought about Nan, and how much I still didn't know about her. Could she have been involved? I really couldn't say one way or the other, something that was very unsettling for me. "I'll keep my eye on her," I said.

"I'm serious, Suzanne."

"So am I," I admitted. The money balanced beautifully, something I was always grateful for, and as I made out the deposit, I asked, "What are we going to do with seventeen donuts?"

"I'll take one off your hands, and some coffee, too, if you have any left," she said.

"Help yourself," I said as I poured her coffee in a to-go cup.

"Why don't we bring the donuts along with us," she said. "You know how good they are at greasing wheels."

"They *are* tough to say no to," I admitted. "We're heading back to Union Square, right?"

"You bet. I want to talk to Henry Lincoln and find out what was going on."

"Do you think he'll open up to us?" I asked. It always amazed me how willing folks were to talk to us about the most intimate things.

"With your donuts as a gift, how can he say no?"

"Mr. Lincoln? Do you have a minute?" We'd driven to Union Square straightaway, and I was relieved to find Peter's former business partner in his office. Lincoln was a short, heavyset man, with a carefully tailored suit that didn't quite manage to hide his build. We'd chased suspects down in the past, and it was never an easy thing to do. Worse yet, after we found some of them, they still refused to answer our questions. Without

222

badges, Grace and I had to rely on our charm, and my donuts, too.

I was always glad when we had the treats with us.

"Are those donuts?" Lincoln asked, spying the dozen I had with me. I'd left the rest in Grace's car, just in case we needed them for something else.

"That's right, and they're all for you."

He wasn't sure what to make of that. "And you're just giving them to me, why exactly?" He looked at us both carefully, and then his gaze lingered on Grace. "I know you. You were Peter's girlfriend, weren't you?"

"I was," she admitted. "I'm sorry for your loss."

"Come in. Sit down," he said. "In all honesty, it was more your loss than mine."

"Does that mean that you're not sorry that he's dead?" I asked.

"I didn't catch your name," he said as he looked at me and frowned slightly.

"I'm Suzanne Hart."

The frown deepened. "Do I know your mother?"

"You do," I answered, keeping my response as simple as I could. The less I said about Momma, the bigger presence she'd have in the conversation.

"Thought so," he said, and then muttered

something else under his breath.

"So," I said, "back to Peter. You didn't sound that upset about him dying."

"Of course I am, but not for such altruistic reasons as your friend there. It turns out Peter was pretty adept at lying, even to his partner. I hope he wasn't that way in his personal life."

"I'm sorry to say that he was," Grace admitted.

Lincoln just shook his head. "The man never knew when to play it straight, and he never realized just how good he had it."

"How exactly did he lie to you?" I asked.

"Where do I start? We were going along fine, making a little money here and there, without any real downside. Then he got the opportunity of a lifetime, and he wanted to cut me in on it. Nice guy, right?"

"What happened?" Grace asked, her voice softening.

"I lost half of everything I had in the world," Lincoln said. "I might as well have married a trophy wife and given it all to her. At least then I would have gotten some companionship out of the deal."

"I'm confused," I said. "How does that make Peter the bad guy? He must have lost money, too."

"That was the impression I got, until three

days ago, that is. I was at a bar drowning my sorrows when the man we'd invested with happened to come in. After a few drinks, he asked me why I didn't pull out when Peter did, when the fund was still making money.

"I nearly spit out my drink. I asked him what he was talking about, and he told me that Peter had pulled out everything he had just before the dive, but that I'd told him that I was going to ride it out no matter what. He screwed me to the wall, but good."

"What good did that do him, though?" Grace asked.

Lincoln sighed heavily. "We had an argument just before it happened, a stupid little thing that didn't mean anything. Well, good old Pete took offense, and he skewered me for disagreeing with him."

"You must have wanted to kill him," I said lightly.

"I'd be lying if I said the thought didn't cross my mind," Lincoln said, and then realized what he was saying. "Hold on a second. You're not trying to hang this on me, are you?"

"Well, you said yourself that you had a motive."

"Maybe so," Lincoln said, "but I wasn't the only one, not by far. The man polarized people more than anyone I've ever known in my life. There must be a list a mile long of folks who wanted to see him dead." He turned to Grace. "I'm sorry, I don't mean to talk about him that way to you."

"I understand," Grace said, something she'd been repeating since we'd started our investigation.

"Could you name anyone besides yourself who might have a motive?" I asked. "Generalities won't do any good. We need names and concrete reasons they should be considered as suspects."

Lincoln leaned back in his chair, and for a second, I worried that it might not take his full weight. "Why should I help you hang some other poor guy? I love donuts as much as the next guy, but they aren't exactly worth throwing somebody under the bus."

"Well," I said with my brightest smile, "there's always my mother."

He sat up at that point, and the frown suddenly reappeared. "There's that, but do you have anything else besides donuts to make it worth my while talking to you?"

"Funny, I thought you'd be eager to give us names of folks we could investigate besides you," I said with a smile.

"What makes you two think you can catch a killer, anyway?" he asked. "Neither one of you is a cop."

I shrugged, trying to look as nonchalant as I could. "We've done it before, working with the state police, and on our own." That might have been stretching things a little, but I could justify it if I had to. After all, we'd helped Chief Martin solve cases before, both with Jake's assistance and alone.

That seemed to impress him, at least a little. "At the top of my list would be his brother, Bryan," Lincoln said.

"We've spoken to him already," I said. "Anyone else?"

He nodded as he glanced at Grace, and then quickly looked away. "I don't have too many other details about his personal life."

Grace shook her head. "Mr. Lincoln, if you're worried about hurting me, don't. I know about Peter's dalliances."

"I'm sorry to bring it up," Lincoln said. "But Peter fancied himself a ladies' man. Why he would go out for hamburgers when he had steak at home is beyond me."

Grace didn't react, so it took all I had not to do so myself. Was this man seriously hitting on Grace right after Peter's death? He had nerve, I had to give him that.

"Thank you," Grace said noncommittally. "Are there any names you can share with us?"

Lincoln leaned back again, and then began ticking them off on his fingers. "There was a girl named Leah, another one named Kaye, and a pair of older women he had a few flings with that he bragged about when he was drunk. Peter used to say that no woman could resist him, no matter how young or old. He said just recently that he had dates on the same night with a woman in her early twenties and one in her late forties. He wasn't much of a man, no doubt about it."

"Any idea who the older ladies might be?" I asked.

Lincoln shrugged. "He said something about his landlady, and a friend of hers. Peter bragged that neither one knew he'd been seeing the other. I swear, considering all the women in his life, it's amazing that he ever got anything done." He sat up and pushed away from his desk, creating more open space between us. "That's all I can give you. Sorry I couldn't be of more help, but there's nothing left to say, and I can't imagine why we'd ever need to talk again."

"If you'd like us to take your name off our suspect list once and for all," I said, "it's easy. Just give us your alibi for the night and the next morning when Peter was murdered, and we'll be out of your hair."

He was about to comment on my request when his phone rang. He glanced at the number, and then said, "Sorry, but I've been waiting for this call. It's going to be a while, so there's no need for you to wait."

Grace and I got the hint, and stood up together.

As we did, Lincoln said into his phone, "Hold on one second, please," and didn't say another word until we were gone.

"What do you make of that?" I asked Grace when we were back out in her car.

"I already knew that Peter was a cheat. Now we're just discovering how unfaithful a man he really was."

"Do you really believe that he was having a fling with Rose White?" I asked.

"We've had two people refer to it, so I've got a feeling that it's probably true."

A thought just chilled me. "And her friend? Could he have been talking about Nan? If he was, it gave my new assistant reason of her own to want to see Peter dead."

"It could also explain why their friendship broke up. I guess there's no way to know for sure until you ask her," Grace said.

"That's a conversation I'm not looking forward to," I admitted.

"I could do it myself, if you want me to,"

Grace volunteered.

That was the only scenario worse than me doing it on my own. "Don't worry about it. I'll take care of it. Tomorrow will be soon enough, though, don't you think?"

"Of course," Grace said.

"What do you think of Henry Lincoln? Could he have murdered Peter?"

Grace didn't even need time to consider it. "Peter may well have ruined him, so yes, I think the man has his own reasons for wanting him dead. Besides, we don't have an alibi for him, so there's no way to check whether he has someone covering for him or not. Until we find out where he was when Peter was murdered, his name stays on our list."

"Agreed," I said. "In the meantime, who do we talk to next?"

I thought about it, and then realized there was one name that kept coming back to the top of my list. "I think we should find Bryan and see just how deeply his hatred for his brother ran."

"I'm game if you are, but I've got to warn you, I doubt he'll be pleasant."

"You mean he could be ruder than he was before?" I asked.

"Trust me, he was on his best behavior then," Grace said.

"Oh, boy. I can't wait. Do you know where he lives?"

"Actually, it's not that far from here," Grace said.

"Then let's go."

We found Bryan working in his driveway. He had portable tables set up under a canvas canopy with plain metal legs and a sand-colored top that blocked the sun. Under the tables were the bags and boxes of things we'd taken from Peter's apartment, and he was currently sorting through the bags that Grace and I both knew contained nothing but trash.

"So, you got it after all. Good," I said as we approached, trying my best to look cheerful. "We were hoping that Rose would change her mind."

"Rose had nothing to do with it," Bryan said smugly. "My lawyer went over there with me and made her turn it over. I'm the executor of his estate, so I'm in charge, not her, and not anyone else."

If he was looking for a fight, I wasn't about to give him one. I was there for answers, not a verbal sparring match. I looked over the garbage and asked in a voice as interested as I could make it, "So, have you found anything?"

He looked disgusted by the piles, and I could see that he'd at least laid layers of newspapers down before he'd gotten started. "No, you were right about that," he conceded grudgingly. "It's all garbage."

"Hey, you never know. You might have found something important that the rest of us missed," I said. "It was smart of you to double-check after us." I was doing all I could to appease the man, and Grace caught on.

She smiled at him and said, "If you're finished with this, we can help you bag it all up again."

"That would be great," Bryan said. Apparently he was pretty amiable when everyone did exactly what he wanted. Then again, who wasn't?

Grace and I grabbed trash bags and started working. We had the mess rebagged in no time. "Where would you like these?"

"Just take 'em to the curb. Tomorrow's trash day."

We did as he asked, and when we got back to the tables, he was wiping them down using spray cleaner and paper towels. Once they were clean, Grace and I dried them off, and I grabbed the first box.

"What are you doing?" Bryan asked.

"We're just trying to help."

He took the box from me, and then he put it back where it had been. "Thanks for your offer, but I'm taking a break before I dig into those."

"Bryan, we've already seen what's in them, remember?" I reminded him.

He nodded. "I know, but this is thirsty work. Either one of you care for a beer?"

I shook my head. "No, but a Coke would be great."

"I just have Pepsi," he said.

"Pepsi's fine," Grace said.

"Be back in a second."

He walked into the house, and as he was retrieving our drinks, I asked Grace, "Any thoughts on how to approach him? How much harder can we push him?"

"Bryan never was one for subtlety," Grace said. "I'm beginning to think that we should tell him what we're doing up front, and ask him to help us find his brother's killer."

I was surprised by the suggestion. "Do you think he'd actually respond to that?"

"Not a chance," Grace said, laughing just a little. "But how is he going to be able to refuse us, unless he's the killer himself? We might not get anything out of him, but we might just get some answers."

"That's a smart idea," I said.

"I have my moments."

Bryan walked back out with four cans: two sodas for us, and two beers for him. "It's getting kind of warm out here," he said.

"April does that," I answered. After we'd all taken drinks, I said, "You're probably wondering why we're here."

"You're snooping," he said, and then took another sip.

I was about to protest, when Grace spoke up. "That's right," she agreed. "We're going to find out who killed your brother, and we came to you for help. You probably want the murderer found even more than we do."

Bryan took a drink, whether because he was thirsty, or because he wanted to buy some time to think, I didn't know. After he finished a long swallow, he said, "Sure, of course I do. What can I do to help?"

"Who do you know who might have wanted to see your brother dead?" Grace asked softly.

"Who didn't? Seriously, between his business and his love life, the man was a mess. I don't know why our folks always thought that he was the one who would turn out the best. I'm going to miss him, there's no doubt about that. But I don't have any names for you. Sorry, there's really nothing I can do."

"Well, you can let us take your name off

234

our list so we can focus on who really killed your brother," I said. "Do you have an alibi for the night he was murdered, and the early morning hours afterward?"

Bryan looked at me angrily. "Are you harping on that again? I can't believe you think I'd kill my own brother."

"It happens, no matter how much people don't like to acknowledge it," I said. "So, where were you?"

"I was with a friend of mine all night until six the next morning," Bryan said.

"A woman?" I asked him.

"It sure wasn't a dude," Bryan said with a bit of a laugh.

"Tell us her name," Grace said. "And we can clear it up in a heartbeat."

"It's not that easy," Bryan said. "She doesn't want me spreading her name around any more than I have to. I already told the cops. If you want to find out, go ask them."

This was all news to me, but then again, the chief of police didn't exactly keep me updated on how his murder investigations were progressing, despite how much I wished that he would. "If you told him, you can share it with us. We're discreet," I said.

Bryan shook his head. "Listen, she's ticked off at me enough already without having you two snooping around in this mess." He looked at the boxes, and then said, "Now, if you don't mind, I'll tackle the rest of these myself."

"We'd be glad to help," I said, but Bryan just shook his head.

"No, thanks. I'm good."

After we left Bryan to his boxes, we made our way out of the neighborhood.

I asked Grace, "Is it just me, or do you feel we're being stonewalled everywhere we turn? Why won't people give us their alibis? All they seem to want to do is point fingers at everyone else."

"Can you really blame them?" Grace asked. "Most of them probably don't even have alibis. Peter was last seen when, exactly?"

"The last I heard, it was between ten at night and five the next morning when the police found him," I said.

"Now, think about how many people are home alone during those hours. Not everyone keeps your crazy schedule, so they probably weren't all asleep, but I'm guessing most of them were home alone. It's a tough alibi to prove or disprove."

"Maybe we're going about this the wrong way," I said, struck by sudden inspiration. "Who was the last person who admitted to seeing Peter alive?"

"Do you mean besides me? I'm guessing that has to be Trish. She threw him out of the Boxcar Grill for being drunk and disorderly." Grace paused, and then asked, "You don't think she had anything to do with Peter's murder, do you?"

"Of course not," I answered, not even giving the question the dignity of the least amount of thought. "If there are four people in the world I know are innocent besides me, she's one of them."

After a moment's hesitation, Grace asked, "Did I make the list?"

"Of course you did," I said, trying my best to reassure her.

"Then who else is on it? I'm just curious, that's all."

"Well, I'm pretty sure that Momma didn't do it, and I could swear under oath that Jake didn't kill him."

Grace whistled as she pulled over to the curb. "And everyone else in town is a suspect?"

I smiled. "Not just in April Springs. I'd have to say that we have a ten-county radius of potential killers."

"That's not going to make it easy finding the murderer then, is it?"

"Hey, don't give up on me. If it were that

easy, everyone would be able to do it," I said.

Grace's car was still idling, and she reached into the backseat, flipped open the donut box lid, and selected one of the last few remaining treats. After she took a bite, she asked, "We're not going to need these, are we?"

"Help yourself," I said. "If you don't mind driving while you eat, why don't we go to the Boxcar Grill and see if we can get Trish alone? I want to hear every detail about what happened when she threw Peter out, and more importantly, who else was at the diner when she did."

"They didn't necessarily have to be eating there," Grace said.

"No, but what good does it do us to assume that it was someone else lurking in the shadows? It's going to be a lot harder to find the killer if they weren't even around the Boxcar the night of the murder, so we might as well work on the assumption that they were there as well."

"Okay, at least it sounds like a plan, but I have another thought."

"Go on, I'm always eager to hear what you've got to say," I said.

"After we get a list of names of folks who were at the Boxcar when it happened, why don't we ask them if they happened to see anyone outside, either when they went in, or when they left?"

"Sounds good to me," I said. "Let's go talk to Trish."

CHAPTER 13

"Trish, I know this isn't the greatest time in the world for you," I said as I looked around the crowded diner, "but when you get a break, can we talk?"

"Are you kidding? I always have time for the two of you. What's up, ladies?" she asked, shaking her ponytail a little as she moved her head toward us. "Is something wrong?" Trish must have noticed Grace's expression, because she quickly added, "Grace, I didn't mean to be so flip. I'm sorry about Peter. In a way, I feel sort of responsible for what happened to him."

"We know you didn't kill him, Trish, so you have nothing to apologize for," Grace said. "From what I've heard, you did what you had to when you threw him out, and if he was as drunk at your business as he was when he came to my place, you did the right thing. I can't imagine anyone blaming you for what happened to Peter."

240

Trish nodded. "That's a relief. I'm glad you feel that way."

"Honestly, if anyone here is to blame, it's me. I threw him out after you did, and I slapped his face in the process and did my best to humiliate him," Grace said.

"You can't blame yourself for any of that," I told her. It was the edge of the breakdown I'd been dreading. The odd thing was, though, she was kind of steely when she said it, and that worried me even more.

"Who do I blame then? It's not Trish's fault, and it's surely not yours," Grace said softly.

"Maybe you shouldn't let me off the hook so easily. I saw a problem, and I ignored it," Trish admitted. "I could have called him a cab, I might have had one of my regular guys take him home, or I could have even let him sleep it off in back. I didn't do any of those things. I threw him out, and the next thing you know, someone killed him. If I'd stepped in and done something, he never would have made it to your place, and he wouldn't have trashed Suzanne's building, either."

Grace reached out and hugged Trish. "So then we both share some of the guilt."

Trish nodded as she pulled away. "I guess so. There's certainly enough of it to go

241

around."

I moved toward them and said, "Ladies, let's not forget one important fact. None of us hit Peter in the back of the head. His killer did that, and that's who's responsible for his death, not any of us."

Grace nodded. "You're right. That *is* what's important. Trish, we're going to solve this, and then Suzanne and I are going to wallow and try to drown our grief in ice cream and donuts."

"Count me in," Trish said. "I can mourn with the best of them." She hesitated, and then said flatly, "That's not why you're here, though, is it?"

"We need your help, but it's pretty clear we came at a bad time."

"It's always a bad time, if you let it be," Trish said. "Hang on. I'll be right back." Trish disappeared into the kitchen just as local blacksmith James Settle approached the register to pay his bill. Without giving it another thought, I stepped behind the register, took the bill, rang up the sale, and then gave James his change.

"I didn't know you were moonlighting here, Suzanne," he said.

"I try not to make a habit of it, but you never know where I might pop up next," I answered with a grin. The two of us had gotten off to a rough start when he'd tried to pull up the old train rails that ran through the park and near my converted depot, but we'd worked things out, and now I counted him as one of my newest friends.

James just laughed, and after he was gone, Trish came back to the register with Hilda in tow. "She's agreed to handle the front while Gladys cooks."

"I think 'agreed' might be a tad too strong a word," Hilda protested. "You know I hate running the cash register."

"It's not that bad, and you know it. If Suzanne can do it, surely you can handle it yourself," Trish said.

"You saw that?" I asked.

"You'd be amazed by what I can see from the kitchen," Trish admitted.

"Listen, I'm sorry if I stepped over a line."

"Are you kidding? If you do need to moonlight, you've always got a place to work here with me."

I tried to hide the blush I felt coming on. "So, you heard us, too?"

She laughed. "The mighty Trish hears all and sees all. Listen, I bought us about five minutes before Hilda starts to have a breakdown. Let's step outside, and you can tell me what I can do to make your lives easier."

"No one's ever offered to do that before,"

I said with a smile. "What all does that offer cover, exactly?"

"More than you know, less than you can imagine," Trish said. She spied one of the picnic tables she kept in front of the Boxcar for folks who had to wait in line to get in, and she led us to it. "I've been on my feet all day, so this is a nice break for me."

"Again, we're sorry about interrupting you at work," Grace said.

Trish took her hands in hers and said, "Grace, I'm a huge fan of yours, but if you apologize to me one more time today, I'm going to snap. Understand?"

Grace managed a slight smile. "Got it."

"Good, I'm glad that's settled. Now, I know you're both here to ask me about Peter's murder, but I'm afraid I can't help you with any details. I didn't see or hear a thing after I threw him out, and that's the truth."

"We figured as much, but we have a few more questions," I said.

Trish grinned, and I asked, "What's so funny?"

"Chief Martin gave up a lot easier than you two. He asked me a few general things, and then he moved on. I got the distinct impression that his leads were taking him in another direction. How about yours?"

"We're doing the best we can, with our limited resources," I admitted. "Some folks just won't talk to us without a badge behind the questions, and not having George or Jake around doesn't make things any easier, either."

After a moment's pause, she said, "You know, I could always close the diner for a few days and help you do some digging if you're interested."

I knew that Trish depended on her steady income from the diner nearly as much as I did from my donut shop, so it wasn't an offer she made lightly.

"We appreciate that," I said, "but what we really need at the moment is information."

"Then ask away. I'm a regular dictionary of facts."

"Who was eating at the diner when you threw Peter out?" Grace asked gently.

"I didn't physically remove him; you know that, don't you? He was drunk, so it wasn't like I had to manhandle him or anything. I showed him the door, told him to scoot until he sobered up, and he did as he was told. That was the total sum of our interaction, I swear it."

"What we want to know is," I asked, "who else was here when you did it? Did anyone leave right after it happened?"

"And did anyone take off just before you tossed him out?" Grace asked, adding her own follow-up.

Trish took in all of our questions, and then said, "You're trying to see who might have done it, and whether they were here or not when I booted him. It's smart."

"We do have our moments," I said with a grin.

"And great minds think alike. That happens to be one of the few things Chief Martin did ask me."

I felt a little bit deflated knowing that he'd gotten there before me, but at least we were on the same page. "What did you tell him?"

Trish reached into her pocket and pulled out a sheet of paper. "Actually, I had to make him a list. He's coming back to get it in half an hour."

I spied the names, and then asked Grace, "Do you have any paper and a pen on you?"

She supplied them, and I quickly jotted down the names. Sadly, none of them were on my suspect list, but that didn't necessarily mean anything. If a friend of a friend had been there at the time, it would just have taken one telephone call to get the killer onsite while Peter was so obviously helpless.

I was just finished copying the list when I

heard a familiar voice say, "I'll take that, if you don't mind."

Chief Martin had come to collect Trish's list early, and in the process, he'd gotten confirmation that I was indeed digging into his homicide case with both hands.

"Find anything interesting?" he asked as he took Trish's paper from me.

"No, not really. I think it's about what I expected," I said.

"Suzanne, this isn't nearly as amusing as you're making it out to be."

"Trust me," I said. "I know there's nothing funny about it. You don't think I actually *want* to be digging into this murder, do you? It's not exactly a regular thing for me, Chief."

"You sure act like it is sometimes," he said.

Grace said, "Don't blame her, Chief Martin. She's doing all of this for me. I need to know what happened to Peter."

The chief's tone of voice changed into a softer range as he said to her, "Grace, I understand your frustration, but my department is doing everything in its power to find Peter's killer. We've got resources you can only dream about, and we're putting them all to the test."

"But there are people who will talk to us

who won't be candid with you," Grace said. "You've said so yourself in the past."

He shrugged. "Maybe once or twice, but as a matter of course, I'm still the law around here, and I'm the one who investigates any crimes that happen in April Springs."

"Tell you what," Grace said. "We'll let you have that list to yourself for a day. You can talk to anyone you want to and we won't interfere. Right, Suzanne?"

I didn't want to agree to that, not for one second, but Grace had put me in a position where I really didn't have much choice. "I promise."

"Now hang on one second," Chief Martin said. "You two are in no position to try to make bargains with me. I've been willing to give you a little leeway in the past, but it's not something you should ever take for granted."

"I don't know. Their offer sounds reasonable to me," Trish interjected.

"I don't recall asking you your opinion, either, young lady," Martin said.

Trish grinned at him. "Then think about how much better it is when I just volunteer it. Chief, you know these two almost as well as I do. Frankly, I'm amazed they're even giving you a day before they start snooping.

It's got to be a hardship for them, and the only way you're going to stop them is to put them both in jail, and you know that won't work, for more reasons than I should have to explain to you."

Trish had thrown my mother into the mix, no matter how indirectly, and I wasn't sure how the police chief was going to react. I always did my best to tread very lightly when Momma came up in our conversations, since I never wanted my relationship with her jeopardized by something I said to the police chief.

He looked at her narrowly, and then nodded. "It's against my better judgment, and I'll deny it if any of you lunatics ever repeat it, but I'll find a way to live with that."

I stuck out my hand. "Let's shake on it, then."

The chief took my hand briefly, and then dropped it just as quickly.

Before he could get away, though, I asked him something that had been gnawing at me since Peter had been thrown out of Trish's place. "I'm guessing you did an autopsy," I said.

"It's a matter of course, yes," the chief admitted reluctantly.

"Did they happen to check to see if Peter was actually drunk when he was killed?"

Before the chief could answer, Trish said, "Trust me, the man was plowed. I can tell when someone's faking it, and he was the real deal. Besides, what did he have to gain by getting thrown out of my place?"

"With Peter, the only thing that's certain is that you can't take anything for granted. If he thought someone was on his tail, it might have made more sense to him to act more vulnerable than he really was. If he made a public showing of being falling-down drunk, he may have intended to bait his attacker into making his move."

"Actually, that's not a bad thought," the chief said. But before I could let the warm and fuzzy feeling run through me, he added, "But sorry, he was nearly twice over the legal limit of public intoxication."

Whether the chief realized it or not, he'd just given me something I could work with. I'd been thinking about an entirely different line of questioning, but I could forget about that for now.

It was pretty clear that the chief wasn't all that interested in having a question-and-answer session with us, despite a few other things I wanted to ask him. He took the paper I'd given him, folded it up, and put it in his breast pocket. "Now, if you ladies will excuse me, I've got a list of potential witnesses to go over with my force."

After he was gone, Trish said, "Whew, that was a close one. For a second there, I thought we were all going to jail."

As much as I appreciated my friend's help, there was one thing we needed to get cleared up immediately. "Trish, thanks for stepping in, but don't ever use my mother as a lever against that man again. Understand?"

"I'm sorry," Trish said, instantly contrite. "I just couldn't get him to budge, so I thought that might be a handy way to get him to agree."

"If anything like that ever comes up again, trust me; I'll find a way to handle it myself."

"I've got it, and I'm sorry, Suzanne," she said.

I did my best to smile brightly. "It's forgotten."

She nodded, and then asked, "What are you two going to do now, since you have to wait twenty-four hours?"

"Actually, we never promised that," I said. "Grace made it a point to say one day, and as far as I'm concerned, every new day starts at midnight."

Trish shrugged. "Okay, but who are you going to call at that time of night?"

"I don't know. I can't look at the list until

then." I stared at the paper in my hand, knowing full well every name that was printed there, since I'd copied it myself so recently. I wasn't going to use them to pursue any leads, though. A deal was a deal, and if Chief Martin caught me breaking my word to him, all possibilities of cooperation in the future were gone. Not that I'd go back on my word anyway. The way I was raised, a handshake is better than any signed contract, and my good name meant more to me than I could ever explain. In a great many cases, in my opinion, contracts were for cowards who wouldn't keep their word otherwise.

"So, what do we do now?" Grace asked as I folded the list up and put it in my back pocket.

"Well, I've been thinking. I believe we should talk to Rose White and see how much of what we've been hearing about her is true."

Trish stood and brushed off the seat of her jeans. "Well, I'd love to tag along, ladies, but I've got a business to run. Keep me informed, though. I'm interested in what you find."

Grace and I drove to Union Square, but it was all for naught. Rose was gone, or not interested in answering our repeated knocks on her door.

Either way, it didn't appear that we'd be talking to her anytime soon.

"I think we should probably just call it a day," I said as Grace and I headed back to April Springs. We'd been putting in some miles today, but mostly it felt as though we'd been spinning our wheels again. Every time we found something that might be a lead, it just got more and more convoluted. "We can attack that list tomorrow when we're fresh."

"Do you mind if I see it for a second?" Grace asked. I suddenly realized that she hadn't had a chance to read it since I'd copied it down from Trish's original.

I started to hand it to her, but I hesitated as I asked, "You're not going to start digging on your own, are you? We made a promise to the chief of police, Grace."

"I'll abide by what we agreed on," she said, "but that doesn't mean I can't start thinking about the best ways to approach these people first thing tomorrow. They might be a little gun-shy after talking to Chief Martin, so we might not be able to come at them all so directly."

"Okay," I said as I handed the list to her, "but don't do anything without me."

"I wouldn't dream of it," she said.

So, why did I have the feeling that she might, anyway?

I knew that I couldn't babysit her, though. Grace was a grown woman, and if she wanted to do something she thought was right, I couldn't stop her.

I just hoped that she wouldn't.

As we drove home, Grace looked up at the sky and said, "It looks like a storm is on its way, Suzanne."

I glanced up at the quickly darkening sky, and saw flashes of lightning in the distance toward April Springs. We got fierce spring thunderstorms sometimes in our part of North Carolina, blackening the day as though it were nighttime; the lightning was particularly intense at our cottage. Since it was surrounded by so many trees, it wasn't all that unusual to hear the cracks of lightning even as the thunder exploded, and we'd lost a few trees over the years in powerful storms. I would have given just about anything to be safe in my room at the moment, though. I had a bad feeling about just how much of a punch this particular storm might have.

The rain came then, suddenly and in waves, slapping fists of water at the car. I couldn't imagine how Grace was able to drive in it. "Maybe we should pull over and wait this out," I suggested.

"It's fine, Suzanne. I can still see," she said, just a little intensely since she was concentrating so hard on keeping her company car on the road. I could see her hands gripping the steering wheel so tightly that her fingers were nearly white.

Then the hail hit, pounding down within the rain, round balls of ice the size of pennies beating down on us like hammers.

"Pull over," I ordered, having a hard time making myself heard over the sound of the icy attack.

"I'm going to, as soon as I can find a spot!" she answered frantically.

I searched the side of the road as well for some kind of refuge, but the two-lane road was hemmed in by trees on both sides of that stretch. We'd passed the one place where we could have stopped safely two hundred yards back. As Grace slowed her pace, she put her emergency blinkers on, signaling anyone who might be coming that we were on the road as well.

"Up there," I said, pointing through the pounding rain and hail. "There's a spot just ahead."

"I see it," Grace said. "We're going to make it."

And as she slowed and got ready to pull her company car over to the side of the road, I felt the first slam from the back of her car.

Someone had just plowed into us from behind.

The car was still rolling from the impact as I turned around to see who was behind us, but I couldn't make out any details of the driver in the storm. All I could see was a white pickup truck, but it was impossible to make out who was behind the tinted windows with the low level of visibility I had. For some odd reason, it was easier seeing in front of us than it was behind.

"Are you okay?" Grace asked me.

"I'm fine. How about you?"

"Just dandy," she said.

Just about then, the car hit us again, this time much harder, driving us into a stand of trees just shy of where we'd hoped to turn off. The front of Grace's windshield shattered on impacting a low-lying branch, and I felt the airbag explode in my face as we finally came to a full stop.

"Are you all right?" someone said a minute later as he tapped on the passenger side window of the car.

"I think so," I said, turning to look at an older man wearing a bright yellow rain jacket and a matching hat, even though the rain had suddenly, inexplicably, stopped. The storm had passed, leaving behind an eerie green glow in the sky that looked as though a tornado might be nearby.

I took a quick inventory of myself, realized that the airbag had deflated just as suddenly as it had appeared, and found that my ears were ringing and my nose was a little sore; besides that, I was fine.

I looked over at Grace. "How are you doing?"

"I'm not sure," my best friend said, and her voice sounded a little hazy to me through the pounding in my ears. "All I know is that suddenly I've got a splitting headache."

And that's when I saw the blood on her forehead.

PROBABLY NOT THE WORST DONUT IN THE WORLD YOU'LL EVER EAT

I know, high praise, right? The thing about this donut is that it has its fans, enough for me to go to the trouble to make it, but I'm not among them. If I were doing these just for me, I'd double the chocolate, add some butter, and change the buttermilk to chocolate milk instead, but I make these for someone else in my family, so I don't touch the mix.

Ingredients

Mixed
1 egg, beaten
1/2 cup sugar, white granulated
1/2 cup buttermilk
1/2 cup canola oil
1 teaspoon vanilla extract

Sifted
2 cups flour, unbleached all-purpose
1/3 cup cocoa powder
2 teaspoons baking powder
3/4 teaspoon cinnamon
1/4 teaspoon baking soda
A dash of salt

Instructions

In one bowl, beat the egg thoroughly, then add the sugar, buttermilk, canola oil, and vanilla extract. In a separate bowl, sift together the flour, cocoa powder, baking powder, cinnamon, baking soda, and salt. Add the dry ingredients to the wet, mixing well until you have a smooth consistent dough. Knead on a lightly floured board 4–8 minutes, until the dough bounces back at the touch.

Roll the dough out on a lightly floured surface 1/4- to 1/2-inch thick, then cut out donuts and holes with handheld cutter.

Fry the dough in hot canola or peanut oil (370 degrees F) for two to three minutes on each side.

Drain, then top with powdered sugar immediately or eat as they are.

Yield: 8–12 small donuts.

CHAPTER 14

"You're bleeding," I said, searching her head for the wound. A bit of branch covered in leaves was still inside the car right between us, and I had to push it aside to see just how badly Grace was hurt.

She touched her forehead lightly. "It's just a scrape, Suzanne. Another quarter inch and it would have missed me completely."

"Don't either one of you move," the man said through my open window. "I hear sirens coming." He handed me a clean white hand towel and said, "Press that on her wound."

"Let me have it. I can do it myself," Grace said, snatching it from me. She pushed it delicately against her wound, and then said, "Stop fussing over me. There's nothing I've got that a Band-Aid and an aspirin won't cure." She pushed at her door to open it, but it wouldn't budge. I glanced over and saw that she was wedged up against a tree, a sapling, really. A foot either way and we would have had to deal with hitting a pair of large hickory trees, some of the toughest wood around. As it was, we'd gotten lucky.

I started to open my door when the kind stranger said, "Stay right here."

"You shouldn't blame yourself. That storm was pretty bad, and the road conditions were horrible. It wasn't your fault," I said.

"Did you hit your head?" he asked me as he looked me over. "I don't see anything, but you can't be too careful."

"I'm fine," I said. "I just don't want you to feel as though you're responsible."

He shook his head. "Lady, I don't know what you're talking about. I was driving in the other direction when I saw you go off the road. I wasn't the one who clipped you."

"You weren't driving the white pickup?" I asked, thoroughly confused now.

"I drive an old blue station wagon," he admitted. "But I saw the pickup. After he hit you, he just kept on driving. If it's any consolation, he nearly ran me off the road, too."

"Did you happen to get a look at the driver?" I asked.

"No, it all happened too fast, and his windshield had a pretty dark tint on it. I didn't think they allowed those things in North Carolina."

The first ambulance arrived on the scene two seconds later, and the old man was brushed aside as the emergency workers saw to us. After confirming that we were all right and not too much worse for wear, they let us both out through my side of her car. I was a little wobbly at first, but I managed to hold myself up with the side of the vehicle.

Grace came out next, and they checked her eyes with a penlight, and then did a thorough inspection of each of us. After pulling the towel away and looking at Grace's wound, the woman dressed in a blue jumpsuit said, "You got lucky. It's just a scratch."

"Thank you. That's what I've been telling everyone, but nobody seems to want to believe me," Grace said.

"Don't get too excited. We're still taking you ladies to the hospital," the tech said. "You both need a real checkup."

"It's really not necessary," Grace said.

"Whether it is or not, we're going, so you might as well stop fighting it."

"Grab my purse, Suzanne," Grace said, resigned to the fact that we were going to take a ride in the ambulance.

"I'll get it." The older man heard her and

retrieved it just as a police car from April Springs drove onto the scene. I found myself hoping that it was anybody but our chief of police, but this wasn't my lucky day in too many ways.

As Chief Martin got out of his car, he asked the EMT, "Are they okay?"

"We think so, but we're transporting them to the hospital so they can get full exams."

He nodded, clearly relieved that we were all right, and then he asked in that pointed voice of his, "What have you two gotten yourselves into this time?"

I was spared the need to answer when the EMT spoke up for me. "You can interview them at the hospital after they're finished with their examinations."

The chief of police just nodded. "Believe me, I will. I won't be far behind you."

We started to get in the back of the ambulance when Grace looked back at her car. "How in the world am I going to explain that to my boss?"

That's when I finally got the feeling that she was going to be all right. As we made our way to County Hospital, I wondered if what had happened to us had been an accident with a hit-and-run driver, or if the intent had been more malicious than that.

■ ■ ■ ■

"Okay, what have we got?" a familiar voice said as the back doors of the ambulance opened up. We were in the hospital bay of the emergency room, and I was glad to see that my friend Penny Parsons was on duty.

"What's happened?" she snapped again as she immediately sprang into action.

As the EMT started to tell her, I knew that we were in good hands.

An hour and a half later, Grace and I were both being released from the hospital when Chief Martin showed up, with my mother beside him.

She hugged me fiercely, and though the woman was barely five feet tall, I could swear I felt a few of my ribs crack under the pressure. "Hey, take it easy on me," I said. "I was just in an accident, remember?"

"Are you hurt?" she asked, the concern heavy on her face.

"Not from the wreck, but I think your bear hug just broke two ribs."

She eased her grip, and then my mother smiled at me. As she brushed a strand of hair out of my face, Momma said, "I'm so glad you're not injured."

She turned to Grace and added, "Oh, dear. That looks dreadful."

Grace touched the bandage on her forehead lightly. "I'm sure it looks worse than it is. It wasn't that big a scratch. I'm guessing they ran out of Band-Aids, so they had to pull out the big bandages."

"Young lady, you are coming home with us," Momma said, using a tone of voice that nobody would dispute. "And I don't want to hear another word about it. Do you understand?"

Grace nodded solemnly. "Yes, ma'am, I do. Thank you."

She turned to me and said, "And as for you, Suzanne, your shop will be closed tomorrow."

"Momma, I have to earn a living. And besides, I wasn't hurt at all."

"Trust me, you'll be sore tomorrow; you both will," the chief said. "You need to take it easy. One day off won't kill your bottom line, Suzanne."

It was a testament to how shaken I must have still been from the accident that I didn't even fight them on it. "Fine. Somebody needs to call Nan, and then put a sign up in the window."

"I'll take care of it," Chief Martin said. "Now, let's get you two home."

"I thought you needed to interrogate us," I said.

He shook his head. "Interview, not interrogate, and thankfully, Luke Davenport gave me just about all I needed to hear. I've got an APB out on white pickups with damaged grills, but that's most of them on the road in these parts, if you ask me. I've got a feeling we won't be able to find who hit you from behind. I still can't believe he left the scene of an accident like that."

As we got into the squad car, I said, "I'm not all that sure it was an accident. What do you think, Grace?"

"The road conditions were pretty rough," she admitted, "But I'm not saying it couldn't have been on purpose. Do you think that truck was *trying* to hit us?"

I suddenly realized that there had been no doubt in my mind. "Why would they run away, then?"

The police chief said, "I can think of a handful of reasons that don't have anything to do with malicious intent. The driver could have been drinking, he could have had an expired tag, or maybe even no driver's license or insurance at all. I can't just assume that it was on purpose."

"But he hit us twice," I said a little louder than I'd meant to.

"Suzanne, the road had hail on it, along with standing water, and the rain was still pounding down, from what the witness told me at the scene. It's a miracle that truck didn't hit you three or four times. If it had, I doubt you both would have walked away from that car."

"How bad is it?" Grace asked.

"Well, I didn't hear the doctor's report, but I'm assuming you're both okay if they let you walk out together."

"Not us," she said. "My car."

Chief Martin whistled softly before answering. "That I'm not so sure about. If it's ever on the road again, it's going to take a lot of work. But my guess is that it's totaled."

Grace just shrugged. "So, they'll probably just issue me another one."

"Just like that?" I asked, jealous of my friend's company, and the support she got from them.

"Well, I'm a supervisor, so I'm allowed to take my car out when I'm on vacation or after business hours. It's all covered under their plan."

"Does that mean that you weren't covered before?" I asked, remembering how many miles we'd put on it in the past in search of clues and not doing business for the cosmet-

267

ics company.

"Let's just say that it was a gray area then, but it's all covered completely now. Don't worry about me. I'll be driving something soon enough."

"Not too soon, though," Momma said. "You need to recover from this first."

"It's not nearly as bad as it looks. It's just a scrape," she repeated.

"But it could have been worse," Momma said. Her mothering instincts were out in full force, and Grace was caught in the same web that I was. "I'm surprised that the two of you were out on the road when the conditions were so bad."

I was about to explain when Grace said, "We didn't have much choice. We were just trying to get home."

Momma hesitated, and then said, "Well, I can't fault you for that. The important thing is that you're both going to be all right."

Once the police chief got us home, he left to call Nan and put a sign in the window at Donut Hearts. Grace and I settled on the couch while Momma made us some of her famous chicken noodle soup, a meal that she swore could bring dead men back to life.

As we sat together, I asked, "Do you really think it was just an accident?"

"I don't know," Grace admitted. "I'm not sure I want to consider the possibility that someone did it on purpose."

I knew what she meant. It wasn't a good feeling knowing that there was someone out there who wouldn't mind seeing both of us dead.

"But who could we have made mad enough or desperate enough to try to kill us?" I asked.

"I'd think we'd have to assign numbers, the way we've been nosing around the past few days."

"Grace, we need to be on our toes," I said firmly. "Just in case this wasn't an accident like everyone else so clearly wants to believe."

"Hey, you've just about convinced me," she said, and her hand went back to her head.

I was about to say something more when someone knocked on the front door, and when Momma answered it, I saw that it was Jake.

Then I lost my breath as I made it to my feet just in time to be wrapped in his embrace.

This time I didn't mind the pressure on my chest nearly so much.

If he wanted to break a rib or two of mine,

he was welcome to it.

"I'm so glad you're okay," he said as he finally pulled away. "What happened to you two?"

"We were run off the road," I said.

He looked surprised by my answer. "That's odd. I heard it was an accident. You were out driving in a rainstorm and your car went off the road."

Grace shrugged. "Honestly, I'm not sure exactly what happened."

He looked at her bandage. "Did you get hit very hard?"

She shook her head. "No, it's just a scratch. I didn't forget anything. Like I said, though, I'm just not sure what happened."

Jake grabbed a nearby chair and I rejoined Grace on the couch. "Go on. Tell me exactly what happened, and don't leave anything out, no matter how trivial it might seem to you."

After we brought him up to date, Jake asked, "Is Martin out looking for the truck? If nothing else, the driver left the scene of an accident." My boyfriend looked angry, and I saw the cop's expression on his face, one that was cold and hard, built of steel. I'd seen that look before, and knew that Jake was in his full state police inspector's mode; I pitied the man who'd tried to kill us if

Jake ever caught up with him.

"He's got an APB out on it," I explained, "but like he told us, how many trucks around here are white and have some damage on them? It's not exactly 'needle in a haystack' material."

Jake sat back. "That's true. He hit you twice, you say?"

"The second shot was harder than the first one," I admitted.

Jake turned to Grace. "And you're really not sure that it was deliberate?"

"I'm not calling Suzanne a liar," she said defensively.

Jake took a deep breath, and when he spoke again, his voice softened. "Of course not. The reason I'm asking is that the driver would have a better idea than her passenger if it was all done maliciously." As he said it, he leaned forward and squeezed my hand.

"Hey, I'm not upset by the question," I said. "Maybe I'm just hoping it was meant to scare us off. At least that might mean that we were getting somewhere digging into Peter's murder."

My boyfriend smiled at me wryly. "Suzanne, only you would take it as a good sign when someone tries to kill you."

"I don't know that they wanted us dead," I amended. "It didn't feel that way. After

271

all, we were both pretty vulnerable after the wreck, and if the pickup driver wanted to kill us, one more hit could have done it. This was just a warning."

"Or an accident in bad weather," Grace added.

Jake nodded. "Well, I've driven a pickup in the rain before, and if there's no weight in back, or if the tire treads are worn down just a little, or if one of a thousand other things happened, it could have been an accident." I started to say something when he added, "Then again, it could have been a warning for the two of you to back off." He hesitated, and then looked at me wryly. "Any chance you two will do what they want, if that's the case?"

I grinned at him. "What do you think?"

He smiled warmly in return. "That I just wasted my breath asking the question." Jake paused a moment, stood, and then got his phone out. "Excuse me, ladies, but I've got to call my boss."

I stood as well and put my hand on his shoulder to steady myself. "What are you going to do, Jake?"

"One way or the other, I need to get off this case so I can help the two of you."

I could see where this was going, and I didn't like it. "Jake, that's truly sweet of you, but I still don't think you need to do that."

"Suzanne, I appreciate what you're saying, but ultimately it's my decision. I'm going to step away from this, even if it means I have to turn in my resignation to do it."

I knew how much of Jake's identity was tied into what he did, and I wasn't about to let him throw that away for me. "You can't. I won't let you."

"I'm not sure you have the right to forbid me from doing anything," Jake said, his voice creeping into the cold zone.

I don't know what I would have said if Momma hadn't just come out of the kitchen. She looked at Jake and said, "Would you like to join us for some chicken soup? I'm making plenty." Then she took in the tension in the room, and looked squarely at me. "Suzanne Hart, what have you done this time?"

"Jake's threatening to quit his job to help us on this case just because he's worried about me."

"And why wouldn't he be?" Momma asked.

"Not you, too," I said. "I'm a grown woman, you two. I can take care of myself."

"Of course you can," Momma said. She turned to Jake, and then took his phone gently from his hands. I wouldn't have tried that myself, but Momma had a way about her, and he let her take it without raising an eyebrow. "I'll just hold on to this until you come to your senses."

"You don't want me looking out for her?" he asked gently.

Momma laughed. "Oh, no, I'm not stepping into that bear trap. I just don't want you doing something that I'm certain you will regret. You knew that Suzanne liked snooping into murder when you first met her, agreed?"

"Yes," he acknowledged.

"So, what's changed since then?"

He bit his lip, then shrugged. "I don't know."

Momma smiled brightly. "I do. You love her now, and you don't want to lose her."

He nodded. "That's it. Of course it is."

"So, do you think you'll win any points shadowing her every move, trying to wrap her in bubble wrap to keep her safe all of the time?"

Jake shook his head. "Of course not. I'd never do that."

"Then you need to know that whatever happens, Suzanne is doing what she wants, or feels that she needs to do. You've got an important job to do, Jake, and you love it. Throwing that away for my daughter, no matter how altruistic your motives are, is just plain stupid, and you're not dumb. Now, may I give your telephone back to you, or do I need to keep it a little while longer?"

Jake sheepishly reached a hand out for it. "No, ma'am. I'm good now. Thank you."

"It's my pleasure," she said. After Jake had his phone back, she pulled him down to her level and kissed his cheek, and I could swear I saw the tough old bear blush. No doubt about it, my momma had a way with people. "Now, how about that soup? Surely you have that much time to spare before you go back to work?"

"That would be great," he said.

She nodded. "I'll make some of my famous grilled cheese sandwiches as well, and there's some pie left over from yesterday. We'll have ourselves a regular feast."

"What just happened?" Jake asked as Momma disappeared into the kitchen. "She took that phone from me as though I were a kindergartner with a toy that didn't belong to him."

"Don't feel bad," Grace said. "She's focused her magic on me before, and there's just no way to say no to her."

"Don't look at me," I added. "I've been around her my entire life, and she can still do it to me when she sets her mind to it. It's kind of unnerving, isn't it?"

We all agreed, and Jake and I took our seats again, waiting to be summoned into the dining room.

After a moment, Jake asked tentatively, "Suzanne, are you planning on opening the donut shop tomorrow?"

"Why do you ask?"

"Well, I may be overstepping my boundaries again, but unless I miss my guess, you two are going to be pretty sore tomorrow. It might not hurt to take a day off." He looked as though he were waiting for an explosion, and I felt sorry for the poor man. He'd taken enough beatings tonight, and I wasn't about to add to them. "I'll close the shop, then."

"Listen, I know it's none of my business, but I really . . . Hang on. What did you just say? Did you actually agree with me?"

Grace laughed. "Don't take too much credit for it. She's already been persuaded. Donut Hearts will remain dark tomorrow."

Jake looked at me closely. "Are you sure you didn't hit your head?"

I reached back for a pillow and threw it at him. He plucked it deftly out of the air, and then laughed. "I'm just saying," Jake added with a grin.

"Okay, maybe I am a bit of a workaholic, but then again, so is my boyfriend."

"Agreed," Jake said.

"Don't look at me," Grace chimed in. "We all know that I goof off every chance I get."

As Grace said it, her cell phone rang, and she grimaced. "It's my boss. I'd better take this outside. It might require some major tap dancing on my part."

Grace stood up, a little unsteady at first, and then walked out onto the front porch.

Jake stood, moved to my couch, and then kissed me soundly. "It's about time. I thought she'd never leave."

CHAPTER 15

I grinned up at him after his welcoming kiss. "If I'd known what you were waiting for, I would have thrown her out when you first walked in the door." I kissed him again, and then said, "Listen to me, you big lunk. I'll promise to be careful and not take any chances I don't have to, but you have to promise me you'll stop trying to protect me from the world and myself. Okay?"

"It's a deal," he said as he brushed a bit of hair out of my face. I thrilled to his touch, such a gentle gesture that left me feeling so loved. "I promise."

Of course, Momma chose that moment to come out of the kitchen. "I'm sorry, I'll come back later," she said as she started backpedaling. "Dinner is ready whenever you are."

"It's fine, Momma," I said. Jake steadied me as we stood. "Grace is on a phone call with her boss, so I'm not sure when she'll be back in."

Just as I said it, the front door opened and Grace came back in with a puzzled expression on her face.

I immediately jumped to the worst conclusion. "She didn't fire you, did she?"

"Actually, she seemed pretty happy that I was okay. She said they've been meaning to upgrade my company car for months, and this will give them the perfect opportunity to do it."

"So, you're not in trouble at all?" I asked, amazed by Grace's continuing ability to fall into a barrel of mud and come out dressed for the prom.

"No, she said everything was fine on our end. Remind me to give Chief Martin a big kiss the next time I see him."

"Why is that?" Momma asked, a sentiment I echoed. I wasn't sure that I'd heard her correctly myself.

"He found my emergency contact info, and since my boss was on the list, along with you and your mother, he thought he'd save me some grief. He called my boss, explained to her that the accident wasn't my fault, and that I was lucky to be alive. Somehow he made everything right."

Momma nodded. "I told you all that Phillip has a good heart."

"He must. He chose you, didn't he?" I asked, and then I hugged my mother.

"What was that for? I didn't do anything," she said, a little confused.

"Pass that on to your boyfriend for me, would you? I'm not sure I could do it face-to-face myself," I said with a grin.

She just nodded. "I'll do it, and add a little interest as well. Now, who's hungry?"

We all admitted that we were, and Momma led us into the dining room, where she'd laid out our best china and silver.

As we took our seats, I said, "This is a little fancy for chicken noodle soup and grilled cheese sandwiches."

"Your grandmother always used to say that the plainer the meal, the finer the china should be," Momma replied.

"Funny, I never heard her say that," I protested.

Grace laughed at me. "It still makes for a good story, though, doesn't it?" She turned to my mother and added, "Thank you for taking me in, yet again."

Momma hugged her. "Grace, I couldn't love you more if you were one of my own." She turned to me, and said, "You know what I mean, Suzanne, I intend no offense to you by saying it."

"Hey, I agree, Grace is a part of the family."

Grace looked a little embarrassed by the outpouring of emotion. To deflect the attention, she looked at my boyfriend and said, "Don't feel bad not being included."

Jake held both hands up as though he were defending himself. "Are you kidding? I'm just happy to be here right now, sharing a great meal with three such lovely and classy ladies. How could I possibly feel bad about anything?"

I looked around the room. "Is there someone else here I don't know about?"

"Suzanne," Momma scolded me lightly, though I could see her suppressed smile.

"Momma," I replied, mimicking her tone perfectly.

She laughed outright then, and spread her hands. "Shall we say grace, and then eat?"

Grace and I both said, "Grace," so nearly perfectly in timing that it sounded as though we'd used one voice.

Momma looked at Jake and said, "See what I put up with?"

"I don't know how you do it," he said. "You are a saint, no doubt about it."

As we ate, we enjoyed the delicious, simple, and yet very hearty meal. Though the food was excellent, the company meant even more. After the soup and sandwiches, we each had a hefty portion of pie, but when it was finally all gone, Jake stood and stretched. "That was delicious. I hate to eat and run, but I'd better get back."

"If you'd like to spend the night, you're welcome to our couch," Momma said.

"Thanks, but I'd better be heading back if I'm going to wrap this case up so I can get back here." He took my mother's hand, kissed it lightly, and then said solemnly, "Thank you for everything."

Momma beamed. "You are most welcome. Grace, why don't you take a seat on the couch and I'll take care of the dishes while Suzanne shows her young man out?"

"I've got a better idea," Grace said. "You've done enough for us tonight. Why don't I start the dishes, and after Suzanne's said her good-byes, she can help me."

"You've both had a rather eventful day, and tomorrow is going to be difficult enough as it is," Momma protested.

"All the more reason to help out now while we can move with relative ease," Grace insisted.

"At least let me help a little now," Momma said.

Grace could clearly see that she wasn't going to win that battle, so she did the smart thing and agreed.

They were just starting the dishes when I walked Jake out onto the porch. "Isn't that sweet? They wanted to give us some privacy so we could say good night."

He grinned, and then said, "Let's not waste it then, shall we?"

After a deep and satisfying kiss, he said, "I'd better go while I still have the will-power."

"I've never known you to crumble before," I said with a grin.

"Well, I've never come so close to losing you once I found you, either."

"I'll be okay. I've been in some tough jams before, remember?"

He nodded, and then hugged me tighter. "That doesn't make it any easier, though."

"Call me when you get back to Spruce Pine," I said as he put one foot on the step.

"I promise," he said, and then Jake was gone.

When I got to the kitchen, the dishes were nearly finished. "Hey, I wasn't gone that long, was I?" I asked as I picked up a dish towel and dried the remaining dishes.

"What can I say? Your mother and I work well as a team," Grace said.

Once we were finished, I caught myself yawning. "What's next?"

"You sound as though you could use some sleep."

"I'm too full to sleep," I said just as the telephone rang. Since I was standing closest to it, I started to reach for it as I said, "I'll get it."

Somehow Momma beat me to it, though. I listened as she told whoever was calling to phone back tomorrow after lunch, and then she hung up.

"Who was that?" I asked, naturally curious.

"Another friend of you two girls calling to see how you're doing. I've told them all to call again tomorrow after lunch, but a few apparently didn't get the message."

"That's a relief," I said.

"Why is that?" Momma asked.

"I was beginning to think that no one cared," I said.

"Trust me, dear girls, it is only out of respect for me that they haven't flooded the cottage by now with their well-wishes."

"It's either that, or they're afraid of you," I said with a grin.

"I'll allow that, since I'm not above using it as a motivating factor."

"You don't have to tell me," I answered.

She swatted me with a towel, and then said, "I'm putting you two in my bedroom, and I'll take your room, Suzanne."

"I can sleep on the couch," Grace volunteered. "I don't want to displace either one of you."

Momma answered, "Nonsense. I need a minute to put on fresh sheets, and then I suggest you both try to get some sleep. It will be just like old times. Grace, I swear, sometimes you were here more as a child than you were at your own home."

"That's because my mother couldn't feed me nearly as well as you could," she said with a grin.

Momma returned the smile. "I loved your mother dearly, but she could burn water, couldn't she?"

We all laughed at that with fond memories of someone now gone, and Grace and I stopped protesting about the sleeping arrangements. The last few eventful days since the murder, plus the accident, had taken a great deal out of both of us, and I had a feeling that neither one of us would have any trouble at all falling asleep tonight.

I woke up at my usual time, though, started to climb out of bed more out of habit than anything else, and every muscle in my body screamed out in protest. The wreck must have jarred me more than I'd realized. I'd planned to get up, sneak out of the house, and open the donut shop as usual, despite everyone else's expectations.

That clearly wasn't happening, though. I'd be lucky to be able to do it tomorrow, judging by the way I felt at the moment.

I settled back into sleep without much trouble, and heard the reassuring sound of Grace snoring softly beside me.

I woke up again to the smell of fresh pancakes, not a bad way to start any day, in my opinion. Grace was still asleep, but as I got up and stretched, I must have woken her up. Shots of pain ran through me as I moved, and I realized that everyone had been right. I felt as though I'd been worked over by someone who knew what they were doing.

"Sorry," I said. "Go back to sleep if you can."

Grace sat up in bed, and then gasped a little. "Tell me you're hurting at least as much as I am," she said as she rubbed her neck gingerly.

"I feel like I got hit by a bus," I admitted as I put on my robe.

"Or a pickup truck," she amended. "Wow, I thought everyone was exaggerating."

"So did I. It smells like Momma's making

breakfast, but if you want to stay in bed, I'll make your excuses."

"No, I've got to face getting up sooner or later," she said. "The faster we start moving around, the sooner this stiffness is going away." Grace managed to get out of bed, and after putting on one of my robes, which she absolutely swam in, we walked out into the living room.

Momma was smiling brightly as we moved into the dining room, flitting among platters of pancakes, bacon, sausage, and eggs.

"Who else is coming by for breakfast?" I asked as I surveyed the layout.

"It's just the three of us," she said. "I wanted to be sure you both got whatever you wanted today."

"Do we have anything for pain?" I asked, still marveling at just how sore I was.

"Coming right up," Momma said as she presented a tray full of bottles of aspirin, pain relievers, and other meds, along with two large bottles of water and a pair of glasses already topped off.

As I grabbed two pills and a glass, I said, "Wow, you were really ready for us."

"I wanted to be prepared," she said.

After Grace took a dose as well, Momma said, "I hope you're hungry."

I wasn't sure that I would be, but to my

surprise, I found my stomach growling at the sight and smell of all of that food. "This all looks great." I grabbed a plate and started dishing out goodies, with Grace just behind me.

I noticed that Momma wasn't eating, though. "Aren't you going to join us?"

She laughed. "Goodness, I ate hours ago. Suzanne, did you even glance at a clock when you got up?"

"No, it never even occurred to me," I admitted as I peeked into the living room.

It was after ten.

"I can't believe I slept that long," I admitted. "Why didn't you wake me?"

"Are you kidding? I'm impressed by how long you stayed in bed. You must have needed it, or you wouldn't have been able to do it."

"I tried to get up at my regular time," I admitted. "I was going to open the donut shop, but I just couldn't do it."

"I'm glad you resisted the temptation," she said. "April Springs will somehow be able to manage without their donuts for one day."

"I suppose you're right," I admitted. I felt a little guilty, but it was too late to do anything about it now. If Emma had been my assistant, she and her mother could have

288

opened for me, but there was no way I would ever ask Nan to do it. "This smells wonderful."

"Well, dig in," she said.

I didn't have to be told twice. I ate the heartiest breakfast I'd had since I'd opened Donut Hearts, and there wasn't a sugary confection on the table. As much as I loved donuts, it was a nice change of pace having Momma's country feast instead.

"Wow, I'm stuffed," I said as I finally pushed away from the table. "Momma, you outdid yourself."

"It was my pleasure. Grace, did you get enough to eat?"

"I'm as full as I've been in years," my best friend said. "I can't thank you enough for taking me in like this."

"No thanks needed," she said as the doorbell rang. "Now, who could that be? I distinctly told everyone that no one was to come by until after twelve."

"Show them in anyway," I said. "We're fine with seeing whoever's out there."

"Not until you've each had a chance to take a long soak in the tub and have some time to get ready for company. They'll go away, and come back when I say," Momma said resolutely. I knew that no one was going to get past that gatekeeper. "After you've done as I've suggested, then we'll see."

I knew better than to fight her on it.

She left to answer the door. Grace and I both tried to stand, and then settled back down onto our chairs.

"I don't know about you, but I think I'll stay right here a while," I said.

"My thoughts exactly," Grace replied.

Momma came back a few seconds later with a frown on her face.

"What's wrong?" I asked her.

"I'm not sure if you'd like to see who's out there, but I couldn't just turn them away, not given the circumstances."

Wow, that was something. Who could break down Momma's will? "Go on. Show them in," I said.

"Better yet, we'll see them in the living room," Grace said.

"Are you sure about that?" I asked.

"Suzanne, we have to get up sometime," Grace answered with a smile. "It might as well be now. Come on, I'll give you a hand if you need it."

"No way," I replied with a smile of my own. "If you can get up, so can I."

We stood, each of us fighting our grimaces. "There," Grace said, "that wasn't so hard. Whoever is out there better be worth it, though."

As we walked out into the living room, I realized that there was no doubt about that.

"Emma, what are you doing here?" I asked as I hugged my former assistant, despite the pain it caused. "I thought you'd be getting settled into school by now."

She hugged me back, gently, I was relieved to find, and as she pulled away, I saw that there were tears in her eyes. "Suzanne, I missed you so much."

I wiped a few of her tears away and said, "Hey, it's okay. We're both fine. There's no need to cry."

"I'm glad you're not hurt, but that's not it," she said. "I never should have left April Springs. I made a huge mistake when I went away to school. Would you take me back at Donut Hearts?"

I settled down onto the couch, and Grace took one of the chairs so Emma could join me. "Emma, what happened? I thought that going away to college was exactly what you wanted." She'd certainly told me enough times how she couldn't wait to put April Springs behind her, and the sudden change of heart was puzzling.

"Nothing went right," she admitted, clearly fighting the urge to cry. "I hated the professors, the classes, my roommates, everything. Suzanne, I never dreamed how

291

great I had it here. I just couldn't take it."

"You're just homesick," I said as I touched her shoulder lightly. "It's understandable, and I know that it will get better. You just have to give it some time."

She shook her head. "I can't do it. I'm miserable there. Home is where I belong, at least for now. Whether I can come back to work for you or not, I'm moving back home. Mom and Dad packed the truck with my stuff, and I didn't hear about the accident until I read it in Dad's newspaper this morning. He didn't say a word to me when they picked me up, can you believe it?" Emma's father, Ray Blake, owned and operated the *April Springs Sentinel*. Of course he'd run a story about our accident. There wasn't that much hard news to cover in our small town, but I'd never even considered the fact that he'd do a story on what had happened to us.

"He was just trying to protect you, I'm sure," I said. "He's like that, remember? Are you certain that you want to come back home without giving school a fair chance?"

"Suzanne," she asked, her voice quivering a little, "don't you want me to come back to April Springs?"

"Of course I do, Emma," I said, and it was nothing but the truth. "I just don't want you to give up on your dream."

"Dreams change," she said. "Besides, I can go back next year if I change my mind. There are still plenty of classes I can take at the community college that will transfer." She looked at me tentatively as she asked, "How's the donut shop going? Is Nan working out okay?"

I had forgotten all about my new assistant. "She's doing fine," I admitted, "but she's not you. Emma, if your heart's set on leaving school, I won't try to change your mind, but I can't just fire Nan because you came back. It wouldn't be right. You see that, don't you?"

It was pretty clear from her expression that that was exactly what she'd been hoping for, and I felt like a complete heel, but I couldn't cut Nan loose just because Emma was back.

"I understand," she said. "If it doesn't work out with her, though, would you keep me in mind as her replacement?"

I stood, feeling a little better, whether from the meal or the pills I'd taken, and hugged her. "Emma, you know I will. As a matter of fact, if you're interested, you can come in and work the day Nan takes off every week. I know it's not much, but it's the best I can do. How does that sound?"

"Great," she said, though only halfheartedly.

"I'm sorry I can't offer you more."

"Don't worry about it. It's perfect. Honestly, I'm just glad that both of you are okay." She finally looked at Grace and asked, "How are you feeling?"

"I'm as sore as I can be, but other than that, I'll make it just fine."

"I'm sorry about Peter," Emma added, and I felt a slight chill come into the room.

"So am I," Grace said, though what she meant exactly was hard to determine.

"Well, I'll let you two rest," Emma said as she headed for the door. "I just wanted to pop in and say hello." She lowered her voice, and then added, "I'm coming back later during your regular visiting hours, per your mother's request."

I grinned as she said it. Why wasn't I surprised?

"Your first shift starts in three days," I said. "And Emma?"

"Yes?"

"I really am glad to see you again," I said.

"Me, too."

After she was gone, Momma came out of the dining room, and I didn't doubt for one second that she'd heard the entire exchange.

"Am I doing the right thing keeping Nan

on?" I asked her and Grace.

They both nodded, which made me feel better instantly.

Momma said, "Suzanne, you made a commitment to Nan, and she's doing her job. I'm sorry Emma is out in the cold, but you did what you had to do."

"Do you really agree, Grace?" I asked.

"I don't see that you had any choice. Don't be too tough on Emma for coming home, though. I had two roommates who did the exact same thing, and they're both doing great now. Going away to school just isn't for everyone."

"I hope she follows through with what she said and keeps up with getting her education," I said.

"She took classes at the community college before, and if I know Ray Blake, she'll be enrolled again come the fall. In the meantime, we need to get dressed. I'll just run home, take a quick shower and change, and then I'll be right back."

"Would you like me to go with you?" I volunteered.

"No, I may be a little feeble at the moment, but I think I can make it on my own," she said with a smile. "Besides, I want to take that bath in my own tub."

Something occurred to me just then.

"How are you going to get home? Are you really up to walking that far?"

Grace's expression changed in a heartbeat. "That's right, my car's gone."

"Oh, I almost forgot. There was a rental car dropped off for you this morning," Momma said as she walked into the room. "It's a nice one, too."

Grace nodded. "It doesn't surprise me one bit. My boss never was one to take half measures, and she must have found out from Chief Martin where I was staying."

Still, Grace hesitated, and I had to wonder if she wasn't quite ready to drive again after what had happened the day before. It might take a little time to get her confidence back behind the wheel after the accident. I said, "Tell you what. I know you're a big girl and all, but if you give me ten minutes to get ready, I'll go with you."

"You don't have to do that," she said, though I could hear in her voice that was exactly what she wanted.

"I know that I don't have to. I want to," I said as I made my way up the stairs. "In the meantime, sit tight on the couch and I'll be right down." I turned to Momma and added, "I'll take that bath tonight. Deal? For now, the shower will be perfect."

She got it instantly, which was one of the

things I loved about my momma. "That sounds like a splendid plan," she said.

I tried to hurry, but the hot water felt too good beating down on my sore body. I must have overstayed my allotted time, but by the time I was dressed in fresh jeans and a new T-shirt, I was closer to being ready to take on the world than I had been since the accident.

To my relief, Grace was still there.

"Here I am, clean as a whistle and ready to go," I said with a smile.

"How was your shower?"

"Better than it had a right to be," I said.

"I'm looking forward to that myself," she replied.

"Then let's go."

I called out to Momma, who must have gone in the kitchen after I left to get cleaned up, and said, "We'll be back a little later."

She popped her head out of the other room. "Take your time, but there is going to be a flood of visitors precisely at twelve, and I'd hate to disappoint them."

I glanced at the clock and saw that we had plenty of time, even if Grace decided to take twice as long as I had getting ready. "Don't worry about us. We'll be here."

"Good. And bring your appetites with you. I have another feast planned."

I groaned a little at the thought of another of her big meals so close on the heels of the last one. "Just make it something light, okay?"

"Sorry, we both know that's not in my vocabulary," she said with a smile. "Can you smell that aroma?"

I took a big whiff of the air and didn't need to guess. "It's your famous lemon chicken," I said. It was a recipe my mother was known for far and wide, and rightly so.

"Maybe I can spare a little room for a bite or two," I said with a grin.

Momma laughed. "I thought you might. Now shoo, you two. I've got work to do."

As we closed the front door behind us, I whistled when I saw Grace's rental. It was quite a bit nicer than the Jeep I drove every day, and it was even a little better than Grace's wrecked company car. "My, my, my. We're traveling in style, aren't we?" I asked with a grin.

Grace didn't return my smile, though. She was staring at the new car as though she thought that it meant to hurt us.

I added, "Hey, I'd be happy to drive, if you're not ready to get behind the wheel again."

"No, I can do it," she said, taking one firm step after another toward the car. "I've got to face it again sometime, so it might as well be now."

"Are you sure?"

She allowed herself a quick laugh. "It's less than three football fields away to my place. I'd better be able to do that, since so much of my job these days is driving from one rep's territory to another."

I hadn't thought about that. "You don't have to go back to work right away, though, right? You still have some time on your leave."

"Don't worry," Grace said as she got into the car. "By the time I go back to work, I'll be fine. Come on, let's see how this baby handles."

We drove the brief route without incident, and as Grace pulled to a stop in her driveway, she stroked the steering wheel lightly. "You know what? I could get used to this."

"And think," I said as we got out. "This is just the rental. Your new one is going to be nicer than this one." I laughed as I added, "Sometimes life just isn't fair."

"And sometimes it's just right," she said with a smile.

A BAKED OLD-TIMEY SPIN

A great many donut recipes use very similar ingredients, so sometimes I like to take an old favorite and play with it. Not all the experiments work out, but some are good enough to add to the family list of recipe possibilities, and this is one of them. The taste is different from what you might expect in a donut, and some love it as much as others don't. If you've got a rainy day and feel like playing, this one's worth a try.

Ingredients

Mixed
1 egg, beaten
1/2 cup sugar, white granulated
1/2 cup buttermilk
1/4 cup whole milk
1 tablespoon butter, melted
1 teaspoon orange juice

Sifted
1 1/2 cups flour, unbleached all-purpose
1 teaspoon baking powder
1 teaspoon pumpkin pie spice mix
A dash of salt

Instructions

In one bowl, beat the egg thoroughly, then add the sugar, buttermilk, whole milk, melted butter, and orange juice. In a separate bowl, sift together the flour, baking powder, pumpkin pie spice mix, and salt. Add the dry ingredients to the wet, mixing well until you have a smooth consistent batter.

Using a cookie scoop, drop walnut-sized portions of batter into small muffin tins or your donut maker, and bake at 360 degrees F for 8–12 minutes, or until golden brown.

Yield: 8–12 small donuts.

CHAPTER 16

"What's all this?" Grace asked as we drove back to the cottage I shared with my mother. She'd taken a little longer than I had to shower and change, but then again, I didn't have a bandage on my head to protect from the water. I hoped that she'd be able to downsize it soon. It made her scratch look much worse than it actually was. There were two cars already parked in the driveway besides mine and Momma's, so Grace had trouble finding a place to park. She ended up edging off into the grass, the only space she could have taken without blocking our visitors in.

"That's Emma's car," I said as I pointed to it, "and the other one belongs to George. Since Momma told her that she couldn't stay long this morning, she came back to find out what really happened yesterday."

She looked at me for a second and frowned. "How many times are we going to have to retell this story over the next few weeks?"

"More than either one of us is going to want, I'm willing to bet," I said. "Should we make a run for it while we can?"

"I'm feeling better after that shower, but not good enough to go on the lam," Grace answered with a smile. "After all, they *are* our friends."

"I know." I opened the passenger side door, but Grace put a hand on mine. "Suzanne, we need to talk before we go in."

"Why is that never a good thing to hear?" I asked.

"Nothing's wrong. I just think we should get our stories straight. Now don't take offense, but are you positive that the wreck was intentional? Because if you are, I've got your back. Just say the word, and I'm on board. We can tell the same story, and let folks believe what they choose to."

I looked at the sincerity in her gaze, and realized that I could have no better friend. "I've been thinking about it, and honestly, I believe it might serve us better to say that it was an accident after all."

She looked startled by my statement. "You were so sure, though."

"I still am," I admitted. "But what good does it do us to stir up any more trouble than we've already got? Besides, if we tell everyone that it was an accident, maybe the killer will get sloppy again and make another run at us."

She shook her head. "We're taking an awfully big chance here, aren't we?"

"Hey, we can stop anytime. You just say the word."

Grace frowned, and then asked, "You'd really do that? I know how you are when you get your teeth into a case."

I grinned at her. "You got me. It's doubtful that I could stop now even if I wanted to, which I don't. Grace, I understand your reticence, but we need to see this through to the end."

"No matter what?" she asked solemnly.

"No matter what."

"Then let's go inside. The quicker we can get rid of our well-wishers, the faster we can pick up our investigation. I've got a feeling we need a new sense of urgency for finding the killer."

"Why do you say that?"

"Think about it, Suzanne. When whoever it was who ran us off the road realizes that we aren't taking the warning to heart, they're going to come after us again, and next time, they might not stop with just trying to scare us off. It would be a great deal better if we found out who they were first."

"It's a deal," I said as Momma came out onto the porch.

"Are you two going to sit out there all day, or are you planning to come inside at some point? We've got company."

"We're coming," I called out, and Grace and I soon joined her.

"What were you two nattering on about?" she asked as we approached.

"You know us," I said with a grin. "What won't we talk about?"

Momma had no trouble reading me, so she had to know that I was avoiding her question intentionally. She decided to accept that as she stepped aside. "Well, go on in. They're waiting for you."

We walked in the door, and I saw that Momma had outdone herself. She must have emptied the freezer entirely, putting out a spread that would have been fitting for a state visit from the president. There were chicken, ham, meat loaf, green beans, fresh mashed potatoes, cranberry sauce, and three kinds of pie.

"Who is going to eat all of this?" I asked, amazed by the splendor myself.

"Well, I can't handle all of it," George said with a grin, "but I'll do my best to take more than my fair share." He studied us, each in turn, and then asked, "How are you two doing?"

"A little sore," I answered for both of us, "but we're making a remarkable recovery."

"That's what I told them before." Emma turned back to me and asked, "And the guy just hit you out of the blue?"

I saw that Momma was about to reply when I stepped on her next line. "What can I say? The weather was the worst I've ever seen it, and no one should have been out on the highway, including us. They call them accidents for a reason."

Momma looked cryptically at me, and I nodded ever so slightly. She just shrugged, but I knew she'd caught on. "May I fix you both plates?" she asked.

"I think I'll wait a bit," I said.

"Suzanne, you have to eat something," Momma said, and I knew that there was no use refusing her. Besides, it did look awfully good, and I hadn't had that big a breakfast, well, not in the scheme of things. It was amazing how adept I'd grown at lying to myself when good food was involved.

I nodded as I took a plate, and Grace followed suit. We both tried to limit our portions, but soon enough, they were both full.

"George, you and Emma need to grab some plates."

"We're right behind you," George said, handing one to Emma before he took a plate for himself.

"You didn't have to wait for us, you know," I said.

Momma's cheeks flushed just a little.

I asked her, "Seriously? You wouldn't let them eat until we showed up?"

"Of course I would," she said. "I did my best to force plates on both of them, but they refused to take a bite until you two were back. You have better friends than you realize, Suzanne."

"Oh, believe me; I know just how good they really are." I turned to them both, and said, "Well, we're here now. Dive in."

"You don't have to tell me twice," George said, and then started heaping his plate with food. Emma took a much more conservative approach, but like us, she quickly added enough to it to visibly fill her plate.

"Your mother thinks I'm too skinny," Emma said.

"Actually, what I really said was that you could use another pound or two," Momma corrected.

"You can have a few of mine if you'd like," I said with a grin.

Momma didn't even shush me for it, a sign that showed she had been worried about me indeed. "I think you're perfect just the way you are," I said. "What do you think, George? Doesn't Emma have a cute figure?"

He looked up from his meat loaf, a bite on his fork suddenly hovering in the air in front of his face. "What? Er, sure, I don't know, what am I supposed to say when someone asks you a question like that?"

I laughed. "Well, one option is that you don't have to answer the question."

"Suzanne," Emma said with a laugh, "you are a wicked, wicked woman."

"What can I say? I do what I can."

After we'd all started eating, George asked, "I've been wondering about something. Did you even see the guy before he hit you?"

"I'm sure they don't want to talk about the accident," Momma scolded. Funny, it worked better on George than it ever had with me. I was probably just used to it from all of my exposure over the years.

"We don't mind," I said. I might as well start getting used to the story I was about to tell. "Honestly, at first it felt deliberate when that truck rammed into us, but with the rain and hail covering the road, it's a miracle he kept from hitting us as long as he managed it. I'm sure it wasn't intentional."

"Then it was a man?" George asked. It was easy to see the cop that was still inside there, just waiting to be let off the leash.

"The rain and hail were coming down strong, and the windshield was tinted pretty dark," I admitted. "Honestly, I have no idea who it was."

"Well, whoever did it should be roasted over a slow fire. I can't believe they just left you like that."

"They probably just panicked," I said. "Help came along soon enough, and we're both fine. That's really all that matters. George, is there anything new with you?"

"No, not off the top of my head," he answered, looking a little quizzically at me. "Why do you ask?"

"I just heard that there were a few women in town who had their sights set on you, and I was wondering if any of them had hit the target yet." I couldn't hide my grin as I said it, and I saw the other women at the table smiling covertly as well.

He dismissed the conjecture with a wave of his hand. "Suzanne, don't listen to rumors around April Springs. Not a single one of them has ever been right, and we all know it."

"Maybe so," I said, "but they're fun to speculate about, aren't they?"

"Not for me. I have enough trouble keeping up with what's actually going on in this crazy little Southern town of ours without adding nuance and innuendo into the mix." He turned to Momma and said, "By the way, I've never properly thanked you for organizing that write-in campaign."

"I assure you, no thanks are welcome," Momma said.

"You've got that right," George said with a grin. "You were clearly smarter than I was. At least you managed to back out before you were elected."

"George," my mother said, "that's because I was ill-suited for the job, and I knew it. The main reason I was running was to throw Cam Hamilton out of office. Once he was no longer in the picture, I realized that someone more qualified than I was deserved to be at the helm."

"And how exactly did my name come to mind?"

She smiled. "What can I say? I hate to see a valuable resource wasted when the town could benefit."

"Hey, I had a full and productive life before I became mayor," he insisted.

I tapped his arm. "Of course you did, but

just look at how much good you're doing now."

He put another bite of meat loaf on his fork, but didn't eat it just yet. "Does that mean you're telling me that you don't need me to help you investigate Peter Morgan's murder?"

"I wouldn't say that we don't need you, but we're trying our best to manage without you."

He looked into my eyes. "You're not trying to con me, Suzanne, are you?"

"No, sir. I'm telling the absolute truth."

He nodded once, accepted the statement, and then popped the bite of meat loaf into his mouth. I was about to say something to Emma when someone rang the front door.

"I'll get it," I said, easing myself up from my chair.

"Suzanne, stay right where you are. You need to rest," Momma said.

"The only way I'm going to get rid of this stiffness is by moving around," I said. "I'll be right back. Don't worry."

I made it to the door, wondering which one of my friends was taking time out of her day to wish Grace and me well.

Only it wasn't exactly a friendly face I found when I opened the door.

It was Henry Lincoln, and what's more,

he had two bouquets of flowers with him.

This was going to be interesting, no doubt about it.

"Hello, Henry. We're having a buffet in the dining room, if you'd like to join us," I said in my most gracious Southern accent.

He thrust the flowers at me, and then took two steps back. "Actually, I was hoping to get a minute alone with you, but if you've got company, we can do this later."

I put the bouquets on the porch swing and turned to him and said, "Nonsense. This is fine. We can speak out here." There was no way Lincoln was getting away from me before he had a chance to talk.

He shrugged, and then looked a little uncomfortable as he said, "Suzanne, first off, I'm truly sorry about the accident."

"You don't happen to have a white truck with a tinted windshield, do you?" I asked with a smile.

"What? No, of course not. Why do you ask?"

"Just making conversation," I said. "So, what would you like to talk about?"

He shrugged, accepting my desire to get to the point, whatever it might be. "When I heard what happened, I felt pretty mulish not giving you my alibi for the night of the murder. I didn't want to drag the woman I was with into it, but you have a right to know."

"Have you told the police yet?" I asked, not sure that it was the right thing to say for my investigation, but knowing that it was important, nonetheless.

"I just left the police station," Henry admitted. "Anyway, I spoke with her this morning and got her permission to tell you. She said her reputation could take the hit, and if it couldn't, she'd find some way to live with it."

"I'll do my best to keep it quiet, but I can't promise something like that."

"She understands that."

"Then I'm listening. Who was she?" A dozen names went through my mind in an instant, but when he told me his paramour's name, it was all I could do to keep my jaw from dropping.

"Rose White," he admitted. "I know, she's a little young for me, but there's something about that woman that makes me feel alive."

"Were you at her place all night, or yours?" I asked.

"As a matter of fact, we were in Raleigh at the Hilton by the interstate. Why?"

"Just curious," I said. So, if Henry's story checked out, he'd just eliminated himself as a suspect, and Rose White as well. I wasn't finished with him, though. "How did you two happen to meet?"

"That's an odd thing. Peter introduced us, if you can believe that," Henry said. "We both ran into her in Union Square one day, and I got her number. Don't worry, a dozen folks must have seen us in Raleigh together, including Denton Wicks from Copper Mill. There's a mayor that anyone would believe. We had a late dinner and caught a show with Denton and his wife, Millie, until midnight, and then I was at the pool when it opened at five A.M. to swim my laps, and I talked Rose into going with me to keep me company on the edge of the pool."

If that was true, neither Henry nor Rose would have been able to get back to April Springs, find and then kill Peter, and still make it back in time for his swim.

"Thanks for confiding in me," I said.

"Well," he said, "I just thought that given what happened, you had a right to know."

"I appreciate that."

He started to leave, and then hesitated. "You know, I really do hope you find the creep who killed Peter. Nobody deserves to get struck down like a rabid dog like that."

"I didn't think you were all that fond of him, Henry."

"I wasn't, but that's beside the point," he said. "Now that he's gone, there's one question that I can't seem to stop thinking about."

"Who killed him?" I asked.

"More like how am I ever going to get my money back now?"

I thought about the three thousand dollars that Grace and I were still holding that we'd found in Peter's apartment, but I wasn't the slightest bit tempted to turn it over to Henry. It wasn't my responsibility, after all, and I'd make Grace turn it over to Bryan as soon as the murder investigation was over. If he hadn't killed his own brother, at any rate.

"Who was that? Henry Lincoln?" Momma asked as she came out on the porch when the man drove away.

"If you know the answer, why do you ask the question?" I asked her with a grin.

Momma glanced down at the flowers. "And he brought gifts as well? That's certainly out of character for him."

"He said he heard about the accident," I admitted.

"Is that the only reason he was here?" Momma asked.

"You're a suspicious person, you know

315

that, don't you?"

"What can I say? I get it from my daughter," she answered without missing a beat.

"I believe that's supposed to be the other way around," I said.

"No matter. What did he want?"

I knew it was futile holding out on her. "It turns out that he was with Rose White in Raleigh the night before and morning of the murder, and he's got some pretty reliable witnesses to back him up."

Momma shook her head. "Why am I not surprised?"

"That he had an alibi?"

"No, that he was with a woman. I often suspected that's why he and Peter got along so well, up until the end. They were both fond of the ladies."

"Well, at least now I can start marking names off my list, since he was with another suspect of ours."

"How many are left, then?" Momma asked.

I thought about it, and then ticked them off on my fingers as I named them. "It's not a short one. We've still got Leah Gentry, Kaye Belson, Bryan Morgan, and as much as I hate to admit it, my new assistant, Nan."

"You really think Nan Winters could have done it?" Momma asked as George, Emma, and Grace joined us outside.

"Think who did what?" Emma asked.

"We were just wondering if Mrs. Orange used a slingshot in the tree house," I said with a smile. There was no way I was going to let myself get roped into that particular conversation.

"None of those things are from the game Clue," George said.

"You always were a good detective," I said as I patted his chest. "I can't slip anything past you."

"That means you're not going to tell us, doesn't it?" Emma asked.

"Wow, hanging around me all this time really taught you to read me pretty well, didn't it?" I asked as I smiled at my friend.

"Well, we're off," George said. "Emma's got some unpacking to do, and I have a meeting with the county planner in ten minutes."

"You two have all of the fun, don't you?" I asked as I hugged and kissed them in turn, Grace and I trading off our thanks. "We appreciate you coming by."

"More than you even realize," Momma added. "George was telling us that to keep from overwhelming you with visitors, everyone else is waiting at city hall for his report."

"Honestly?" I asked.

"I wouldn't lie to you."

"And Dad's going to run a follow-up article tomorrow, with your permission, of course," Emma said. "Folks want to know how you two are doing."

I thought about refusing the idea of an article, but then I realized that Ray would run something anyway, so why not let him get his facts from Emma? At least she knew the truth, no matter what her father ended up doing with it.

"Thanks double, then," I said.

After they were gone, Grace said, "That might work on them, but I want the truth. What happened when you and Henry Lincoln were out here?"

"You two have a chat about it," Momma said. "I'm going to start cleaning up."

"We'll be inside in a sec," I said.

"Take your time. You both need to discuss what you just learned."

After Momma was back inside, I brought Grace up to speed about what Henry Lincoln had told me, and she nodded as I finished.

"I believe it's true," Grace said.

"Based on what? Do you think Henry would ever be with Rose?"

"He hit on me once," Grace admitted, "so

yes, I believe it."

"Did you tell Peter about it? What did he do?"

"Nothing," Grace said. "I'm not sure he even believed me at the time."

"He was a real prince, wasn't he," I said, forgetting for a second how tied in with Peter Grace had been. "Hey, I'm sorry. I shouldn't have said that."

"No matter what he was like at the end, he deserved better than he got."

I hugged her lightly. "Funny, even Henry Lincoln just said the same thing. Grace, I promise you that we're going to do our best to see that he gets it. Momma asked me where our suspect list was now, and I was happy to tell her that it had narrowed considerably."

Grace nodded. "Kaye, Bryan, and Leah are the only ones who are left. That's not bad."

"Don't forget Nan," I said.

"Do you honestly believe that your new helper is a killer?"

"Hey, she has ties with just about everyone involved in this case," I reminded her, "and I know she's been holding out on me. Tomorrow, I'm going to press her until she tells me the truth."

"What if she quits?"

I just shrugged. "I'll worry about that if it happens."

"Besides, you've always got Emma, now that she's back in town."

"That's not why I'm going to press her, Grace. I need her to tell me the truth, especially if we're going to keep working together. If I can't trust the woman, I can't have her helping run the donut shop. It's as simple as that."

"I know. So, if you're going to talk to her tomorrow morning, we only have three folks left on our list. Any ideas about where to start?"

"I'd say we tackle the ladies," I said.

"You're not afraid of Bryan Morgan, are you?" Grace asked gently.

I thought about it for a second, and then I admitted, "I wouldn't say that I'm afraid of him, but then again, I wouldn't want to be alone in a dark alley with him, either. To tell the truth, he kind of gives me the creeps."

"I know what you mean, but that doesn't make him a murderer, does it?"

"No," I acknowledged, "but it doesn't clear him, either."

"So, should we tackle Kaye or Leah first?"

"I vote Leah," I said. "I heard she's already back in town, staying with her uncle again. I guess Ida put too many restrictions on her."

"Great. Nothing like a little family honor to defend. Burt isn't exactly your biggest fan, is he?"

I grinned at her. "That's what makes it so nice. I don't have to tiptoe around him, do I?"

CHAPTER 17

"Is Leah here?" I asked Burt as Grace and I walked into the hardware store.

It was clear that Burt wasn't all that happy to see us, but that was just too bad. He said sharply, "I told you both, she left town, not that you ever bothered respecting me or my family's wishes. My sister told me you were up at her place, so don't try to deny it."

"Why would we? *She* was really nice to us," I said, hoping that he'd get the hint.

"Yeah, well, she always was a softie. Don't make that mistake with me."

"Burt, we're going to find your niece one way or the other, so you might as well help us. The last time we spoke, Leah was really cooperative, and we left things on really good terms."

"I don't know why you think I should believe that, because I don't. Not that it matters. She's not here," he repeated.

"Come on, Suzanne. Let's go," Grace

said, tugging at my arm. "It's no use."

I wasn't about to give up that easily, but something in Grace's expression told me it was time to retreat. I trusted her instincts almost as much as I did my own. "Fine, but we'll be back later, Burt."

"Do what you want. I can't stop you. But I'll be here, you can count on that," he said, and then he dismissed us both.

"What's going on?" I asked Grace as we walked out onto the sidewalk together. "We can't just let him off the hook like that. We need to find Leah."

"I did," she said with a grin. "While you were chatting with Burt, I was looking out the window, and guess who I saw?"

"Leah, I'd wager, but where is she now?" I asked as I glanced up and down Springs Drive. I didn't see any sign of her now.

"She just ducked into the Cutnip, and if we play things right, we might just have a captive audience when we question her."

"That's brilliant," I said as we walked across the street, passed the town clock, and then headed into the beauty parlor to see what we could find out about Leah and her alibi.

"Are you finally coming in for a new hairstyle, Suzanne?" Wilma Gentry asked as

Grace and I walked into Cutnip. Somewhere in her forties, the salon owner was wearing her signature tight black stretch pants and leopard print blouse under her smock. "You know, you could do worse than try mine."

I looked at the giant ball of teased henna on her head, and it was all I could do not to laugh out loud. It wouldn't have been well received, though, especially since there were half a dozen women sitting in chairs waiting patiently to have their own big hair done.

"Thanks for the offer," I said as I spotted Leah getting her hair washed, "but I just need a second with her."

Cynthia Trent, Wilma's most conservative stylist and a woman close to my age, was working on Leah's hair, wetting it under the sink and no doubt cutting off any chance Leah had of hearing our conversation.

"What can I do for you, Suzanne?" Cynthia asked.

"Sorry, I didn't make myself clear. It's Leah I need to speak with."

Cynthia nodded. "It'll be a second. She can't hear a thing right now."

Wilma didn't look all that pleased to see us hovering in front of Cynthia's station, but she didn't say anything. I'd been thrown into her world once when one of her stylists had been murdered, not because of the way

324

she did hair, but because of who she'd been dating.

Cynthia finished soaking Leah's hair, and wrapped it in a towel as Leah sat up.

"We need a minute of your time," I said.

"What?" Leah asked as she first became aware of us. It took a second for it to register. "What's going on, Suzanne? I already told you and Grace everything I know."

"That's not quite true," Grace said as Cynthia quickly toweled off her hair.

"Can't we do this later? I'm kinda busy right now," she said.

"I don't mind if you don't," Cynthia said. I wasn't sure she was enhancing her tip, but I appreciated the fact that she was trying to help me out. Or was she just curious about what we wanted to talk to her client about?

"Go on then, get it over with," Leah said.

"If you need a little privacy, you can use the back room," Cynthia relented, so maybe her motives weren't so base after all. It was tough to miss when Wilma scowled at her. The salon owner cherished gossip nearly as much as she did receipts, and I had a feeling the stylist would be getting scolded for even suggesting we take our conversation somewhere else.

"I've got nothing left to hide," Leah said,

the resignation clear in her voice.

"Wonderful," I said. "All we need is your alibi the night Peter was murdered, and we'll leave you alone about this forever."

Leah didn't look all that pleased with the question. "What do you want from me? I already told you."

"No, as a matter of fact, you didn't," Grace said.

"I was home alone," she said as her eyes shifted around the beauty parlor.

I knew she was lying, but I also realized that she wasn't going to tell me right there in front of everyone else.

"Good enough," I said. "That's all we needed. Thanks for your time."

Grace looked puzzled, but it was nothing compared to Wilma's reaction. "Seriously? You're buying that lame story?"

"Why shouldn't they?" Leah asked. "It's the truth."

Wilma realized she was in danger of offending one of her customers. "Of course it is. I'm sorry, I've just been watching so much truTV that I get caught up in this stuff. It's like the drama's taking over my life, you know?"

"Did you see the case about the missing mom, and they found her in Las Vegas in the middle of her husband's trial for her murder?" one of the clients asked.

"I'd have gone there, too, if I'd been married to that man," another volunteered.

"I would have gone with her," one of the other stylists added.

I broke in before they dragged me into their debate. "Thanks again, Leah. We'll see you'all later."

Grace and I left the building, but instead of going back to her rental car, I sat down on one of the benches by the town clock.

Grace nodded her approval. "We're going to ambush her out here, right?"

I smiled. "I'd like to think of it more as if we're continuing our questioning in a more private setting."

Grace looked around, and then nodded. "You know, there's a very real chance that she might not give us any more of an answer out here than she did in there."

"Look at it this way," I said. "Here, at least there's a chance that she'll tell us the truth. It seems as though Leah cares more about what people think than she lets on. If we get her alone, we might just find out where she really was."

"You don't expect her to tell us anything if it incriminates her, do you?"

I shook my head. "Grace, I'm still not sure if she did it or not. Have you made up your mind already?"

"No," my best friend admitted. "Maybe I just *want* her to be the one."

"It can't be easy hearing all that she's had to say," I said. "But hang in there. We're getting close. I feel it in my bones."

"Well," Grace said with a slight smile, "if it's not Leah, then it's most likely going to be Bryan, Kaye, or Nan."

"If we even have the murderer on our list," I reminded her. "There might be a lead that Chief Martin is following right now that's going to flush out the killer, and we may have never heard of him. Or her," I added, realizing that our own list was heavily slanted toward women.

"I don't care much who catches the murderer," Grace admitted. "I just want this mess to be over."

We waited out on the bench for a long time, and when I looked at the clock above us yet again, it had been nearly an hour. "What's keeping her? She should have been finished by now."

"Should we go check on her?" Grace asked.

"I don't know how we can do that without arousing more suspicion," I said.

"Suzanne, I don't care. I'm going in."

I followed her, wondering what we would

say, but Grace took care of it. "What happened to Leah?" she asked as we walked back in.

"I thought you were done with her," Wilma said, waving her scissors around in the air like a baton.

"We just have one more question for her and then we're finished," Grace said.

Cynthia looked puzzled. "I don't know what to tell you, but she's not here. She slipped out twenty minutes ago."

"That's impossible. We were sitting by the clock the entire time," I confessed.

"I wondered why she wanted to go out the back door," Cynthia said.

"She didn't say where she was going by any chance, did she?" Grace asked.

"Not a word. Sorry."

"Not as sorry as we are," I said.

We left the hair salon, and I told Grace, "She's getting pretty good at eluding us, isn't she?"

"If it were an Olympic event, she'd win the gold medal every time."

I shrugged. "Let's go talk to Bryan. We've been lied to so much lately as people smile at us, it might just be refreshing to have a little open hostility."

"What possible reason could we give him to talk to us, Suzanne?"

I remembered the cash we'd taken from Peter's apartment. "Let's drop by the donut shop, and then I'll tell you what I have in mind."

We drove over, even though we could have easily walked the short distance, and I saw the sign Chief Martin had put in the window. It said simply, CLOSED UNTIL FURTHER NOTICE.

"That's not right," I said. "I'm just shutting down today. This sign makes it look as though I'm going out of business."

"That's why we came by here?" Grace asked. "So you could fix your sign?"

"Of course not," I said as I took it down. "But now that I've seen it, I'm going to put a new one up since we're already here."

Once we were inside, I took a sheet of paper and wrote, OPEN TOMORROW, THURSDAY, BUSINESS AS USUAL and put it in the window from the inside. After I did that, I walked into the back and pulled an old-fashioned donut sign made of raised metal from the wall.

"What are you doing now, redecorating?"

"This is my personal version of a safe," I told her. Once I had the sign down, I started to take the banded cash out that we'd gotten from Peter's place.

"That's pretty creative," Grace admitted.

"I've just got that old safe I don't use in my basement that's tucked under the steps. I should give it to you since I don't use it myself."

"Thanks, but this works fine for me. I never have much cash on hand, but that's where I keep it, if you ever want to rob me," I said with a smile.

"It's so much smarter than most folks could figure out," she commented.

"And economical, too. Who's going to check behind a sign like that for a safe? It's as secure as I need it to be."

"So then, we're giving the money to Bryan," she said when she saw that I had the cash.

"It's the right thing to do, since he's Peter's executor," I said. "Besides, this way, he's bound to talk to us, if for no other reason than to get his hands on the cash."

"We're just going to hand it over to him?" she asked.

"It's not going to be that easy for him. He's going to have to jump through some hoops before we turn it over. Are you okay with that?" I asked as I handed her the banded bills.

"It was never ours to begin with," she said. "I'd just as soon we didn't have it anymore, so let's go."

■ ■ ■ ■

As we drove to Bryan's place, I noticed that Grace had lost a lot of her nervousness about driving.

"This rental car's nice, isn't it?" I asked.

"Better than what I had before. I can't wait to see what I'm getting next."

"It must be nice having a company car," I said.

Grace frowned a bit. "Suzanne, don't kid yourself. I learned early on that if a company gives you a perk like that, you're expected to use it for them. I can't tell you the miles I've logged driving for them, and now that I'm a supervisor, it's just gotten worse."

"You still like what you're doing, though, right?"

"Of course I do, but I haven't ever met anyone who had a perfect job."

"I don't know," I said after a long pause. "I really like what I do for a living."

She took her gaze from the road for a second to look at me. "Are you telling me that you enjoy getting up in the middle of the night while everyone else is sleeping just so you can make them donuts?"

"Okay, I might change the hours if I could," I admitted with a laugh.

"There you go, then."

By the time we got to Bryan's house, we'd come up with a way of dealing with him, but that all went out the window when we arrived. He was standing by his door having a very public argument with someone else we needed to talk to. It appeared that Kaye Belson was paying a visit herself, for what reason, I had no idea.

But I was going to find out.

"Keep low and drive on past his place," I said as Grace started to pull in.

"Why?" she asked, but she ducked down a little as she kept driving.

"Pull over right here," I said, as we passed a row of spruce trees that blocked one side of Bryan's property.

She did as I asked, and that's when I spotted a familiar car just ahead of us, its driver also watching the scene unfold on the porch.

There was no reason in the world I wouldn't recognize it. Grace and I had tried to follow it when we'd been in Montview.

It was Leah's cherry-red Trans Am!

I got out of the car before Grace could even come to a full stop, and hurried toward where Leah was parked. She must have seen me, though, and her car suddenly shot down the street as if she were being chased by demons.

Grace pulled up beside me and asked, "Want me to follow her?"

I shook my head. "You'd never catch her. Why don't you just go ahead and park."

She did as I suggested, and as we got close to the trees, which offered a perfect shield for us, she whispered, "What was Leah doing here, anyway?"

"I'd say that she was stalking Bryan, if I had a guess," I replied softly. "We'll deal with her later, though. I'm more interested in what those two are arguing about at the moment."

We had no trouble hearing either voice from where we hid, since neither one of them was making any effort at all to control their volume, and we could peek through the bushes to watch them as well. It was like live theater, though none of it was scripted, and the element of danger present was real enough.

"I want it, Bryan. It rightfully belongs to me," Kaye yelled, and I could certainly feel the heat from her temper from where we stood.

"I'm telling you, I don't have it," Bryan yelled back, looming over the young girl like a man mountain. "I still don't know what you're talking about." I caught a smug expression on his face as Kaye looked away for a split second, and I had a feeling that Bryan was hiding something from her, and gloating about it as well.

Kaye backed down a little from his presence, taking a step off the porch. Her voice was quite a bit more timid as she added, "Bryan, it's not worth anything to anyone but me. I just want something to remember your brother by."

"Cut out his obituary then, and paste it in your scrapbook," Bryan said. "Now, go away."

"I'm not leaving until I get what is rightfully mine," Kaye said, and I had to admire her courage, if not her common sense. "Call the police, if you have to."

"I don't need them to fight my battles for me," Bryan said as he took a step toward her. "I can deal with you myself."

I was still trying to decide what the best course of action was for us to take when Grace stepped through the trees toward them.

I no longer had an option then, so I followed her.

"Are you sure you want to do that in front of witnesses?" Grace asked.

Bryan's fierce scowl suddenly disappeared. "I'm not doing anything. She won't leave,

335

and I'm tired of asking her."

"I want those letters Peter wrote me. They're bundled up in a packet, and they're mine," Kaye protested.

Bryan looked at me and asked, "Did you find anything like that when you cleaned out his apartment?"

It was a little too close to the truth for my taste. "We didn't find any letters," I replied, hoping neither one of them pushed me on it. "Did you find any letters, Grace?"

"No, there were no letters that I saw," she said, mimicking my answer. In a nearly broken voice, she suddenly asked Kaye, "He really wrote you letters?"

"Seven of them, to be exact," she said, a little too smugly for my taste. Then she pouted a little as she went on to explain, "When he found out that I had kept them, he took them back. But Peter said that he'd keep them safe for me."

"What makes you think he didn't just throw them away as soon as he got them?" Bryan asked, and I had to admit that I'd wondered the same thing myself.

"He wouldn't do that," she said. "If you all aren't lying to me, I still believe that he hid them somewhere."

"I'm telling you, we searched his place, and they weren't there," I said.

"What were you doing there in the first place?" she asked me, the suspicion clear in her voice. "What were *you* looking for?"

"We were helping the landlady, if you really must know," I said, trying to add some irritation to my voice. "Bryan didn't want to face it himself, and who could blame him? Grace and I were around, so we offered to lend a hand. It's as simple as that."

"And I went through the stuff they found, but there weren't any letters," Bryan said. "If that was really all of it."

Before I could stop her, Grace took the bills from her pocket and handed them to Bryan. "As a matter of fact, we found these while we were cleaning the place up. We didn't know who to give them to, but when we found out you were your brother's executor, we wanted you to have it all."

Bryan smiled and grabbed the carefully wrapped bills, then he tore the rubber bands from them. "Three grand, huh? What's the real reason you didn't turn this over to me when you were here the last time?"

I said quickly, "We could have taken that money to the police, but it's not their business, is it?"

He jammed the bills into his pocket, then said, "You did the right thing."

"What about my letters?" she asked us.

"I already told you," I said. "We didn't find them, and that's the truth."

"What else was with the cash, though?" Kaye asked. "Was there a packet there, too? It might not look like letters. You might not know what you had. Did you throw anything out that was with the money?"

"We found the cash, along with a scrap of paper and an old key that might go to anything," I said. "That was all that he hid at his place."

"Let's see the key, and the paper, too," Bryan demanded. "By all rights, they belong to me now."

"They're at my place," Grace said, "but they won't be of any use to you."

"I'll be the judge of that," Bryan said. "I want them, and I mean right now."

"First thing tomorrow is the best we can do," I said. "We have other plans tonight."

Bryan nodded. "Fine. Bring everything with you when you go to your donut shop tomorrow. What time do you open?"

"Six," I said. I wasn't about to admit how early I got there every day. Being alone with Bryan, even with Nan in the other room, was not something I ever desired.

"I just don't understand. There had to be somewhere else he thought would be safe,"

338

Kaye said. She looked at Grace and asked, "Were you keeping anything for him that might belong to me?"

Grace just shook her head. "Are you insane? He wouldn't leave your precious letters with me for safekeeping, now would he?"

"Where does the key fit, then?" she asked petulantly.

"We don't have a clue, and that's the truth."

Kaye took a few steps back, and then looked straight at me. "Suzanne, you're not lying to me, are you?"

"I've told you nothing but the truth," I said, and to my surprise, it was true this time.

"I don't know who to believe," she said, and then Kaye started to cry.

"Are you okay?" I asked her softly. I didn't mean to show one of Grace's rivals any sympathy, but it was tough to just stand there and watch her openly weeping.

"I'm fine," she said through her tears, and then hurried back to her car, which was parked on the street in front of Bryan's place, and drove away.

"Thanks for the cash, and for getting rid of her," Bryan said. "Are you sure there wasn't any more where this came from? You two didn't take a finder's fee or anything, did you?"

"We don't steal," I said, letting my voice grow cold. I didn't like being accused of things I hadn't done.

"Hey, don't get things in a knot. I had to ask," he said. "I'll see you tomorrow, bright and early. I have to take care of some business now, so you two need to go."

He stepped back inside, and I heard the dead bolts locking shut behind him.

It appeared that Bryan Morgan had gotten everything he'd needed from us.

"What do we do now?" Grace asked. "That didn't go as well as I'd hoped it would."

"Well, nobody chased us off with a shotgun, so we've done worse in the past," I said.

"True, but I don't expect we made any friends, either."

"That's okay. We have enough friends," I said. "When we're looking for a murderer, we can't always play nice." I thought again about the prospect of Bryan coming to my donut shop, and then realized that until I got this case sorted out, I didn't want to be alone with any of my suspects. "Do you feel like paying one more visit today?" I asked her.

"Suzanne, you're the one doing me the

favor, remember? I've got as much time as you need," she said. As we got into her car, she added, "All you have to do is tell me where we're going."

"You might think I'm losing it, but I'm suddenly not all that excited about waiting until morning to talk to Nan. I thought we might see if we could catch her at home and clear the air between us right now."

"That makes perfect sense to me," Grace said. "After all, there's safety in numbers."

"Nan, it's Suzanne Hart and Grace Gauge," I said as I knocked on her door for the second time. "May we come in? We need to talk."

I wasn't even certain that she was home, but then she opened the door a crack, the chain firmly still in place. "Suzanne? What happened to you today? I didn't know that we were going to be closed until I read that note on the door. Are you shutting down for good?"

"I'm so sorry," I said. "I thought the chief was going to call you, but he must have gotten distracted. Grace and I were in a car accident yesterday, and I forgot to let you know what was going on."

"Was it bad?" she asked, still standing just behind the partially closed door. Nan looked us both over, and clearly couldn't see anything wrong with us. Was that a hint of suspicion in her expression? Goodness knows I'd seen it enough coming from other people.

"We're fine," I admitted, "but the car's a wreck. May we come in?"

She hesitated, and I wasn't even sure she'd let us in, but ultimately she shut the door, took the chain off, and let us inside. That was the extent of her hospitality, though. She didn't offer us food, drink, or anything else, just two seats on her couch. "What can I do for you?"

"It's about Peter Morgan," I said, and I saw her stiffen.

"What about him?" she asked warily.

"Why didn't you tell me initially that you knew him, Nan?" I asked. "You had plenty of opportunity, and yet I had to practically drag it out of you that you'd been his babysitter once upon a time."

"I know a great many people, Suzanne. Do you feel entitled to know about every last one of them? I should warn you, it's a fairly long list."

"I don't need the names of random strangers," I said, doing my best to ignore her snippy tone, "but you might have mentioned that you knew the murder victim," I said.

"So what? I used to babysit Peter when he was young," Nan said. "Why is that such a big deal? Rose White did, too. Have you interrogated her yet?"

"Rose? How is that possible? It's too far a stretch to believe that both of you watched over the same boy."

"It's not that big a coincidence when you know the reason why," Nan said. "Rose and I are first cousins, and we always used to do those jobs together, especially when the child was a handful. And trust me; Peter was almost too much for both of us together."

"Why didn't you tell me that you were Rose's cousin?" I asked, incredulous about the amount of information that Nan had chosen to keep to herself. "I even asked you about her, and you just said that you'd drifted apart."

"Frankly, I didn't see that it was any of your business," Nan said. "And for your information, family can split up just as much as friends can."

"Did you date Peter, too?" Grace asked so softly that I doubted Nan had heard her.

"What? Have you lost your mind? Of course not." She really did look outraged by the question.

"We already know that Rose did," I said.

"It's natural to figure that you might have done it yourself."

Nan shook her head, looking angrier by the second. "Is that what you think of me? He was just a boy I looked after once. That's sick."

"He didn't stay a boy though, did he? Nan, we're just asking questions, not making accusations," I said as calmly as I could.

"That's not how it sounds to me." She stood, and moved to the door. "Now, if you'll excuse me, this interrogation is over."

"We're not interrogating you," I said as calmly as I could manage. "We're just having a conversation, like where were you the night Peter was killed?"

I knew that I'd pushed her too hard the second I'd said it. "You're accusing me of murder now? I'm on your suspect list?" I thought she might have a stroke, but I couldn't lie to her.

"Nan, you had two important connections we didn't know about, and it looks to the world as though you were hiding both of them from us. Why don't you make this easy and just tell us your alibi, and then you'll be off the hook?"

"And you expect things to just go back to normal if I tell you?" Nan asked. It was her turn to be incredulous.

"Of course I do. We're all adults here. And after all, we're just talking. Nobody's pointing any fingers at anyone else. Why wouldn't things stay the same between us?"

She looked mad enough to spit fire. "Because I've had enough of your questions, your outrageous working hours, and the fact that I constantly smell as though I took a bath in lard."

"We use canola oil in our fryer," I corrected her automatically.

"Good-bye, Suzanne. You may consider this my notice."

Grace and I started to leave, but I couldn't help myself. I paused, and then said, "If you don't mind, I'd still love to hear your alibi."

"I was here, alone, trying to get enough sleep so I didn't cut off a finger working at your donut shop when anyone with any sense at all would be home in bed, alone or otherwise. I'm sure you don't believe me, but frankly, I don't care, since I plan to never take another step inside Donut Hearts as long as I live. Good day."

Once we were out in the hallway, I turned to Grace and asked, "Did she really just quit working for me? What happened to a two-week notice?"

"She didn't work there that long, so you honestly can't expect her to give you any notice at all, after that, can you?"

I shrugged. "What happened to common courtesy?"

"It was never that common to begin with, and if you look at it from her point of view, I'm sure she feels justified acting the way she did. Suzanne, you were kind of rough on her."

"I just can't stand being lied to," I said.

"Welcome to my world," Grace said.

I thought about it, and knew that she was right. I probably had pushed Nan harder than I should have, and someday I'd have to apologize for it. At least if she hadn't been the one to kill Peter. "Hey, on the bright side, Emma can come back full-time now."

Grace stopped me as we walked to her car. "Suzanne, you didn't goad Nan like that on purpose, did you?"

"We needed answers," I admitted. "We can't afford to tiptoe anymore."

Grace wouldn't let it go, though. "That's not what I'm talking about, and you know it. I'm asking if you forced her into quitting so you could have Emma back. Be honest with yourself before you answer me."

"No, it never crossed my mind at the time," I said honestly. "I get so used to Chief Martin asking me intrusive questions that sometimes I forget how it can feel if you're not used to that kind of pressure from someone. If I had it to do over again, I would be quite a bit more subtle, but I stand by what I said. The questions needed to be asked."

"Okay, I can buy that. One question, then. Are we satisfied with her answers?" Grace asked.

"Nan is still a long shot, but I'm willing to take her off the list for now."

"Were her responses that convincing to you?" Grace asked as we started walking to her car again.

"No, but she was as mad as I could ever imagine her being, and she still managed to usher us out of her place without resorting to any threats or violence. I know it's nothing a prosecutor could use in a court case, but it's good enough for me. If I had to guess, I'd say that Nan isn't our killer."

"How nice that might have been to know before you had to slap her around a little bit," Grace said.

"Hey, I didn't lay a finger on her," I protested.

"Not with your hands, but can you say the same thing about your words?"

"Like I said, I'll apologize later and send her a dozen donuts," I said. "Happy?"

"You'd better make it roses, or carnations, or something that blooms."

"You don't think she'd like donuts as a gift after what she said about my treats?" I asked with a smile.

"I'm not sure that you should push it any more than you already have," Grace said. As she did, she stifled a yawn. "I can't believe I'm so tired. To be honest with you, I didn't sleep all that well last night."

"Was it because you were in a strange bed?" I asked as we got into her car. "I slept like a champ myself."

"No, it was more because you fought the covers like they were trying to strangle you, Suzanne, and then you started snoring. I can't do that again. Tonight, I'm sleeping in my own bed."

That was not going to happen, not if I had anything to say about it. "Grace, there's still a killer on the loose. Is that the best idea in the world?"

She nodded firmly. "After we stop and get a bite to eat on the way, I'm taking you home, and then I'm going back to my place for tonight."

I didn't want her to be alone, and I knew that Momma would feel the same way. "Just wait until I pack a bag when we get to the cottage, and I'll come with you."

Grace shrugged. "It's not necessary, you know."

"Let's just say that it's something I want to do," I replied.

"Fine, but you're sleeping in the guest room by yourself. I need my sleep tonight."

"Hey, I'm not the only one who snores."

She smiled and said, "I might, but mine are certainly more delicate than yours."

"You're entitled to your opinion, but I'm not conceding that I'm hard to sleep with, or that I snore, too."

"You don't have to, Suzanne. I'm sure your mother and Max will both testify, if I need to prove it in court."

I gave up. I never thought of myself as someone who snored, but then again, I wouldn't be awake to hear myself doing it, would I? Max had teased me about it when we'd been married, but I hadn't taken him seriously. Evidently the blanket thing was new.

"Okay, let's concede that neither one of us is perfect and leave it at that," I said. "Now, do you want to tell my mother that we won't be eating or sleeping there tonight, because I don't want to make that particular call."

"Coward," Grace said.

"I'm not denying it."

349

She frowned at me, and then pulled her car over into an empty parking lot. "Hand me the telephone before I lose my nerve."

Easy-As-Pie Cherry Treats

When I'm in a rush and don't have the time or energy to make one of my tried-and-true donut recipes, it's amazing how a little puff pastry and some cherry pie filling can do the trick in making a child smile. Try these sometime, even if you're not in a hurry!

Ingredients

1 sheet Pepperidge Farm puff pastry dough (1/2 of 17.3 oz. pack)

1 can (approximately 20 ozs.) cherry pie filling, or your choice of any fruit filling.

1 egg, beaten, combined with 1 tablespoon water.

Instructions

Heat the oven to 400 degrees F. Let the puff pastry dough warm on the counter, and then open. Cut the sheet into matching pairs of your choice, being sure to have the tops and bottoms duplicate in size. You can use fun cookie cutters for these shapes as well. Spread filling out on bottom sections, then cover and crimp the tops to seal. Brush with the egg wash mix, then poke a few holes in the tops of the pastries to let the steam escape as they bake. Bake 20–25 minutes, or until golden brown.

Yield: 4–8 small pastry treats, depending on the sizes and shapes you cut.

CHAPTER 18

"Are you certain you have everything you need?" Momma asked me again as I finished packing a small overnight bag to take with me to Grace's house.

"If I forget anything, I'm just down the road. Are you sure you don't mind being alone tonight? You could always come stay with us. We can make it into a sleepover."

"No, I'll leave that to you two. In all honesty, I don't know how you sleep in that bed of yours. Even the lumps have lumps."

"What can I say? It suits my body."

"And no one else's," Momma said.

As I headed for the door, she caressed my cheek lightly. "You are a good friend to Grace, Suzanne. She's lucky to have you."

"Honestly, I'm lucky to have both of you in my life. Momma, I don't tell you nearly often enough, but I love you. You know that, right?"

"I do," she said, with the trace of a tear in

one eye, "But it's always good to hear, and I never grow tired of it. I love you, too."

"Then I guess I'll go," I said.

"Is Grace waiting for you outside?" Momma asked as we walked down the stairs from my room.

"She was going to, but I sent her on. I have to drive to work in the morning, and I didn't want to walk there in the dark."

"That's prudent of you, but she shouldn't be left alone. Go on now, don't worry about me. I'll be fine."

"There's no doubt in my mind about that," I said.

"And don't forget to call Emma to tell her that she's got her job back."

"It's already taken care of," I said. "She's starting work in the morning."

"Good," Momma said, and I walked out the door. "I'm glad that's been taken care of. Good night, Suzanne."

" 'Night, Momma," I answered.

As I left the house and got into my Jeep, I glanced up at the front porch and saw my mother standing there, framed in the silhouette of the open door, waving to me as though I were going off to the other side of the world and not just down the block. I waved back, and then headed over to Grace's house.

"I put fresh sheets on the guest bed," Grace explained, "and there are towels on the chair if you feel like a shower. If you don't mind, I think I'm going to call it an early night tonight."

"Hey, I'm the one who usually taps out first," I said with a laugh.

"I know, but today took more out of me than I thought it would."

I studied my friend for a second. "Emotionally, or physically?"

"A little of both. In fact, I believe I'm going to take one of those pills the doctor prescribed for me, and you're welcome to one yourself, if you'd like." We'd both been given prescriptions for something stronger to help us sleep, and Grace had filled hers earlier.

"I'm not that bad so far," I said. "I think I'll stick with what I've got."

"Good night then, Suzanne."

"Good night, Grace."

I settled into the guest room, changed into my nightshirt, turned off the light, and tried to sleep. It was just after nine, and ordinarily there might be a hint of light left in the sky, but the overcast clouds had taken care of that. It might as well have been midnight from the lack of light coming in through the shades. I'd had a busy day after a full night's rest, so there was no reason I shouldn't be able to fall right to sleep.

Other than the fact that I was in a strange house, trying to sleep in a bed that wasn't mine, and that my thoughts wouldn't let go of the puzzle I was working on, trying to figure out who had killed Peter Morgan. With Leah, Bryan, and Kaye left on our list, I had to admit that I favored Bryan as the culprit. After all, he'd stood to gain the most by his brother's death, and his temper was certainly no secret. Leah might have felt scorned by Peter, and Kaye was clearly jealous of Peter's other lady friends, but I had to keep in mind that either one of them could have wanted to see Peter dead if they'd felt rejected. Love was a powerful motive, for both good and evil, and it could never be discounted. What might seem trivial to someone looking in from the outside might feel like the end of the world to a person going through the pain.

But which one was the killer? I needed more information, but I wasn't sure how to get it. I believed that Grace and I had pretty much worn out our welcome with our three remaining suspects, so those were dead ends. I finally just got up, reached into my jeans pocket, and retrieved the key we'd found at Peter's apartment, wondering where the safe was that it fit. We'd be turning it over to Bryan tomorrow, for what good it would do him. It had to be the key to more than a safe, though. Were Kaye's love letters hidden away there, or was it something much more explosive? Did it hold the real reason Peter had been murdered?

That's when I heard a creak coming from downstairs. It might have just been Grace's house settling, or something that was perfectly normal, but for some reason, it put me on edge. I slipped on my jeans, stuffed the key back into my pocket, then put on my tennis shoes, keeping the nightshirt on as well. Opening the door, I stuck my head out into the hallway and heard something there again.

Was someone down there? I quietly slipped down the hallway and peeked inside Grace's room. My eyes had grown accustomed to the lack of direct light, and I could make out things well enough to navigate without bumping into anything.

"Grace? Are you awake?" I asked softly.

I knew the answer before I even asked the question. Her slight snores told me that the pill she'd taken had kicked in. Grace was lost to the world, and if I was going to investigate the noises coming from downstairs, I was going to have to do it alone.

I crept back out of her bedroom and briefly went back into the guest room. The downstairs was quiet now, and I wondered if it had just been my imagination. I was well aware of the fact that my mind could manufacture things that weren't really there when I was overly stimulated. For a second, I debated calling Chief Martin, but did I really need him coming over to Grace's to prove to me that I had too active an imagination? I decided to compromise. I'd take my phone with me, along with anything I might be able to use as a weapon, and go downstairs to look around. Chances were good that nothing was wrong, and I could try to go back to sleep.

Then again, if someone were down there, I'd be ready to defend myself and call for help as well.

It seemed like a good plan at the time, anyway.

Back in the guest room, all I could find that I might be able to use as a weapon was the wooden dowel Grace used as a closet rack. It wasn't as good as a baseball bat, but it would have to do. At least the heft of it felt good in my hand.

I crept down the stairs, and made a quick survey of the first floor. I don't think I took a single breath, though I know that I must have.

It was all clear.

"You and your imagination," I said softly to myself, laughing a little about how carried away I'd become.

Then I heard something in the basement. At least I thought I did.

Slowly, I opened the door and peered down into the gloom. I didn't see any movement, or hear a thing. I debated turning the light on, but if someone were there, I didn't want them to know that I'd found them.

I walked down the steps carefully, ever aware of what surrounded me. In the past, Grace's basement had always been just a storage area for the things she didn't need or use every day, but suddenly, it took on a completely different feeling.

When I got to the last step, I decided that there were too many places for someone to hide down there. And then it hit me. Of the last three suspects, only Kaye had been insistent that Peter had hidden something of hers. Had she known about the money, or was there something far more valuable than cash or old love letters? Kaye had been insistent on Bryan's porch when any sane person would have turned and run. She was after something big.

Something important enough to kill for, and those letters had to just be a ruse. It was the only way that every puzzle piece fit together.

I didn't honestly believe that she was really there, but searching the house had allowed my mind to work out the solution.

On a lark, I reached out and flipped on the light.

That's when someone knocked the clothes rod out of my hand.

It appeared that it hadn't been my imagination after all.

I wasn't alone.

"I knew it was you," I said as I looked at the small ladies' handgun Kaye was pointing at me. "There never were any love letters, were there?"

"Very good, Suzanne. Now hand me your cell phone."

I had it still clutched in my other hand, so I couldn't very well deny its existence, or even call Jake to tell him that I needed help. I'd fallen into the trap of believing that modern technology would save me in the end, but I had been wrong. As I handed it over, she tucked it into her jacket pocket with a smug look on her face.

Had I just given her my last hope of surviving this?

"At least tell me what is so valuable that you'd kill for it."

I was afraid that she'd just ignore me, but instead, she chose to indulge my request. "It's easy enough. I just need that key, Suzanne, and I'll show you."

It suddenly burned hot in my pocket, but I wasn't about to let her know that I had it on me. "What good is that going to do you? We don't even know where the safe is. Whatever you're looking for could be any-where."

"No, it's here. I can feel it." Kaye laughed at me then, a sound that raised the hairs on the back of my neck. She was on the edge, there was no doubt about it, and I didn't want to push her over if I could help it. She explained, "Among Peter's many faults was that he was blackmailing a rich business-man in Maple Hollow, and I plan to take the operation over myself now that he's dead."

"How did you find out about it?" I asked. As I did, I saw a slight movement behind her. Had Grace made it down the steps without either one of us seeing her? No, for a brief moment, I saw that it was Leah

361

Gentry standing in the shadows! She must have followed Kaye there. But why wasn't she trying to help me now? Maybe she wasn't any more prepared to confront a killer than I was.

Kaye said, "I was at his apartment one afternoon, and while he was napping, I found the packet duct taped behind the toilet. From what I saw, it was pretty volatile stuff. I didn't get a chance to see it all, though. He woke up and caught me."

"He must have been furious," I said, looking around for something I might use as a weapon. If I had the chance, I was going to fight back. Maybe, with Leah's help, we could overpower her together. If not, I was still going to go down swinging. I might not be able to beat a gun with a more primitive weapon, but if I could mark her in some way, maybe Chief Martin would realize that she was the one who'd killed me. I'd seen people go to their graves without justice, and if there was the slightest chance, I was going to make sure that it didn't happen to me. Kaye might be able to get away with killing all three of us, but she'd bear at least one mark from the battle.

"He grabbed my arms so hard he bruised me," she said, pulling back the sleeve of her jacket to show me. I saw some fading

362

discoloration there, so maybe she was telling me the truth. And why not? What possible reason did she have to lie to me right now?

"What happened to the packet after that?"

"He told me that he had stashed it in a safe place where no one would ever think to look, not even the safe's owner. I didn't get it then, but I do now."

"You aren't making any sense, you know that, right?" I asked, as I saw a thin steel rod left over from a construction project. It was rebar, something used in concrete work, and I knew that Grace's dad had loved playing around with brick and mortar when he'd been alive. But how was I going to get to it? I needed Leah to do something to distract Kaye, if only for a second, but she was frozen in place, listening to our conversation as though she'd lost the ability to move or act.

It looked like I was on my own.

"Peter wasn't making any sense, either, when he died, was he? I followed him that night, you know, watching him get drunk over *her*. When Trish threw him out of the Boxcar, I nearly had him. But then Burt Gentry came out of the diner just as I was about to pull Peter into the shadows, so I couldn't get to him. I thought I'd lost him for good, but he walked over to Grace's, and then got thrown out of here, too. You should have heard the way Grace slapped him. It sounded like the crack of a rifle. That's when he found the paint and decided to redecorate your donut shop. I nearly got caught laughing when he threw that yellow paint on your building. He must have heard me, and I called over to him. That's why he left the bucket right where it was and stumbled to the back of the Boxcar. I told him I had something for him that would ease his pain, and he was so drunk, he didn't even question what I was doing."

"But why did you kill him?" I asked, inching slowly closer and closer to the steel. "Was it all just about the money?"

"The blackmailing is just icing, Suzanne. The drunken fool told me that he never cared about me, or Leah, or any of the other women he'd bedded. He said that Grace was the love of his life, and that he'd ruined it."

"Is that why you tried to kill Grace and me on the road during that wicked storm?"

She looked puzzled by the question. "What are you talking about?"

"So, it really was an accident?"

She laughed. "Boy, you really are paranoid, aren't you? Though it does turn out this time that you were right. Someone is out to get you, and it turns out it's me. In fact, I'm about to get rid of you like I did Peter. He should have known better than to declare his love for someone else."

"And when he did, that's when you hit him with the post." It was all starting to make sense now. Kaye had a temper, and she couldn't believe that Peter would ever choose anyone over her.

"He went down like a bag of sand," she said with the hint of laughter in her voice. "I kept shoving him with it once he hit the ground, trying to make him get up and tell me that he was acting, but he never moved. I searched his pockets, but the only things I found were his wallet and his keys. I went back to his apartment, but I couldn't find the packet anywhere, and I was afraid to make a mess. I didn't want anyone to know that I'd been there."

"But it was wrecked when we opened the door to clean it out," I protested.

"That's because I went back after the cops left. I kept thinking that I must have missed something, and at that point, I didn't care who knew that I'd searched the place this time. I tore it up, but I still didn't find a thing. I've been dying to know. Where did you find the money and the key?"

"It was stuffed up in the range hood," I said, "hidden by the filter."

A look of satisfaction overtook her face. "That was very smart of you, and it brings me back to why I'm here. I've already found Grace's safe, but I still need that key."

It was time to act. I couldn't count on Leah anymore.

I pulled the key out of my pocket, but then I let it slip out of my hand, as though I were clumsy, or more likely, nervous. "Sorry, I guess I'm a little unsteady right now."

"Pick it up," she ordered.

This was it. Maybe a gunshot would trigger something in Leah to make her help me. I just hoped it wouldn't be too late, then.

I reached down to get the key, keeping my gaze on Kaye the entire time.

Then I caught a movement behind her, and saw that Leah was suddenly out of her trance. She threw the nearest thing she could find at Kaye, an old Barbie doll sitting on top of a box of other discards. It wouldn't have done much damage under any circumstances, and I wondered how clearly Leah was thinking to choose that as her weapon, but it did manage to distract Kaye. She swung the gun around and shot at Leah, the explosion bouncing off the concrete block walls of the basement and suddenly filling the air with the unmistakable scent of gunpowder.

I was deafened by the blast, but I couldn't let that stop me.

I grabbed the steel bar and brought it down on Kaye's shoulder, though I'd been aiming for the back of her head, a kind of poetic justice. Either she'd shifted slightly at the last second, though, or my aim was off. Either way, the force of the blow still managed to knock the gun out of her hand. As we both scrambled for it, I managed to get there first, just barely, but we were too close for me to use it against her, not that I was sure that I could, even given the circumstances. Kaye and I struggled for it. She had a strength I never imagined that she might possess, and I knew that I was losing the battle. If I let go of the gun, I knew I'd be dead a few seconds later. Right now, I couldn't worry about Leah, or Grace, or even Jake. I was in the fight of my life, and I knew it. As we wrestled for the weapon, both of us lying on the floor struggling to get final control, I saw a shadow and some movement above us. Had Kaye missed when she'd shot at Leah? Was she running away now, leaving me to die alone? No, the motion was coming down the stairs, I could see that much, but only that.

Then I saw Grace standing near us in her nightgown, the discarded steel bar I'd used now in her hands. She held it as though it were a dagger, and I could see it penetrating Kaye's heart in my mind.

"Don't kill her, Grace," I yelled out. "She's not worth it."

"You can't trick me like that, Suzanne. I'm not stupid," Kaye said.

Grace seemed to realize what I was saying. She turned the bar from a sword to a club, and hit Kaye a little harder than I would have liked.

It did what it had been meant to do, though. Kaye's grip eased as she lost consciousness, and I grabbed the gun before she could come out of it.

If she came out of it.

"What happened to Leah?" I asked as I struggled to stand. "Is she dead?"

Grace and I hurried over to see, and I pulled back when I spotted her on the floor, bleeding from her temple.

"She's dead, isn't she?" I asked through sobs that came unbidden. Leah had tried to help me, and she'd paid for it with her life.

"Hey, don't cry for me just yet, Suzanne. I'm okay," Leah said as she struggled to sit up. "It barely nicked me."

Grace studied the crease on her forehead

and then said, "Head wounds are the worst, aren't they?"

Leah nodded, holding a bit of one of Grace's old ballet costumes firmly to the wound. "What happened to Kaye?"

"She's just knocked out. There's no doubt in my mind that she's going to be okay," I said as I heard her start to moan.

Grace patted her gown, and then said, "Do either one of you have a cell phone on you? Mine's upstairs."

"Mine's in her pocket," I said, not wanting to look for it at the moment.

"I'll call the police," Leah said as she reached for hers.

"Ask for Chief Martin," I said. "He deserves to hear this from us directly."

As we waited for everyone to show up, I asked, "Leah, there's one thing that I haven't figured out yet. Why did you keep running away from us, if you were just trying to solve the case yourself?"

"I knew that no one would believe me. Why should they? I haven't exactly been acting like I should be taken seriously lately, have I? When you were questioning me at Cutnip, I realized that you had all of the bases covered except for Kaye. I'd seen firsthand how crazy she could be when she was jealous, so I decided to start following her around to see where it might lead me."

"That's why you were at Bryan's. We thought that you were spying on him."

"That, too," she admitted. "But mostly Kaye. Honestly, I didn't know that she did it for sure until I heard her tell you."

I reached down and picked up the discarded key. "Should we wait for the police, or go ahead and open the safe ourselves?"

"You can do what you want," Grace said, "but I can tell you right now, there's nothing there."

"So then that means there's no harm in us checking," I said.

I moved to the safe, conveniently cleared by Kaye earlier, and slid the key into the lock. Without hesitation, it went in and turned smoothly.

Inside it was a packet of the information Kaye had been searching for, along with another huge wad of hundreds.

Grace looked at it as though she didn't believe it. "That's not possible," she said as she started to reach for the contents.

I pulled her back. "We don't want any of our fingerprints in there right now," I said, and she pulled her hand back.

"Peter must have taken my key one night and used the safe for his own things. He had a lot of nerve, keeping it here without asking me," she said.

"Doesn't that sum Peter up in a single sentence?" Leah asked. "Grace, I'm truly sorry for what I did to you. I knew better, but that didn't stop me. I'll do whatever I can to make things right with you."

To my surprise, she hugged Leah carefully. "When you saved Suzanne, you cleaned the slate between us, as far as I'm concerned."

"I didn't do much of anything," Leah protested, though it was clear that she was happy with the resolution.

"Don't sell yourself short," I said. "You distracted Kaye when I needed it, and that's the only way we managed to beat her."

"With a Barbie doll," Leah said wryly.

"Hey, whatever works," I said as I could hear the police sirens nearing the house. Kaye must have heard them coming for her, too, because she started to try to stand up.

I put a tennis shoe on her back and shoved her back down onto the concrete floor. "The only place you're going is to jail."

CHAPTER 19

"Pass the milk shake pitcher," Trish said the next evening as we all sat in the living room. "I'm getting low."

I did as she asked, and then I looked around at the other women gathered together there. Along with Trish, Grace was there as the guest of honor, and we'd decided to invite Leah as well. After all, without her, we might not be having this particular party.

Momma was out on a date with Chief Martin, and Jake was due in tomorrow.

For the second, and unprecedented, day in a row, Donut Hearts had been closed for business. Emma and I would reopen tomorrow, but right now, I was there for Grace, and in a way, Leah as well.

"Everyone, fill up your glasses," I said as I stood. The other women joined me, and I hoisted my own glass in the air. "This was supposed to be a time for Grace to grieve,"

I said, "but I propose that we change tonight's theme to strong women sticking together in times of crisis. Anyone else agree?"

"I do, but I'd like to add something else of my own, if you don't mind," Grace said, tapping her glass to mine.

"By all means," I said as I touched my glass back to hers.

Grace added, "To friendship."

"To loyalty," Leah added.

"To us," Trish finished with a smile, and we all drank deeply.